FAST FOCUS

FAST FOCUS

•

Cheryl Cooke Harrington
&
Anne Norman

AVALON BOOKS
THOMAS BOUREGY AND COMPANY, INC.
401 LAFAYETTE STREET
NEW YORK, NEW YORK 10003

PRINTED IN THE UNITED STATES OF AMERICA
ON ACID-FREE PAPER
BY HADDON CRAFTSMEN, BLOOMSBURG, PENNSYLVANIA

To the men in my life,
thanks for believing
—Cheryl

and

To Dr. Stuart Connolly,
with gratitude
—Anne

Chapter One

They flew past him in twos and threes. Wing-footed lunatics with nothing better to do on a glorious spring day than work up a sweat running laps in the park.

It didn't seem to matter where he went in this city, the rat race never stopped. *Slow down!* he wanted to shout. *Look around you!* But the natives kept right on running. He gazed in wonder, and with considerable longing, at the cool, shimmering waters of the Pond, pink with the reflection of cherry trees in bloom. The warm air was sweet with the scent of countless blossoms, the path underfoot littered with new-fallen petals. It was hard to remember, in this idyllic setting, that he was right at the center of a city teeming with seven million people; that the traffic, noise, and endless bustle of Fifth Avenue waited, just a few hundred yards to his left.

Brushing the tangle of sweaty hair from his eyes, he stared into the distance and groaned in dismay. Alexandra Frost, in her bright red T-shirt, bobbed effortlessly to the crest of the hill ahead, moving as if that bulky backpack slung over her shoulder were utterly weightless. He forced his leaden feet to follow, wondering why on earth he hadn't rented himself a bike instead. What with all her other fit-freak habits, he should have known the woman would be into marathon running.

"Stop," he muttered, breathlessly directing his plea to the back of her ponytailed head. "Oh, please, take a break." But the perky red T-shirt sailed blithely around the corner. He followed, eyes locked to the spot where she'd disappeared from view, heart pounding, lungs straining from the unaccustomed effort. *Don't lose her.* The tramp of his feet on the hard-packed earth faded to a distant echo, drowned out by the deafening rush of blood in his ears. *Don't lose her!*

1

*   *   *

A quick glance over her shoulder confirmed it. Still there—well, just barely. The man who'd been shadowing her for the last twenty minutes was obviously *not* a seasoned runner. Shortening her stride, Lexie jogged to a halt and knelt to tighten her shoelaces.

The tall, dark-haired man lurched around the curve seconds later, stumbling to a standstill only a few yards away. Neatly avoiding eye contact, he turned abruptly, bending to rest with his hands on his knees.

He was good, she thought grudgingly. If she hadn't seen him lurking around before, she'd really have to wonder if she wasn't imagining things.

Thinking back, Lexie was almost certain she'd seen him in the shop on Monday morning, and then yesterday he'd appeared outside the big front windows of the Broome Street Gym. Leaning nonchalantly against a lamppost, he'd pretended to read the *Times* as he watched her work out on the Nautilus. He'd been nowhere to be seen by the time she'd left for home, but all the way there, she'd had the most uncomfortable feeling that she wasn't alone. He'd been following her, all right. Now all she had to do was figure out why.

She let the backpack slip to the ground, reaching stealthily inside to retrieve her camera. It was an old-fashioned clunker, one of the first pieces of professional equipment she'd ever owned, and really far too heavy to run with. But she had no desire to tempt fate, or muggers, by flaunting one of her expensive new ultra-lights. And Lexie Frost had a rule. *Never* get caught without a loaded camera. There was simply no way of knowing when the shot of your dreams might materialize. And so the old Nikon went along for the ride, tucked into an army surplus backpack, just in case. And this was *definitely* one of those ''cases.'' Cradling it furtively in the crook of her arm, she squeezed off a few frames of the stranger. His annoyingly handsome face was one she wouldn't soon forget.

Keeping a covert watch on the man as she stood, Lexie employed a little sleight of hand to return the heavy camera to her bag. She almost had to feel sorry for him, doubled over and panting the way he was. Not bad looking . . . for a pervert, that is. Dark, straight hair, flecked with hints of copper, straggled damply across his forehead and into his eyes. An obviously brand-new shirt clung fast to his sweat-drenched shoulders and back. His back and shoulders were rather pleasantly contoured, too, she mused, as he gave in to a violent spasm of coughing.

She sighed. The poor guy was really hurting. Lexie adjusted her backpack and allowed herself a wicked little grin. It wouldn't be much of a challenge to lose him at all.

Stretching once or twice, as if she were in no particular hurry, she waited until the stranger glanced wistfully out across the Pond, then sprinted down the path just as fast as she possibly could. She'd rounded the next bend before he'd even discovered she was gone.

"This *can't* be happening," he said with a groan, pumping legs that felt more like rubber than flesh and bone. She must've figured it out. And if she knew he was following her . . .

Plunging into the tangle of shrubbery that bordered the path, he battled his way uphill and cross-country, shortcutting the long curve of the pathway and, with any luck, cutting short the time it would take to catch up to Miss Alexandra Frost. He burst out of the brush a few seconds later, just beyond the bend, and scanned the path to the left and right. Her red T-shirt was nowhere to be seen.

"Hey, mister!"

A slight, olive-skinned boy stepped out from behind a gaily canopied pushcart, waving both hands in the air and then pointing directly at him.

"Me?" he asked, with a dubious frown.

"Yeah. You. C'mere, will ya?"

The boy wore a yellow canvas cap and apron, decorated with images of juice-squirting oranges, plump red berries, and thick black letters that spelled out the words *Juice Louie*. And the boy was laughing, as if he'd just heard a really good joke.

"Did . . . did you . . . see . . . a . . . a woman . . . red . . . red T-shirt . . . running?"

The boy laughed again, even harder this time. "Nice lady." He grinned. "She say, give you this." He offered a huge bottle of frosty-cold papaya juice. "She say, man with 'I Heart New York' shirt need a drink." The boy chuckled. "Lady say, tell man to work on his approach." He was almost doubled over now with laughter. "She say, she . . . she don't date perverts. Ha!"

"Where . . . which way did she go?" he demanded, heaving a deep breath as he snatched the cold drink from the boy's hand.

He was met by a stubbornly blank stare.

"Where?" he snarled, narrowing his eyes and leaning to within an inch of the boy's suddenly solemn face. "Listen to me, kid. Your 'nice lady' could be in *real* trouble. *Tell me!*"

"There." The boy pointed a trembling finger southward. "That way."

Rocking back on her heels, Lexie breathed a long, silent sigh of relief. For a moment there, it had looked as if she'd have to rescue "Juice Louie" from the irate clutches of Mr. Pervert, but the kid had given in at last, pointing him in the right direction down the path. Not that it would do him the least bit of good, she thought with a quiet snicker. She was the one doing the following now.

She watched from behind the broad, weathered trunk of an old sycamore tree, as the stranger ventured along the main path to the next bend, then doubled back to investigate a little-used side track. Dodging from tree to tree, Lexie followed until, at last, the man threw up his arms in a dismal gesture of defeat. He limped into the shade beneath a little stone bridge and stared, for a long moment, at her gift of papaya nectar. She wondered what he might be thinking as a wry smile played across his face. Leaning heavily against the cool, moss-covered stonework, he rolled the frosty bottle dejectedly back and forth across his temples before twisting off the cap to drain it dry.

"You're welcome," murmured Lexie, feeling inexplicably sorry for the man all over again. What was it about him? she wondered, studying him thoughtfully. Whatever it was, it was really quite irritating. She wanted to be angry—*furious*—with this enigmatic stranger who'd insinuated himself, uninvited, into her perfectly well-ordered life. She knew she should probably be terrified, or at least a little bit nervous, but her gut instincts kept insisting that he posed no threat at all.

Giving in to a little snort of annoyance, she crept closer, keeping safely out of sight in the tangle of new spring greenery. There was just something about him, an undefinable "something" that cut right through her naturally suspicious nature; right through all the big-city street smarts she'd acquired growing up in Manhattan; right through every lick of good sense she'd ever had; and left her considering the possibility of walking boldly up to the man and introducing herself. Not now, of course. Not here, with nobody else around. But if she—

The loud snap of a twig and sudden motion in the trees caught Lexie's attention. She watched, rooted firmly to the spot, as a second man, squat and scruffy, stepped onto the path directly opposite her hiding place. He'd pulled the brim of his old fedora low across his face, as if to hide himself—but from what? Or who? And why, she wondered, was his heavy trench coat buttoned firmly to the neck, on a day so warm it felt more like mid-July than early May?

He didn't see her crouching among the shrubs, only inches from his feet, and turned to skulk menacingly along the path, one hand shoved deep into the pocket of his coat. *Seedy little character,* she thought, studying him uneasily. What was he up to? He was a bit too clean to pass for homeless. Shifty and unshaven, yes, but that coat of his looked new, and expensive. The shoes, too. If this were a movie, he'd turn out to be some sort of hit man, or gangster. He'd have a loaded gun in that pocket, and he'd—

Lexie felt a chill prickle ominously up her spine. She glanced quickly along the path. Deserted. Not a soul to hear if she yelled for help. No one but Seedy Man and her own personal pervert. But to Lexie's dismay, her pervert had both eyes closed at the moment, still recovering from their marathon run around the Pond. And Seedy Man was inching closer and closer to his resting place under the bridge. A little too close . . .

Lexie was on her feet the instant he eased the gun out of his pocket. She watched in horror as the man took slow, careful aim—

"No!" Crashing through the brush and onto the path, Lexie covered the few yards between them in mere seconds, but to her eyes, the world had slowed to a painful crawl.

Seedy Man turned, lifting his head to reveal dark slits of eyes and a wide, flat nose beneath the brim of his big hat. She saw his lips twist into a cold smile, saw the gun in his hand point directly at her, and she shrieked again. Ripping the backpack from her shoulders, she swung, leaning her whole body into the force of the strike. The heavy camera found its mark with a sickening thud, and the seedy little man crumpled limply to his knees.

"He's got a gun!" she screamed, swinging again. The man groaned as his face hit the dirt.

The stranger appeared at her side in an instant, kicking the gun from Seedy Man's lifeless hand; bending to feel for a pulse at his thick, stubbled neck; rifling efficiently through his pockets. Cool and calm, as if he'd done that sort of thing before. Lexie stared down at him, incredulous. This guy was no pervert, she thought in a flash of comprehension. He was a cop!

"I wondered when this lowlife was going to show up again," he muttered, miraculously producing a pair of handcuffs from somewhere behind his back. He hobbled the unconscious man, wrist to ankle, then straightened abruptly, touching Lexie's arm as if he'd known her forever. "Are you all right?" he asked gently.

Was she all right? He wanted to know if she was all right? Folding her arms around the old backpack, Lexie held tight to keep her hands from shaking. Another of her cardinal rules— *never* let them know what you're thinking.

"Who are you?" she demanded, certain he could hear the terrible pounding of her heart. "And why've you been following me? And . . . and who's he? And why was he following you? And . . ." She gulped a deep breath and backed slowly away. "Did . . . did I . . . kill him?"

The pervert/cop laughed—a low, chuckling, familiar sort of

laugh that made Lexie very uncomfortable. "Don't worry," he said calmly. "He's not dead. Yet."

She felt her eyes widen as he stepped closer. The pervert/ cop was sliding his hand under the waistband of his sweatpants. Did he have a gun, too?

Lexie sidestepped, moving just beyond his reach, and readying the trusty old Nikon for another assault. "Stop! Or . . . or I'll kill you, too."

He edged even closer, his brown eyes twinkling with amusement.

"Give me one good reason why I shouldn't," she snarled. At least, she tried to snarl, tried her best to sound dangerous— the crazed camera guerrilla. But fright, and a major adrenaline rush, had reduced her voice to a mousy, insignificant little squeak.

Her eyes widened again as his hand reappeared. He was holding a badge.

"Ward," he announced, instantly poker-faced. "FBI."

Was it the real thing, or a dime-store fake? Lexie took another giant step away from him. "I want to see some real ID. Right now. Or . . . or I'm going to start screaming!"

He shrugged, eyeing her quizzically. The seemingly endless stash in his pants yielded photo ID, and he stepped closer, holding the officially signed and sealed document under his chin. His lips curled into an annoying little smirk. "Satisfied?"

Reilly Ward, it said, in large, black, official-looking script. *Federal Bureau of Investigation.* Lexie studied it carefully. It looked like the genuine article, although she'd often wondered how an ordinary citizen was supposed to judge the validity of such things.

"Well . . . I guess. But you've got some major explaining to do, Federal Agent Reilly Ward. Or is it Ward Reilly? Did you know you've got two last names, there?"

His eyebrows lurched upward. "Let's get out of here," he muttered, taking a firm grip on her arm to drag her back along the path.

"Hey! Let go of me!" Lexie dug in her heels. "I'm not going anywhere with you. And anyway, what about him?"

Slowly regaining his senses, the seedy little man moaned loudly, as if on cue.

"Leave him. I'll clean up your mess later." Ward scanned the trees anxiously. "We've got to move. *Now!*"

"Not until I get some answers. Why've you been following me?"

"Following you? I haven't been following you. I've been following that dirt bag you clobbered—nice shot, by the way."

"Oh, well, you're very welcome, I'm sure. I guess I did save your life, didn't I? But from where I stood, he was the one doing the following. Not too good at your job, are you, Ward Reilly? Not too good at lying, either. I've seen you twice before, at Shutterbugs, and at the gym on Broome Street."

Slinging the backpack over her shoulder again, she planted both hands firmly on her hips and stared him down. "You have been following me, and I want to know why."

"Okay, okay," he said with a groan, glancing over his shoulder as if he half expected another ambush. "I'll tell you all about it, I promise. But first, we need to get out of here." Ward gripped her arm tightly once again. "That guy has a partner," he said, through clenched teeth. *"Now, move!"*

The prospect of facing down another armed assassin set Lexie's feet in motion and she quickly took the lead, pulling Reilly Ward along with her. It was worse than running with Rufus, she thought, suddenly very thankful that she'd left the big dog at home. Who knew she'd wind up dragging her pervert/agent instead?

"Sit," he gasped, stopping short at a bench on the Plaza. He walked a small circle around Lexie, carefully surveying the crowds of sun-starved New Yorkers streaming into the park to enjoy the day.

She chuckled sympathetically. *"You* sit. Before you fall over. I'll just stand, if it's all the same to you. I need to stretch, or I'll seize up." She snickered again as he collapsed onto the bench with a miserable little grunt. "You might want to try it sometime, Ward Reilly. Works wonders."

Bracing her foot against the top rung of the bench back, Lexie leaned into a long, easy stretch, all the while keeping a close watch on Agent Reilly Ward. He seemed just a little too interested in the slim, lightly tanned leg extended gracefully beside him. "Y'know, Ward Reilly," she murmured, briefly catching his eye, "I had you figured for a pervert . . . now I'm sure. Wipe that look off your face, mister, and mind your own business."

He smiled, looking up to meet the challenging gaze of her intensely violet eyes. That freshly scrubbed face of hers glowed with the warmth of recent exercise. Little wisps of jet-black hair had escaped from her neatly tied ponytail, and now played around her forehead in the gentle breeze. Nimbly switching sides, she eased into another willowy stretch. About five-four, he guessed, and a good part of that taken up with those amazingly supple legs. Interesting lady, this Alexandra Frost. Too bad. He squared his shoulders, remembering the promise he'd made to himself. Mixing business with pleasure was a good way to get somebody killed. And that wasn't part of the plan.

"It's Ward," he said, trying his best to sound matter-of-fact as those violet eyes flashed again. "Reilly Ward. And the look on my face is abject misery, Miss Frost. Pure and simple. What possible pleasure can you find in running up hills at high speed for hours on end?"

"Ward? Reilly Ward? Hmmm. Just like Bond. James Bond." *Oops!* Obviously, Agent Ward had heard that one before. He looked none too pleased. Time to change the subject. "It's good for the soul—running, I mean. Not to mention good for the body. Kind of a natural high."

He looked skeptical. Lexie rounded the bench and sat down beside him, one leg curled beneath her. "All right, Ward, you're safe. Nobody'd be stupid enough to try something with all these witnesses around. So?" She stared fixedly into his surprisingly gentle brown eyes. "What's going on?"

The man was suddenly all business. "Like I said, Miss Frost, you're mistaken. That little weasel's been hanging around your shop, and the gym, for weeks. You must have seen him before." He sighed when Lexie shook her head. "Well, we've had him under surveillance. You don't want to know why."

"Oh yes I do. I want to know everything."

"Well, I'd love to stay and chat," he said, struggling to his feet, "but that creep needs a baby-sitter. You're not in any danger; don't worry. Everything's okay now."

"Hey! You can't—"

"Go to work, Miss Frost." He glanced back over his shoulder wearing a terribly charming, lopsided grin. "You're late, aren't you? I'll be in touch, never fear." Adroitly weaving through the crowds, Federal Agent Reilly Ward tossed a quick wave in her direction before vanishing into the trees.

"Ex-cuuuuse me?" Tommy Angell drummed loudly on the counter, harrumphing indignantly. "You haven't heard a single word I've said, have you, Lexie Frost?"

"Sorry, Angell." Pushing all thoughts of the mysterious Agent Ward far to the back of her mind, she smiled her very sweetest smile. No sense in offending the only man in the city who might actually have the genius to repair the damage Seedy Man's head had wrought on her beloved Nikon. "Did you? Er . . . say something?"

"Indeed I did!" Tommy fondled the old camera with loving hands. "What have you done this time? Look at this! Cameras are delicate instruments, y'know. And this one's practically an antique. You really should be more careful. What did you do, drop it or something?"

Grinning, she leaned across the counter to tousle his tawny, fine-as-corn-silk hair. "Believe me, you don't want to know. So? Can you fix it or not?"

Tommy pursed his lips into a tight frown, sending waves of worry lines rippling up his forehead. "What about that big assignment of yours tomorrow? Can I trust you with the Hasselblad?" His voice held a definite challenge, but he didn't give Lexie a chance to reply. "I mean, you may well be the fabulous talent everyone says you are—Mr. B's new wunderkind—but I'm responsible for his equipment, y'know? Shutterbugs can't afford your careless ways. *CityArt* magazine or not, Lexie Frost, you'd better watch your step."

Gathering the old camera's bits and pieces into the tail of his shirt, Tommy disappeared into the back room, shuffling his feet and muttering woefully under his breath. ". . . criminal the way she treats a sensitive instrument . . . ought to be a law, if you ask me. How could anybody let this happen . . . ?"

"You wouldn't believe it, Angell," she murmured, with a fond smile at his retreating back. Tommy was all bluster and no bite when it came to her, and she knew it. Lexie curled her fingers around the roll of film tucked deep in the pocket of her blue Shutterbugs lab coat. She wasn't even sure she believed it herself, but she had her proof, right there in her hand. Federal Agent Reilly Ward, captured for posterity in glorious, living color.

What on earth had she been thinking, letting Ward walk away from her like that? He knew her name. He even knew she was late for work. She should've stayed with him . . . should've insisted on a proper explanation. And what about Seedy Man? What if she'd really hurt him? She should've gone back . . . should've made sure he was okay. *Should have.* Too late now to think about what should have been, but Reilly Ward owed her—big time.

"You can run," she said, stalking across the shop to stare out the window, "but you can't hide. I'm gonna find you. And when I do, mister, you've got some explaining to do." She snickered at the memory of his abysmal performance in the park. "I take it back, Ward. You can't run, either."

Chapter Two

" "Aunt Lila?!" Lexie took the long flight of stairs two steps at a stride. The unmistakable fragrance of Chanel lingered in the air and that could only mean one thing—Lila was back in town.

Lexie's loft apartment in the Frost Building was home base whenever the great lady breezed through Manhattan, and it had been much too long since her last visit. Momentarily forgetting Reilly Ward, and the incriminating roll of film shoved deep in her pocket, she burst through the door with a broad smile. "Lila! Welcome home!"

Clothes flew up in the air, erupting in a multicolored volcano from Lila Frost-Heslop's enormous suitcase. The only word that might possibly come close to describing the woman's endless wardrobe was "loud." No muted color would dare to enter the room when Lila was around—why, there'd even been documented cases of color-induced nausea in fainthearted individuals.

"Lexie! That blasted beast has got to go! The great slobbering brute has stolen my brand-new scarf right out of my bag—and it's Italian silk! Hand-painted!" Lila's heavily ringed fingers clutched at her throat in an Oscar-winning gesture. "I feel quite ill, just thinking about that beautiful object masticated in the jaws of that . . . that canine behemoth of yours."

She sat dramatically, her flowing emerald-green and lilac tunic and palazzo pants billowing around her tall, angular form. Her thinning, silvery hair was held in place, as always, by a vibrantly colored headband, in this case, bright purple. The scowl on her usually smiling face was almost comical to behold.

Lexie groaned as she watched Rufus slink effortlessly under

her bed. For a dog so large, so ungainly, he seemed to have no trouble at all sliding into the smallest, most difficult-to-reach places. This was bound to be a battle of wills between her and the "canine behemoth," an Airedale/wolfhound cross who really did fit Aunt Lila's description.

"Rufus," she said sternly, "you come here right now."

No response. Only the sound of her aunt's muttered outrage, which would certainly go on endlessly if Lexie didn't remedy the situation.

She dropped to the floor, commando-style, crawling rapidly toward, and then under, the bed. "Rufus! Gimme that!" Her voice was muffled somewhat by the blankets hanging over her face, but her intent was perfectly clear. Even Rufus would have to pay attention, she thought.

"Grrrrrrrrrrrrr," was the only sound for the next several seconds, and it didn't come from Lexie.

Perched anxiously on the edge of the couch, Aunt Lila fluttered a multicolored silk fan in front of her face. "Lexie? Dear? Have you got my scarf yet? It's Italian silk, I don't know if I mentioned that. And what is that positively dreadful noise?"

"Got it!" Lexie emerged victorious, scrambling out from beneath the bed holding a small object in her hand. She paused to check her frontal view, and frowned to find herself liberally covered with dog hair and dust. "I really ought to clean under there more often," she muttered, thrusting the tiny, dark object in the general direction of her loudly dressed relative. It was pretty much impossible to identify just what that object might be.

Aunt Lila stopped fanning herself for a moment. She leaned forward on the couch, wafting an almost visible cloud of Chanel over Lexie, who quietly choked on the fumes. Aunt Lila smiled at her niece in a somewhat puzzled fashion. Leaning forward a little further, she squinted, then raised her eyebrows, causing the purple headband to do an impromptu rumba on her forehead.

"Lexie, dear," she said, after a moment, "whatever is that tiny thing you're holding? Is it something I really need to see?"

"Aw, come on, Lila, are you going to tell me that you don't recognize this slightly damp article as your new Italian silk scarf?'' She chuckled at the expression of revolted disbelief on Lila's face.

''Canine behemoth,'' she grumbled, setting the fan in motion once again, and shooting a dark glance toward Rufus, still in retreat under the bed. His tail thumped a gentle apology.

''Lila, really! Look, I'll just straighten it out for you.'' Lexie made a face as she pulled at the sodden silk, untangling it as best she could. ''Oh . . . well . . . okay, so it's not as good as new. But I'll hand wash it for you and you'll never know the difference.'' She chuckled. ''I'm sorry about Rufus, but that's just the way he is. He only takes your things because he adores you, y'know.''

''Hmph. I'd just as soon he detested me, if it's all the same to you, dear. And, Lexie, why don't you just keep the scarf? I don't think I'd ever be able to feel comfortable wearing it again, knowing that it's been gnawed by that revolting creature.''

Lexie blew out an exasperated breath. ''Anything for you, Lila. Not that I believe, for one second, that your scarf is irreparably damaged.'' She thought for a moment, musing over the scarf situation, before a wicked grin took shape on her face. ''Hey! Got any other stuff that might look good on me? I'll just give it to Rufus and then you won't need it anymore.''

Lila laughed, a tasteful, tinkling-bell laugh that was strangely at odds with her wild taste in clothing. ''Oh, Lexie, you'll be the death of me.'' She wiped her eyes with a tiny lace handkerchief. ''You do have to admit that your dog is an awful lot more trouble than he's worth. Jack has such good taste in everything else. I can't imagine how he came to saddle you with such a monstrous eating machine.'' She shook her head in a woebegone gesture and fanned herself again, watching as Lexie walked to the kitchen, or at least, to the area that served as the kitchen. The loft was one big open space, wonderfully light and airy, divided into ''rooms'' by the clever arrangement of furniture—by a long, comfortable-to-lean-on counter running the full length of the kitchen, and by several colorfully painted Oriental screens. Only the darkroom and bathroom facilities were properly walled off—or properly private—as far as Lila was concerned. But the place made her only niece happy, and that made it worth putting up with a little inconvenience.

Lexie sighed. "Now, Lila," she said, running tepid water into the sink to wash the scarf, "you know how Jack Gillespie—the original 'Mr. Cautious'—feels about a 'girl' living on her own." She paused for a second, reflecting on the many foibles of her ex-fiancé. Jack was a successful stockbroker, three-piece suits all the way. And even though he was a perfectly lovely man, he was a hopelessly chronic worrier, and he could never come to grips with the fact that Lexie traveled everywhere and anywhere with her camera. She should have listened to her friend René, amateur astrologer extraordinaire, who had always maintained that what Lexie needed was a good Taurus man. Not that she really believed in all that stuff but, well, you just never knew. And Mr. Jack Gillespie was a Pisces, and certainly *not* the right man for Alexandra Frost. The fact that she was a professional photographer—and a darned good one—seemed an irrelevant detail to him. He just worried endlessly, as if she were totally incapable of looking out for herself. One Christmas, he'd arranged a series of self-defense lessons for her. She'd even gone to a few of the classes, just to humor him. The next year, he'd presented her with Rufus. A perfectly adorable, and completely useless, puppy. "For protection, once he grows up." She'd been too softhearted to give the puppy back, and even though he was still completely useless, she'd grown very fond of old Rufus. Well, most of the time, anyway.

"There! Good as new." Lexie congratulated herself as she fluffed Lila's scarf onto the counter to dry. Pulling a bottle of spring water from the fridge, she turned to find her aunt heaving a long-suffering sigh. Rufus had hauled himself out from underneath the bed and was sitting beside Lila, leaning heavily against her colorful palazzo pants, and gazing adoringly up into her face.

Lexie sputtered mirthfully on a mouthful of water. Rufus's devotion to Aunt Lila was really quite touching—to everyone except the object of his affection. She found him to be nothing more than an enormous pain in the posterior.

"Come on, big guy, leave your favorite aunt alone." Lexie

grabbed Rufus by the collar, pulling him to a spot on the carpet with enough open area to accommodate his bulk. "Now, stay put. I'll take you out for your walk in a while, I promise." He lay down grudgingly, and eyed Lexie with obvious annoyance, beginning a slow crawl back to Lila's side as soon as her back was turned.

"Really, dear, I do wish you wouldn't refer to me as having any possible connection to that creature. Someone might think I have something to do with him." Lila shuddered at the thought.

Lexie flopped into a huge, overstuffed chair and dangled her long legs carelessly over the side, taking another sip from her bottle of Evian. "Not much chance of that. It's pretty easy to see how you feel about him. Poor boy. His feelings are probably hurt."

"What feelings? That animal has all the sensitivity of a sack of flour."

Lexie laughed. "Well, you might have something there. But you know I can't get rid of him. And, no, not just because Jack gave him to me! I mean, who else would put up with him? He refuses to walk with the leash, so I have to drag him for a walk. And he insists on eating absolutely everything in sight. But even so," she finished, half-defiantly, "I like him!" Lexie glanced affectionately in Rufus's direction. The big dog rolled over on his back, all four paws in the air, and thumped his tail on the floor.

Aunt Lila sighed, sinking back against the couch and gazing sorrowfully at Lexie. "Now, Lexie dear, you know I only want the best for you. I've always done my very best to look out for you, ever since . . . well, you know." She sighed. "I've often wondered if I've spent enough time with you over the years. And I've wondered if, maybe, that's the reason you're so ferocious about your independence."

Strange, thought Lexie, that even after all these years, the two of them practically bent over backward to avoid any mention of that awful day—the day that changed everything. They should probably talk about it. *Someday.* She forced a smile. "Oh, come on, Lila, I was a pain in the neck long before Mom and Dad died, and you know it. You're just ticked off because I wouldn't marry Jack Gillespie and settle down to some humdrum existence as Mrs. Stockbroker of the Year, or something.'' She laughed. ''Not in this lifetime!''

''Really, Lexie, you do have the most irreverent attitude toward everything. Most disconcerting. And get off my foot!'' This last remark was directed at Rufus, who'd been gradually inching closer and closer to his favorite person, as the conversation progressed.

''Oh, Lila, I know you're very fond of Jack, and so am I. But I have to tell you, he's not the man for me.'' Lexie paused thoughtfully, draining the last swig from her water bottle. ''Right now, I'm not sure I want any man in my life.''

Lila looked pained. ''It's just that I worry about you sometimes, dear.'' She reached to pat Lexie's hand. ''I'm afraid I can't help it. And Jack really cares for you, that much you have to admit.''

''I'll give you that. But he . . . Lila, I *love* what I do. That *Newsweek* cover last year may just have been a case of being in the right place at the right time but, hey, it got me noticed. People ask for *me* now.'' Lexie grinned. ''I'm doing a shoot for *CityArt* magazine tomorrow. Big time. I've been fighting for this kind of recognition for years. But my career doesn't fit with Jack's idea of the perfect wife. He still thinks I'm going to 'come to my senses,' but I just can't be who he wants me to be.'' To herself, she added, *No way, and never again.* She'd had her fill of men, always wanting things their way. From now on, her life would be her own. She had a few things to prove, and speaking of proof . . .

''That reminds me,'' she said, springing out of her chair to hurry across the room. ''I've got some film to develop and I really need to get it done today.'' Swinging open the darkroom door, she paused to add, ''Won't take me long, honest.''

Lila gasped, revolted by the pungent chemical odors emanating from the small room. ''Really, dear, however do you stand that smell?'' She held her Chanel-soaked handkerchief up to her face. ''I feel quite faint. And we haven't even had a proper chance to talk. I'm only here for the night, you know, off to London first thing tomorrow for the International Antiquarians' Convention.'' Her lips curled into a pout. ''I wanted to tell you all about my trip to Mexico, before I got sidetracked by that hairy baboon.'' She glared at Rufus, who thumped his tail adoringly.

''You can tell me all about it when I come out. Won't be too long, really, and then we can sit and have a good long talk—about anything other than Jack Gillespie.''

Lila stared at her niece, hesitating in the still-open doorway, obviously itching to get into her darkroom, and letting that dreadful smell waft around the entire apartment. Deciding to let Lexie off the hook, and save her own sinuses in the bargain, she sighed. It was the sigh of a much heavier and more robust woman. ''Very well, go ahead, I'll just sit out here with this revolting creature until you're done.''

Lexie grinned widely. ''Thanks, Lila, you're the greatest.''

''Yes, well . . .'' Lila realized she was talking to herself. The door to the darkroom was already shut fast, the red ''keep out'' light glowing its warning from the transom. ''Fine. Now I have some time to think.'' She glared at Rufus, who was doing absolutely nothing. ''You,'' she told him sternly, ''you stay put.''

With exaggerated care, Lila eased herself off the couch and moved across the room to her suitcase. Noiselessly lifting the lid, she rummaged through the inner pockets, and smiled with satisfaction as she withdrew a small lingerie bag. She clutched it tightly against her chest and shot another intimidating glare at Rufus, who was watching with great fascination.

Lila stopped for a second, cocking her head in the direction of the darkroom, listening for any hint that Lexie might emerge without warning. After a moment's delay, she crept slowly and carefully toward a small teak table, sitting alone on a worn, but still valuable, antique Indian rug. It was a table that Lexie would never think of moving, as it held a beautiful pink African violet with double blooms, and the plant seemed to thrive in that exact location. The table looked to have formed its own permanent dents in the rug.

Taking the utmost care, Lila moved the plant to the pine blanket box that served as a coffee table. Then she lifted the little table and moved it silently to one side, keeping an eye on the darkroom door at all times. Moving with astonishing rapidity, her clothing swirling colorfully around her, she knelt to roll back the rug, exposing the floorboards.

It only took her a few seconds to lift up a loose board, and pull out a small, suede bag from its hiding place beneath the floor. Then, it was only a matter of a few more seconds to take a brown cloth pouch from her lingerie bag, and to transfer it to the suede one. The entire operation took less than thirty seconds.

Glancing hastily toward the darkroom, Lila replaced the board, and rolled back the rug. Holding the lingerie bag tucked under her elbow, she quickly moved the little table back to its exact position on the worn carpet, then returned the African violet to the same spot it had occupied before her clandestine maneuver. Rufus thumped his tail and uttered an encouraging gurgle.

Lila snapped at him. "Quiet, you idiotic hound!" Rufus pulled himself up to a sitting position, the better to gaze upon the person he adored.

"Honestly, I'm talking to a dog." Lila shook her head distastefully as she moved rapidly back to her suitcase and shoved the lingerie bag inside. With an expression of great satisfaction, she closed the lid firmly, obviously well pleased with her endeavors.

She made her way back to the couch with the hint of a swagger in her step, sighing resignedly as Rufus edged close enough to rest his head on her open-toed shoes. Now there'd be dog slobber all over her Italian sandals. The thought made her shudder, but her mood was so bright that even Rufus, and all that was annoying about him—and that was absolutely everything—couldn't upset her. She chose one of Lexie's photographic magazines from the pile on the coffee table and began to leaf through it.

"All done. And I got some great shots. Really terrific." Nodding enthusiastically to emphasize her point, Lexie emerged from the darkroom with a loud slam of the door. Reilly Ward, it turned out, was extremely photogenic. "Wanna see?"

Lila, after jerking upright when Lexie came shooting through the door, pushed Rufus aside unceremoniously. "Blast this enormous beast, anyway!'' She examined her shoes for slobber marks. ''Thank you, Lexie, but no. I just know I'd pass right out from the noxious fumes in there. Are you sure you're not damaging your health, dealing with all those chemicals?''

Lexie grinned. ''Yep, I'm doing myself irreparable harm, Lila.'' She looked down at her shirt in mock horror. ''Oops! I must have forgotten to put on my radioactive protection suit before I went in this time. Oh, no!'' Clutching at her throat, she staggered toward the couch, collapsing over the end in a pretend faint. ''Save yourself,'' she gasped. ''Don't worry about me.''

The dramatic effect was marred a little by the fact that Rufus felt obliged to charge across the room and stick his large and hairy muzzle into Lexie's face. ''Yuck! Rufus! Can't you see I'm doing my death scene here?'' Lexie made spitting noises as she affectionately pushed the big dog away.

Lila was indulgent. ''Really, dear, there's no need for the melodrama. I'm simply stating that it *stinks* in there. Is that being too critical? Just say the word, and I'll never mention it again.'' She fanned herself vigorously, and scowled a warning at Rufus, who had turned his watchful gaze in her direction.

Lexie regarded the older woman from an upside-down pose on the end of the couch. ''Want some tea now, Lila? I, for one, am absolutely parched. Must be from breathing all that developing fluid.'' She got up and strode to the kitchen, winking at her aunt as she passed. ''Don't bother objecting. I know you've got to be having some sort of tea withdrawal by now. I think it's time for us to catch up on all your news. Why don't you dig out your snapshots while I get the tea stuff ready?'' She rattled comfortably around the kitchen, smiling over her shoulder at Lila, who was already rummaging in her purse for the photos.

''Well, if you insist, dear. I do happen to have one or two little pictures here.'' After a few seconds, she drew out three envelopes of photographs, twenty-four shots to the package.

Lexie laughed. ''I know you can't resist taking the odd photograph. And I do mean odd.''

By the time the tray was set on the coffee table and their tea poured, Lila had already begun to describe her trip to Mexico.

"You should have seen the colors, my dear. And you know, there's no one who appreciates color the way I do." She thrust a handful of photographs under Lexie's nose. "Just look at these fabrics I found at one of the markets. Aren't they incredible?"

Lexie took a long swallow of hot tea and surveyed the photos with interest. "You sure know how to find the 'local color,' Lila, in every sense of the word." She took the package of pictures from her aunt and scrutinized them closely. No one would call Lila a photographer, not with the best possible intentions. Still, she snapped so many pictures that some of them, by accident if not by design, actually showed some points of interest. The local markets, the children, the sunny beaches, the inside of Lila's hotel room—nothing escaped photographic mention. When you put the whole mess of pictures together, it was possible to get the feeling that the place had been properly visited. And that the visit had been a grand success.

"What's this, Lila? It looks as though you were in some kind of jewelry store or something. Must've been some great bargains to be had."

Lila pursed her lips, as if she had to give the matter some serious thought. Then, laughing, she could contain her news no longer. "You're absolutely right there, dear. Why, I found some positively gorgeous stones that are so perfect looking, you can't tell them from the real thing. Perfect for my jewelry designing, let me tell you."

Lila's passion was costume jewelry, and she designed her own line of fashion accessories, which did very nicely for her as a sideline. Not that she needed the money. She was wealthier than Lexie had ever been able to imagine, what with all the Frost family property, and her partnership in the antique business—not to mention the hefty inheritance from the estate of her late, beloved husband. Still, it gave a point to Lila's travels, and she truly loved making the jewelry and seeing people wear her creations.

Lexie smiled at her aunt's enthusiasm, settling herself back into the overstuffed couch, and curling her long legs up underneath her. "Tell me all about it, Lila."

"Well, I have some terrific ideas for the most spectacular earrings and necklaces. They'll sell like hotcakes, I just know it. Here. I took a few pictures of the local styles. I want to adapt them for the market here. It's going to be so much fun! Maybe," she continued, with a thoughtful half-smile, "maybe I'll see Julian about it, while I'm in London."

"Ah, the charming and talented Julian St. James. What a perfect excuse for a visit. But aren't you afraid Buddy might be jealous?" Lexie winked suggestively and laughed at the immediate blush that colored her aunt's face and spread quickly upward from her cheeks to the roots of her silvery hair.

"Really, Lexie!" Lila fanned herself and sputtered indignantly. "Julian is an old and dear friend. And you know perfectly well that Buddy is my business partner. I don't know why you insist on reading anything more into it."

"Well, that very attractive blush you're wearing might have something to do with it, Lila. But I wouldn't dream of making you uncomfortable, so if you don't want to confide in me . . .," Lexie winked again and studied her aunt's photos. "These Mexican necklaces really are very unusual. I'll bet your new designs will be all the rage."

Lila leaned toward her niece, unleashing a cloud of Chanel that pretty much ruined the cup of tea Lexie was drinking. "I think so, too. And you're going to get one of the prototypes, my dear. I've already drawn up my rough designs. Oh, I do hope you'll like them."

Lexie was touched, as much by the gesture as by the unspoken affection expressed. She wore very little jewelry, and when she did, only the simplest designs—a fact that always seemed to escape her aunt's notice. But she made it a point to wear all of Lila's gifts at least once. "You know something, Lila, I can't wait to see them." She placed her teacup on the tray and folded herself into the corner again.

"Now, what was that other thing you wanted to talk to me about?" she asked, feeling pretty sure she already knew the answer.

Lila smiled gently. "Now, Lexie, you know I'm just a doting old aunt. Not that I look like one, mind you. But you know that I am one. And I know that a young woman like you must have her eye on some handsome young man. It's only natural." She fixed a sharp look at Lexie, as though daring her to deny it.

Lexie laughed, not altogether comfortably. "Now, Lila, just because I'm not engaged anymore doesn't mean that I have to be out prowling the streets, looking for eligible bachelors. I mean, sometimes being involved with someone is more trouble than it's worth. And don't give me that look." She shook a playfully warning finger. "It's okay to be single. You're single."

Lila harrumphed impatiently. "My dear girl, I was married to Mr. Heslop for thirty-two wonderful years. I'd like to see the same for you."

"Well, Lila, I'm keeping my eyes open. But d'you know what? I haven't seen anything that makes me want to change my mind." *Except for Reilly Ward,* a little voice inside her said. Not that she was interested. Certainly not! But he was well worth taking a second, long hard look at, and maybe even a third. Lexie tried her best to appear indignant, but her aunt had known her all her life and wasn't so easily fooled.

"Ah, so there is someone. Good. Well, I won't pry. Just so long as you haven't decided to abandon all hope, I'm satisfied." Lila smiled a tiny secret smile. "Pass the tea, dear, I'm in dire need of another cup."

About to deny all, Lexie decided instead to leave well enough alone. Shaking her head, she reached for the teapot, and turned her attention back to Lila's pictures of Mexico.

Chapter Three

"   "Alex-ahh-ndra. Mmmmm. Alex-ahh-ndra." Bracing his hand against the wall above her head, the man leaned even closer. "Such a beautiful name, Alex-ahh-ndra."

His breath smelled of anisette, or licorice—cloyingly sweet—and something about the way Vincent Urbano rolled his tongue around her name left Lexie feeling doubly anxious to finish the photo shoot and make her escape. She ducked quickly out of reach.

"Just a couple more shots should do it, Vincent. Let's go out front. I'd like to get one at the entrance. It'd make a good opener for the piece, don't you think? The Urbano Experience at MOPA."

Just keep talking, she told herself. *Keep moving. Keep the man busy.* She dove through the door and out onto the busy sidewalk, waving Urbano into position while keeping him safely at arm's length.

An elegantly simple glass block pillar stood curbside, enticing visitors with a taste of current exhibits or promises of things to come at the Museum of Popular Art. Exactly how the posters and objets d'art found their way inside the apparently seamless obelisk defied explanation, and it had become somewhat of an attraction in itself. "Perfect!" Lexie exclaimed, as Urbano slithered his arms around the column of glass. *Experience Urbano's New York,* screamed the puce-green neon poster displayed within.

"Oh, it's you!" purred Lexie, urging him to ever more outrageous poses, and capturing frame after frame of his black-clad figure as she circled him on the sidewalk. Coiled as if ready to strike, Urbano flicked his tongue across pencil-thin lips.

"That's it, Vincent, thanks." Lexie settled the sleek black Hasselblad into its case. "I'll let you get back to your work."

"Alex-ahh-ndra! You leave me so soon?" Urbano arranged his face into a definitive pout. "A drink, perhaps? Or dinner? No?"

"Sorry, Vincent." Pasting on her best imitation of a smile, she lied through her teeth. "I'm due at another shoot."

"Then afterward, Alex," he coaxed, stepping closer. "You could come to my studio, see my exquisite new project. It's—"

"I'm afraid my fiancé wouldn't approve." *That is, if I still had such a thing,* she added to herself, imagining what Jack's reaction would have been. Once upon a time, the devil in her might have accepted, just to drive the poor man crazy.

"Fiancé?" Urbano pretended a moment's disappointment, then smiled. "Well, if you're sure . . ."

Drawing a deep breath, she said firmly, "I'm late. Listen, good luck with your show. I think you'll be pleased with the *CityArt* spread."

"Remember me, Alex," he called, as she hurried away. "We *will* meet again."

Lexie darted across the street, nimbly dodging rush-hour traffic. She wasn't likely to forget, unfortunately. Urbano's New York was a dark and terrible place. An entire wall in the great hall, taken up by something he called "Riverside," had looked and smelled like something dredged up from the depths of the Hudson. In another room, he'd mounted the entire outer wall of an old subway car, complete with gang graffiti and the squealing sound effects of a speeding express train.

She had to admit, however grudgingly, that the man did have a certain, well, "talent." He'd almost managed to make her believe, for just a moment, that she was standing on the platform at South Ferry.

The absolute worst of the lot, as far as Lexie was concerned, was the piece Urbano called his "Memory Room." She hadn't even made it past the door before the smell of . . . well, she wasn't exactly certain what the smell was, but she was absolutely positive that she didn't want to find out.

"But Alex," Urbano had whined, imploring her to "expe-

rience'' the piece. "This is life! This is real!" He'd scuttled
along after her as she ran from the room. "Truth in art, Alexandra. That's what I'm all about!"

She shuddered. Vincent Urbano's "art" was bound to look
even worse in the dull, red light of the darkroom. Maybe she
could figure out a way to develop the film with her eyes closed.
Gulping a deep breath of the cool afternoon air, she glanced
quickly over her shoulder. Urbano had turned his back, and
disappeared through MOPA's big glass doors as she watched.
She heaved a sigh of relief to be rid of him, at last. But the
chill that prickled slowly up her spine as she rounded the corner
had nothing to do with Vincent Urbano. Was someone else
watching?

Lexie ducked into a doorway. Pretending to admire the glorious display of orchids in the little shop's front window, she
carefully scanned the street. Federal Agent Reilly Ward had
been conspicuously absent since his hasty departure in Central
Park yesterday morning. Was he telling the truth? she wondered. Was he really following Seedy Man all along? Did that
mean Seedy Man was following her? She could see no sign of
either of them on the busy street, but that meant nothing. They
didn't want to be seen.

A kernel of fear began to niggle at the back of her mind.
They could be anywhere, watching, waiting for the right moment to . . . to what? Impatient, she shook the feeling off, striding bravely back onto the sidewalk. But she couldn't shake the
memory of what Ward had said in the park. *"That guy has a
partner."* She could almost hear his voice again, flinty with
tension. *"Now move!"* And she could see the concern on his
face. Lexie walked a little faster. *Just another few blocks,* she
told herself, clutching the camera bag tight to her side. Another
few blocks, and she'd be safe at home.

The walk south through SoHo could almost always lift her
spirits, no matter how badly things had been going up till then.
But today, she barely noticed the wonderful old cast-iron buildings on Greene Street. She paid no heed to the crowds of people
who shared the sidewalk—yuppie Wall Streeters heading north
for happy hour, a lively group of buskers crooning an a cappella

doo-wop, the fearless bicycle courier with spiked orange hair and an attitude to match—even the sight of Lila's curlicued neon sign in the front window of the Frost Building didn't bring the customary smile to her lips. Poor Jack had been scandalized the first time he'd seen it. "It . . . it's so . . . garish," he'd said with a groan and a roll of his eyes. Of course, his reaction had only served to further endear the elaborate marquis to Lexie's heart. *Mystiques by Frost.* It glowed a brilliant crimson in the darkened window of the store as she hurried past. *Buddy must've closed up shop early today,* she thought, feeling even more alone and vulnerable. She checked her watch. Five-thirty. *Of course,* she thought with a sigh, *he'd have gone home hours ago.*

Buddy always closed early midweek, making up for it on Saturdays and Sundays by staying open as long as the customers kept coming. It was a choice location, he'd told her repeatedly. Just close enough to Broadway and Grand to draw crowds from the SoHo Antiques Fair every weekend. And nobody worked a crowd like Buddy Fine. He'd been Lila's partner and front man in the antique business for as long as Lexie could remember. And more recently, she suspected, Lila's secret beau, as well. He could always be counted on for a friendly smile and some good, fatherly advice. Ah well, no comforting cup of tea with good old Buddy today.

Trudging forlornly up the steps, Lexie wondered, for just a moment, if Jack might have been right to worry about how isolated she was, all alone in the big, deserted building every night. What would she do if . . . ?

Knock it off! Jack Gillespie was a *major* wuss. And if she didn't watch it, she'd wind up in the same boat. Might as well have married the man after all. She chuckled. Mrs. Jack Gillespie. Lunch at the club, anyone? Ho-hum. Humdrum. No way!

She felt much brighter as she turned the key in the lock and braced for the inevitable, bone-wrenching thud as the rear end of Rufus met the back side of the door, full speed ahead.

Strange. No thud.

Lexie eased the door open a crack. "Rufus?" she whispered,

stepping cautiously inside. Late-afternoon sun streamed through
the skylight, bathing the loft in a warm, orange glow. Nothing
seemed amiss, but it was eerily quiet and something felt, well,
just not quite right. And no wonder. It was the first time in
their three years together that Rufus had failed to greet her,
slobbering and wagging, at the door. She imagined Jack's nagging voice in her ear. *"It's not safe there, Lexie. Nobody would
hear you if you called for help."*

With a shiver of apprehension, Lexie carefully eased the
camera bag off her shoulder and onto the floor, scanning the
room for something she could use as a weapon. The baseball
bat. She snatched it from its resting place in Lila's old ele-
phant's foot umbrella stand. In the next instant, the faint clink
of glass on glass froze her in her tracks. She held her breath,
turning slowly back to face the darkroom door. "Ruf—" Her
throat tightened, cutting off the word mid-whisper. She couldn't
have left it open this morning . . . could she? A moment's panic
at the thought of the big dog on the loose in there, happily
gnawing his way through strip after strip of irreplaceable neg-
atives and slobbering all over the print paper, was quickly dis-
missed. She pictured his great, hairy face, lips curled back over
his teeth in a canine grimace, all because she'd once tried to
pat him with developing fluid on her hands. He'd never go in
there. He hated the smell almost as much as Lila did. And it
couldn't be Lila, either, because she'd left for London hours
ago. Then what . . . ?

A wash of red light spilled across the floor, escaping through
the finger-sized crack around the slightly ajar door. There really
was somebody in there! And he'd turned on the light!

Her sharp intake of breath seemed to echo in the empty apartment. She was being ridiculous, letting her imagination run
wild. She'd probably left that light on herself, by mistake.
There couldn't be anyone in there. The loft door had been
locked, and the street door, too. It was a mouse, she decided.
Just a tiny, helpless little mouse looking for crumbs.

Not quite able to accept her own explanation of the faint, but
growing, disturbance beyond the darkroom door, Lexie curled

her fingers tightly around the bat, lifting it menacingly over her head.

A mouse, she thought again, aching to believe it. Rufus had probably seen it. He'd seen it run across the room, and now he was cowering under the bed like the big, brave, guard dog he really was.

She gulped a deep breath. Reilly Ward and his seedy little man had her spooked, that was all. And Urbano's twisted version of life in the city hadn't helped one bit. "Rufus," she hissed again, still holding her voice to the merest of whispers. "C'mere, you big baby, it's just a mouse."

A shadow loomed ominously behind the door, flickering briefly across the thin red line of light, then retreating. That was one *big* mouse. Lexie felt her hands turn to ice and her mouth grow cottony-dry. Picturing Seedy Man's gun aimed squarely between her eyes, her first thought was to run, to escape before it was too late. But she'd have to cross in front of the darkroom, where he'd be certain to see her—if he hadn't already. Either that, or hightail it to the far end of the loft and risk the clatter, bump, and grind of the rickety old freight elevator, assuming it was working at all this week.

The phone! She could call for help, dial 911. Frantic, she scanned the room. The darn phone was never where it should be. There! On the bed . . . but so far away. She tried to swallow the enormous lump that had formed in her throat. The loft seemed terribly large all of a sudden, and her usually nimble feet had turned to stone.

Lexie's flesh prickled with fear as the shadow moved again and the darkroom door swung slowly open. "Rufus! Help me!" Striking out blindly with the baseball bat, she dove for the exit—too late! Powerful hands caught her wrists, almost wrenching her off her feet. "Rufus!" she screamed again. *"Rufus!"*

In desperation, Lexie angled her hip toward the intruder, neatly sweeping the unsuspecting man right off his feet. But he still held fast to her wrists. Landing hard on top of him, she pressed the bat against his windpipe, trying her best to keep him pinned to the floor. "Rufus! *Kill!*"

"Ow," groaned a vaguely familiar voice. "That hurts."

Lexie's hair had tumbled across her face in the scuffle. She shook her head, clearing the tangle of black curls from her eyes. "Ward?"

Deftly twisting the bat from her hands, Reilly Ward looked up at her and grinned. "None other."

"You! How . . . ? You broke in!" Lexie drove her fists into his chest. "How dare you frighten me like that!"

Nonchalantly folding both hands behind his neck, Ward mumbled something that might have been an apology, then smiled again. "I, um . . . I guess you're wondering what I'm doing here?"

"You'd be right about that." Lexie scrambled to her feet. "What the heck do you think you're doing?" she demanded, skirting around his still-prone body to get to her darkroom. "You didn't touch anything in there, did you?"

Ward rolled lazily onto his elbow. "I 'touched' just about everything, Miss Frost. That's what a search is all about, y'know? Didn't damage anything, though. Honest." He pushed to his feet.

"Where is he?" Lexie felt herself tremble as she spoke. Not that she was frightened. Certainly not. It was just the flood of adrenaline coursing through her veins. But she tucked her hands out of sight anyway, impatiently folding her arms across her chest. No sense giving him the wrong idea.

"Where's who?" He cast a questioning glance over his shoulder. "I'm alone, Miss Frost, er, that is, working solo."

"What have you done to Rufus?"

"Now just a darned minute!" He took a couple of steps back, putting a little space between them. Violet eyes flashing, Miss Frost looked ready to do bodily harm to someone, and after her thoroughly impressive display of self-defense a moment ago, he didn't doubt that she could do exactly that. "I didn't 'do' anything to anybody. Who the heck is Rufus?"

Bright flashes of red marked her cheeks as she pushed angrily past him. "Rufus?" she called, gently clapping her hands. "C'mere, big guy. It's okay."

The answer, a hesitant thump-thump-thump, sounded from the far corner of the loft.

"Rufus is . . . he's . . . well, he's my . . . my bodyguard," she mumbled, as the big dog crawled out from under the bed. "Must've gone to the same training school as you, Agent Reilly Ward. Seems I'm always coming to the rescue of one or the other of you." Lexie flopped wearily onto the couch. "C'mere, you useless bag of bones. Did the big, bad agent scare you?"

Rufus slunk sheepishly across the room, giving wide berth to the big, bad agent. With a halfhearted wag of his tail, he leaned heavily against Lexie's leg and licked her hand in greeting.

If dogs could feel embarrassed, thought Reilly, he'd have to say this one was completely humiliated. Rufus glared at him, slowly curling back his lips in what pretended to be a ferocious growl. Hmmm. Big teeth.

Lexie's whoop of laughter broke the tension. "Oh, *now* you decide to defend me!" She grinned, throwing her arms around the dog's neck and tussling his ears affectionately. "Time to put your best foot forward, big guy. Rufus, meet Federal Agent Reilly Ward. He says he's one of the good guys. Agent Ward, meet Rufus—keeper of the loft, defender of helpless women."

"Hey there, Rufus."

The dog eyed him suspiciously, dropping to the floor at Lexie's feet with a disgruntled "woof."

"Okay, Ward," said Lexie, the smile quickly fading from her lips. "Exactly what are you doing here? And by the way, where's your warrant?"

Reilly made himself comfortable at the far end of the couch. A warrant. One of those irksome little details that always seemed to slip his mind—unintentionally, of course. He studied the young woman. How much should he tell her? How much to keep her safe?

Perched on the very edge of her seat, she watched him expectantly. Waiting for her explanation. Daring him to make another mistake. He stifled a smile. She was doing her best to seem calm and in control. But she wasn't. Far from it. The bloom of red, high on her cheeks, and the trembling of her hand as she twisted her long, dark hair into a knot around one finger, betrayed her. That, and the fact that her heart was racing out of control. He could see its frantic rhythm echoed in the faint motion of the simple silver pendant she wore around her neck. It fluttered like a wounded bird against the soft cotton fabric of her white shirt. He sighed. The truth wasn't likely to put her mind at ease—even if he could make her believe it.

"Well?" she demanded, her impatience growing more obvious by the second.

"You'll have to give me a minute to recover, I'm afraid." Plunking both feet onto the coffee table, he folded his arms across his chest. "After all, Miss Frost, you did try to decapitate me with that baseball bat of yours. Huh. Guess I should consider myself lucky. Could've been the killer camera." He chuckled, rubbing the back of his head, as if imagining how it might feel to be hit by a Nikon. "Your other 'victim' is going to be just fine, by the way. Now, how about a cup of coffee, y'know, to settle my nerves?"

Lexie rose slowly to her feet. Only moments ago, in the depths of a dark and dreadful terror, she'd truly believed that her life was about to come to an abrupt and gruesome end; that Seedy Man or one of his equally heinous partners would leap from the red light of the darkroom, gun in hand, to do good-ness-knows-what, while she screamed and screamed and screamed . . . and no one would hear.

The incredible relief of discovering Reilly Ward behind that door instead, must have temporarily addled her brains. What was he doing, snooping around in her personal space? What possible interest could the FBI have in a struggling, next-to-unknown photographer and an out-of-the-way loft in TriBeCa? She backed slowly away.

"Miss Frost?" He lurched upright, planting his feet on the floor with a thud.

This was a very different Reilly Ward, she thought, inching closer to the bed. Another second and she'd have the phone in her hand. Another second and the police would be rushing to her rescue. They'd be very interested in *this* Reilly Ward. This was not the panting, red-faced bumbler she'd met in the park.

Neatly dressed in well-worn jeans and a button-down shirt, this Ward seemed thoroughly competent. And thoroughly unflappable. He stood, watching thoughtfully as she edged away. The intensity of his gaze made her skin crawl. She felt exposed, as if the man knew exactly what she was thinking.

He crossed the room in an instant, catching her hand in his as she bent to retrieve the phone. Jerking her knee sharply upward, she feigned a defensive attack.

"Hey!" Ward instinctively blocked what could have been a painful blow, and Lexie seized the opportunity to skip out of reach, quickly engaging the phone.

"Don't!"

"What're you afraid of, Ward? I'm calling the police. If you're really who you claim to be, it shouldn't be a problem. If not . . . well, I'm sure the NYPD will be very interested to know that there's an armed intruder at large in the Frost Building. I assume you're armed?" The phone's high-pitched tones broke the uncomfortable silence that followed. Nine—one—

Reilly covered the distance between them in a single bound, pinning Lexie against the counter and wresting the phone from her hand. His voice was icily cold. "Don't do that. This is Bureau business. You'll get your answers, Miss Frost. As soon as I get my coffee." He smiled again in an obvious attempt to diffuse the tension between them. "Do you think that might be sometime tonight?"

"Make your own darned coffee," she snapped, plopping herself onto the couch. "You seem to know your way around the place."

She tried to ignore the comfortably domestic sounds that emanated from the little kitchen as Agent Ward set about making their coffee. He'd probably gone through the whole apartment, drawer by drawer, before she surprised him in the darkroom, because he certainly didn't seem to be having any trouble finding things.

"I like your work, Miss Frost," he said at last. "Particularly the shots of that good-looking guy by the Pond in Central Park."

"Huh. Maybe you'd like some prints for your wallet." Lexie

allowed herself a sly smile. She only wished she could have seen his face when he found them. Of all the words she could think of to describe the photographic record of Reilly Ward's debacle in the park, ''humiliating'' was the one that kept coming to mind.

Reilly was ignoring her. ''Those shots of the street musicians are first-rate,'' he continued, pleasantly. ''Are you a jazz buff?''

Lexie fumed. She could hear him rummaging through the cupboards, finding mugs and sugar and spoons. He appeared at her side with a tray, setting it carefully on the couch and then bustling away to the kitchen again. She gave it a quick, sideways glance. Lila would have been impressed. Neatly folded napkins, sugar with two spoons, cream in a little glass carafe—even a plate of cookies graced the black lacquered tray. And his coffee, still bubbling away behind her, smelled absolutely wonderful.

Reilly leaned on the kitchen counter, patiently waiting for the last drops of water to filter through the coffee grounds, and admiring the thick mane of raven hair that tumbled, in mad disarray, around Alexandra Frost's lovely shoulders. She remained stubbornly silent, despite his best attempts at friendly conversation. He sighed. She looked so small—almost fragile—curled into the corner of that enormous couch. It wasn't going to be easy to keep this case impersonal. He was already beginning to feel something for the feisty little lady with her independent attitude and sarcastic wit, not to mention those incredibly expressive eyes of hers. But, he reminded himself, he knew all too well what could happen when things got personal. Tempting or not, there was no room in his life for a woman like Alexandra Frost—no room in hers for someone like him. She didn't need that kind of trouble.

The coffeepot gurgled noisily, as if to remind him of why he was there. He surveyed the room once more. It was doubtful that anyone else had searched the place—yet. Those hired thugs didn't strike him as careful types. They'd have made a real mess. And apparently nothing was out of place. Miss Frost would have been sure to give him an earful about that. No, everything was just as it should be, he thought. Homey. Warm and inviting.

The entire west wall, all eighty or more feet of it, was windowed. And those windows abounded with plants of all descriptions. Plants with lush, green foliage, unlike the withered, sorry-looking specimen that graced his windowsill at home in Washington. Not that it was much of a home. Just a boring, bachelor apartment with boring, rented furniture and a spectacular view of open Dumpsters in the alley below.

Nothing boring about Miss Frost's place, though. Her big, overstuffed sofa and chairs looked, and felt, relaxed and well used. Richly patterned oriental rugs were scattered here and there over a worn, wood plank floor that glowed with the warm patina of aged wax.

She'd painted the walls in a delicate shade of café-au-lait, trimmed with white. Antique Tiffany lamps, of every imaginable shape and color, hung from the high, stamped-metal ceiling. A well-organized galley kitchen stretched half the length of the east wall, framed by a long, oak counter. Its top was cluttered with magazines, unopened mail, and an odd assortment of knickknacks—everything from a miniature grass-skirted Hawaiian doll, to a cobalt-blue butterfly mounted under glass. Everything except the elusive items he'd hoped to find. Nevertheless, he'd examined it all—woven baskets full of seashells, a boomerang, an ostrich egg painted with scenes of the African plains, a smiling jade Buddha, and candles. More candles than he'd ever seen in one place at one time. Enough to burn the Frost Building to the ground, he'd wager, if she ever lit them all at once.

At the far end of the room, a big brass bed, piled high with pillows and brightly patterned quilts, was partially hidden from view by a trio of Chinese screens. A hodgepodge of antique dressers, bureaus, and tables lined the walls, their tops covered with plants, or books, or framed photos of family and friends. On the far wall, an elegant grandfather clock stood guard at the ornately gated entrance to an old freight elevator. He had jimmied the gate, thoroughly inspected the shaft, and, from there, the antique store and showrooms below. He shook his head. If there was anything here, it had been very well hidden.

The coffeepot sputtered its last—a little reminder that it was time to face the music. Reilly filled two mugs, delivering them to the couch without spilling a drop. "Sugar, Miss Frost? Or cream?"

"I can take care of myself, Agent Ward." She glared at him over the rim of her mug. "All right. You've got your coffee. Now, where's my explanation?"

The man acted as if he hadn't heard a single word she'd said. Gingerly sipping his coffee, he smiled and leaned back on the couch, heaving a very contented sigh. "Mmmm, good. Special blend?"

Lexie sputtered into her mug. What was it with this guy? He'd got himself caught in the act, but now . . . She gulped another mouthful of his perfectly brewed coffee. How could he sit there and be so . . . so darned pleasant. Darned annoying. Not to mention darned good-looking.

The coppery flecks in his chestnut-brown hair glinted almost irresistibly in the soft light of the setting sun. Lexie actually had to fight the temptation to reach across and brush it away from his eyes. And that boyishly lopsided grin of his seemed to be having the most unusual effect on her. She wanted to see it again.

"Okay," she said, taking a deep breath and forcing her face into something approaching a pleasant expression. "Time's up. Tell me what's going on."

Reilly straightened his shoulders. "You've been very patient," he said quietly. "And I certainly don't blame you for being upset."

Lexie bit down sharply on her lip. Patient? Upset? She wanted to grab him by his neat, blue, button-down collar, and shake an explanation out of him. Carefully adjusting her pleasant smile, she met his gaze with an air of calm forbearance. *Spit it out,* she thought, quickly approaching the end of her rope.

He studied her seriously for a moment, as if deciding, right then and there, exactly what he should tell her. He seemed about to speak.

Rufus, who'd been napping contentedly with his chin on Lexie's foot, chose that moment to lurch upright. Cocking his head toward the door, the big dog began a low, rumbling growl as the hackles on the back of his neck spiked to attention. Then, as if shot from a cannon, he launched himself at the door, barking a menacing challenge.

Reilly was suddenly all business. "Expecting anyone?"

Lexie shook her head. "No."

"Get down!" he ordered, pulling a gun from a holster at his ankle. "And be quiet!"

She hit the floor, covering her head with her hands and squeezing her eyes shut. With all that had happened in the last two days, obeying the guy with the gun seemed a prudent response.

Easing one eye open, Lexie watched as he crossed the room in two swift, silent strides. Rufus lunged angrily at the door, teeth bared.

"Shut up!" hissed a very annoyed male voice, from somewhere beyond the door. "It's me. It's Jack. Rufus! *Be quiet!*"

Lexie recognized Jack Gillespie's irritated tone a split second too late. Reilly had already thrown open the door, catching the unsuspecting man on his way up the stairs. "Freeze!" he bellowed, taking careful aim with the gun.

"Ward! No!" Lexie scrambled to her feet. "It's okay!" she yelled, running to the door. "Don't! Don't shoot! I know him. It's okay. Jack?" She paused in the doorway to stare down at her ex-fiancé. Jack Gillespie's face was the color of cold oatmeal. Staring down the barrel of a loaded gun had stopped him, mid-stride and openmouthed, on the third step from the top. His lips had completely disappeared.

"Jack?" Lexie ran to his rescue. "It's okay, Jack. We . . . we thought you were someone else. Come on in." Gently taking his arm, she led him into the loft, past Reilly Ward and the still-snarling Rufus, and eased him onto a chair.

"He . . . he's got . . . he's got a . . . a gun." Jack's voice trembled. Tiny beads of perspiration prickled across his lip as he glanced uneasily from Lexie, to Rufus, to the armed and deadly stranger who now calmly strode across the room, folded himself comfortably onto the couch, and picked up a cup of coffee.

Lexie gave Jack's arm a reassuring pat. "I'd like you to meet Reilly Ward," she said, flashing a warning glance in Reilly's direction and trusting he'd be discreet. "Ward, this is Jack Gillespie. He's my . . . a friend."

Retreating to her corner of the couch, she curled her legs beneath her and studied the two men as they tried to size each other up. It was painfully obvious that they didn't think much of each other. Jack was easy to read. The contemptuous expression taking shape on his face said, in no uncertain terms, that his narrow little mind was already made up about Reilly Ward.

Rufus growled again, drawing a threatening glance from Jack. "Knock it off!" snapped Jack. The big dog fell instantly silent when Reilly's finger touched his nose.

"Sorry about the, er, misunderstanding, Jack. Hope you won't hold it against me," said Reilly, extending his hand. "How about a cup of coffee? It's fresh, and very good, if I do say so myself."

"No! Uh, that is . . . I don't think, er . . . no. No coffee. Thanks." The color was quickly returning to Jack's cheeks. He did not shake hands.

Reilly sank back onto the couch with a whispered endearment for Rufus. The big dog dropped to the floor at his feet with a satisfied grunt.

Lexie hid behind her coffee mug, choking back a laugh. Apparently Rufus had made a new friend. *Smart dog. Choose backup with a gun.*

"So, er, Ward is it?" Jack eyed the other man suspiciously. "How long have you known Lexie? Where did you meet? What kind of work do you do?"

"Jack!" Lexie scowled. "You sound like somebody's nervous father."

"That's all right." Reilly smiled agreeably. "I don't mind, really. We met in the park. Jogging. I've had my eye on the lovely lady for quite a while, though.'' He chuckled, winking slyly at Lexie. ''What else did you—oh yes, my work. Nothing very exciting, I'm afraid. Just a boring government job. How about you, Jack?''

Lexie interrupted. ''Jack's a stockbroker, Ward. Very successful, too. We've known each other for ages.'' She caught Jack's eye and grimly shook her head. ''You really should call first, Jack, before you drop by. I thought we'd had that talk before.''

Jack settled himself in the chair and crossed his legs, as if he planned to stay for a very long time. ''I was in the neighborhood, Lexie. Believe me, if I'd known the sort of greeting you had prepared, I'd have kept right on going.'' He turned an accusatory frown on Reilly. ''Who the heck did you think I was, anyway?''

''Didn't know, Jack,'' Reilly smiled mysteriously. ''But in my line of work, you learn to ask questions later.'' He adjusted his gun in its holster, gave the dog an affectionate pat, and stood. ''I've got to be going, I'm afraid.''

Rufus sprang instantly to attention, gazing hopefully up at his new friend.

Reilly chuckled. ''I'll just take the old boy out for his constitutional before I leave—save you the bother later.''

The big dog bounded across the room, staring back at him from the door, tail wagging, feet dancing, tongue lolling out of his mouth in an expression of almost puppylike delirium.

Lexie scowled. What a revolting display. ''Please, don't bother.'' She managed a halfhearted smile as she crossed the room, catching Reilly's sleeve before he turned away.

''Oh, no bother. I don't mind at all, really.'' He patted Lexie's hand. ''You two old friends must have a lot of catching up to do. We'll just leave you to your visit.'' Grabbing the leash from the end of the kitchen counter, he hustled Rufus out the door, as if they'd done it a hundred times before.

Lexie stared after them, almost forgetting, for a moment, that Jack was still in the room.

''Well,'' he snapped, an abrupt reminder that she wasn't alone, ''he seems to feel quite at home.''

"Don't start with me, Jack."

"Don't start with you?" He sprang to the edge of his seat. "Don't start with you? Oh, no, no, no. Don't *you* start with me. I want an explanation—right now!" He waggled a long finger at Lexie as she turned slowly to face him. "This is a new one, even for you. Your boyfriend shoved that . . . that weapon of his right in my face. What's going on?"

"He probably thought you were breaking in, Jack. I guess you should've called first."

Jack glared at her. She could almost see the steam beginning to shoot out of his ears. "Did you really pick him up in the park?"

"That's right, Jack. I 'picked him up.' I went out looking for a guy with a gun, and I came back with Reilly Ward." She planted both hands firmly on her hips and glared right back at him. "Last week, I found a really great guy in the subway— he had some nice red wine in a brown bag. And before that—"

"Knock it off, Lexie." He looked pained. "You know how I feel about you. And I . . . I can't help worrying—"

"Don't. I'm fine. We're not together anymore, Jack. And we're not going to be." She drew a deep breath at the sight of his wounded expression. "I'm sorry, Jack," she said quietly. "You need to find somebody else to love. Somebody who likes being pampered and worried about. Somebody who can make you happy. You deserve to be happy, Jack. We both do."

"But, Lexie. I only—"

"Er, excuse me." Reilly poked his head through the door. "Don't let me interrupt. Just returning the 'keeper of the loft.' In you go, Rufus old buddy." He took a couple of paces into the room, just far enough to toss the leash back onto the end of the counter. "Nice meeting you, Jack." Turning briefly toward Lexie, he gave a knowing wink. "Good night. Be seeing you."

"Wait! Don't go! We haven't—"

"Sorry," he interrupted. "I've got things to do."

"But, Ward—"

She glanced sideways. Jack was staring at her, the most disgusted expression clouding his face. What must this look like to him? Little love-struck Lexie chasing after the new boy-friend? Squaring her shoulders, she followed the very slippery Agent Ward to the door.

"Thanks for the coffee," he said, smiling that endearingly crooked little smile once more. "We'll have to do it again."

"Soon!" hissed Lexie, leaning out the door to claim the last word. "You're not off the hook, mister—I've got your number."

"You sure have, honey." He chuckled under his breath. "You sure have."

He circled the building twice, on foot, checking and rechecking every door and every window. Satisfied, at last, that the place was secure, Reilly pulled his rented car into the alley and slid low behind the wheel.

It was going to be another long night. He sighed, twisting the cap off his thermos to pour the first of many cups of strong, black coffee, and raising his hand in a silent toast to Alexandra Frost, safe in her loft behind those brightly lit windows. He chuckled, quite pleased to have slipped off the hook once again. She was spitting mad, though, and saddled with one heap of explaining to do to her ex.

Reilly reached under his seat, withdrawing a slim metal brief-case. He placed it carefully on the seat beside him and opened the lid. The case held an array of electronic equipment. He flipped a switch, activating the listening device he'd left behind in the loft apartment. Slipping on the headphones, he smiled again. Receiving loud and clear.

Jack Gillespie sounded livid. "Government job? The guy's a mobster, if you ask me."

"Which I didn't, Jack. My life is none of your business."

Reilly dropped the headphones onto the dashboard and thoughtfully sipped his coffee. He'd never been comfortable with this sort of eavesdropping and, even though it was for her own protection—even though there was no other way to be certain she was safe—the thought of one day having to confess this invasion to Alexandra Frost didn't sit well. She deserved a little privacy to deal with her past. He owed her that much, at least.

Lexie appeared at the window as he watched, angrily shaking her head. She paused for a moment, then stalked away, tossing up her hands in a gesture of complete exasperation.

Moments later Jack Gillespie's expensive car roared off down the street. Reilly smiled. ''Good riddance!'' Well, what the heck? Even the dog didn't like him.

Chapter Four

Rinnnnnnng! Lexie groaned and rolled over in the enormous old four-poster bed, tangling herself up in what seemed to be acres of fabric.

Rinnnnnnng! What *was* that noise? To her semiconscious brain, it sounded like a preset timer, loudly protesting that time was indeed up. Surely the darkroom timer wasn't dinging away at this ridiculous hour. She half sat up in bed, pulling grumpily at the covers. What ridiculous hour *was* it, anyway?

Rinnnnnng! Ah, the telephone. Suddenly, things began to make sense. She was sleeping. The phone was ringing. The time was . . . She squinted through the tangled mass of hair obscuring her view of the clock. The time was . . . 4:03 A.M.?

Rinnnnnnnnng! "All right, already. I'm awake," she muttered, fumbling for the receiver, finally knocking it off the table and under a pillow. This was way too much trouble, she decided, resting her head briefly on the pillow as she groped for the phone.

"Hello?"

"Lexie, is that you, dear?" There was an echoey sound along the phone line. Lila's voice sounded as though it came from the bottom of a well. "I'm in London, dear, and I know it's horribly early to call you. It's just after nine in the morning here, and I . . . well, I just *couldn't* wait any longer."

Lexie had a fleeting impression of her aunt stifling a sob. She sat up, hard, against the back of the bed, and gripped the receiver tightly, as if that would help her to get a grip on the situation.

"Never mind the time, Lila, I don't mind at all. Just tell me what's going on."

"Oh, Lexie, they detained me at Customs. Like a common

criminal! They went through all my luggage—*everything.* My makeup, my jewelry, my magnifying glasses, my scarves. Even my . . . my dainties. Well! I have never been so humiliated in all my life!''

Lexie let out a pent-up breath. What a relief. Only Lila's feelings were in danger—and that was something that she could remedy, simply by being a sympathetic listener. Plumping up a couple of pillows behind her, she settled down into a comfortable slouched position. ''Go on, Lila,'' she urged gently. ''Tell me all about it.''

Lila took a deep breath, audible even at a distance of three thousand miles, and began to speak, her voice becoming less strained with each sentence. ''Well, my dear, I just can't get myself settled down. I mean, they treated me so abruptly. And when I asked what they were looking for, they wouldn't even deign to answer. It's the most dreadful situation, it truly is.''

''Well . . . maybe there'd been a bomb threat or something. Maybe they were just being extra careful with everyone. You weren't the only one singled out, I'm sure.''

''That's where you're wrong—quite, quite wrong, Lexie.'' Lila's voice rose shrilly. ''They absolutely had me targeted as a guilty party. I was the only one on the flight who was detained. Imagine my embarrassment. *Me,* Lexie, who's been traveling my whole life, first class, and never stepped outside of the law—ever. Why, I even called the embassy but they said they couldn't do a thing for me.'' She gave an exhausted sigh. ''It's just too, *too* much to bear. I may have to take one of my pills.''

Lexie grinned. This last, melodramatic statement indicated very clearly that Lila was about to get over her ordeal. Her pills were the mildest tranquilizers available, and she'd been carrying them with her for about ten years. If they had any remaining therapeutic value at all, it had to be negligible. More than likely, their only virtue lay in Lila's fertile imagination.

They spoke for a few more minutes, discussing such details as the weather, the thickness of the hotel towels, and the quality of the food, then Lila rang off, seemingly mollified.

Lexie found herself wide awake, however, and vaguely unsettled by the call. Maybe it was just the fact that she'd been dragged from sleep at such an obscenely early hour, but something at the back of her mind insisted that it was much more than that. Something in Lila's story didn't seem quite right. She tumbled out of bed, leaving a trail of blankets in her wake. Rufus looked sleepily up at her as she stepped over him on her way to the bathroom. *You're getting up now?* his look seemed to imply. Giving an almost human shudder, he grunted and rolled over, falling instantly back into blissful, doggy sleep.

Standing in front of the bathroom mirror, she examined her reflection critically. Sleepy eyes, cranky expression, wild black hair straggling over her face and sticking out at rakish angles all over her head. "Yuck. Good thing I don't have to be anywhere soon."

Lexie sighed. Now was as good a time as any to develop those films for the *CityArt* piece. Probably best to revisit "Urbano's New York" on an empty stomach, she thought, and sighed again at the prospect. Still, clicking the darkroom door shut behind her, she had to smile. She was entering her own world, and she loved it there—no matter how unpleasant the subject of her photos might be. Within seconds, she was humming away to herself (slightly off-key, as usual), getting out the chemicals, readying the developing drum, lining up the trays and tongs, and wondering why on earth she didn't get up this early every morning.

Lost in her work, Lexie was completely unaware of the passage of time. She couldn't help remembering the days when she'd had to develop her film in a tray in the bathtub, kneeling on the cold tile floor. She'd had to tape heavy black paper over the window to block out the sun, and change the red light bulb every time she wanted to use the mirror to brush her hair. Not exactly the good old days, but still, she remembered them fondly.

Lila would gladly have paid for the renovations, would even have set her up with a shop of her own—an upscale competitor for Shutterbugs—but her career was something she'd always felt she had to do for herself. Now, the knowledge that she'd done it on her own made every accomplishment that much more rewarding. And right at the moment, everything was just as it should be. She scrutinized the slowly emerging pictures of Urbano's MOPA exhibit. The photographs looked great, despite the utterly revolting subject matter.

The phone began to ring again as Lexie developed the last of the photos. *Drat!* She'd left the darn thing out on the bed, and there was no way she could open the darkroom door until the prints were in the fixer. Drat! What if it was Lila calling back?

It occurred to her that it didn't really matter who was phoning at this ridiculously early hour—why, even if it were an editor from *Photo World,* calling to say they couldn't possibly send the next issue to press without a cover by Frost, he'd just have to wait. No, there was nothing in the world that could make her open the darkroom door until it was prudent to do so. There were valuable prints in the trays—delicate articles, still unprepared to see the light of day. Time was what they needed, and there was no way of speeding up the process. It was as simple as that.

Silence, at last. The phone had finally stopped pestering her to answer, and she examined the fruits of her labor—quite possibly, award-winning shots, if she did say so herself.

Her work completed, she snapped off the safelight and opened the darkroom door, groaning as her eyes met the bright sunlight that streamed through the loft's huge windows. "Ow! My eyes!" She grumbled loudly enough to disturb Rufus, who looked up at her in tired surprise. Lexie fixed him with a stern glare as she rushed to check the answering machine. "Knock it off, Rufe. You ought to be up, anyway."

No message. She sighed with relief. It couldn't have been Lila who called. If it had been, the entire tape would have been filled. Well, whoever had been rude enough to phone at such an early hour, could just plain—

A knock sounded at the door. A self-assured, confident knock. A knock that Lexie didn't even have time to answer. She stood, gaping with surprise and outrage, as Reilly Ward strolled into the room, holding aloft a cardboard tray with two large coffees and a bag of wonderfully fragrant, fresh-baked bagels.

"Special delivery breakfast," he announced, grinning widely. "I tried to call, honest, but you didn't answer. Thought I better get over here as soon as possible, just to make sure you were all right. And, while I was at it, I figured I might as well stop for a little nourishment." He deposited the tray on the coffee table with a flourish. "Hey, Rufus, old buddy, how's it going?"

To Lexie's great annoyance, the canine behemoth hauled himself to his feet and lumbered over to lean, heavily and deliriously, against his new best friend. Darned annoying. All the same, she couldn't help noticing that the man looked mighty appealing, dressed as he was in the same, but slightly more rumpled, blue button-down shirt and slim-fitting jeans he'd worn yesterday. Had he slept in his clothes? she wondered.

His tousled brown hair hung rakishly close to his eyebrows, and his warm eyes crinkled at the corners as he favored her with another of those heart-stopping, lopsided grins.

She scowled, resisting his all-too-obvious attempts to be charming. "Now, look here, Ward, you can't just come and go as you please. What the devil do you mean by waltzing into my building and my apartment as if you own the place? I really am going to phone the cops. Enough is enough." Reilly seemed completely unaffected by her tirade.

"Nice outfit," he commented. "Really, quite fetching."

Lexie looked down. The comfortable but threadbare red kimono, gray sweatpants, and pink fuzzy slippers were just right for the darkroom, but now she felt at a definite disadvantage. "Well . . . I wasn't expecting company. Especially not your company." Not the greatest comeback ever, but it was the best she could do, under the circumstances.

Reilly tore back the lid on one of the coffee cups and tried to imagine what her reaction would be if she knew he'd heard every single word of her conversation with Lila, not to mention her off-key caterwauling in the darkroom. And then, as her violet eyes flashed dangerously, he decided that he really didn't want to find out. He took a sip of his coffee and made a face. "Ah, good stuff."

Rufus was sniffing hopefully at the bag of bagels. "None for you, pal, you'll ruin your figure." Reilly said this to the dog but his gaze never strayed from the owner. Her figure was in no danger of being ruined, he thought. Not even that outrageous costume could disguise that fact.

"The police won't be necessary," he said calmly, ripping a chunk off a poppy-seed bagel and gesturing to her with it. "Here, you may as well sit down and have some free breakfast. I've brought your explanation, and I thought that might be reason enough for you to talk to me." He popped the bagel chunk into his mouth and chewed slowly, watching her as he made himself comfortable on the couch. It seemed that the combination of coffee and bagels, along with the possibility of having her curiosity satisfied, was more than Lexie could bear. Shrugging, she plunked herself down at the far end of the couch and reached for the other cup of coffee.

"Fine. Hand me a bagel and start talking. No guarantee I'll believe a word you say, but give it your best shot."

"Please, I only shoot when it's absolutely necessary. But, okay, here's what's happening." He paused to shove another chunk of bagel into his mouth, and chewed thoughtfully for a few seconds, fully aware that he was pressing his luck.

"First of all, why don't you tell me a little bit about your aunt's business? Kind of fill me in on this end so everything's nice and clear."

She glared at him. "My aunt's affairs are none of your business. And anyway, there's no way you're going to get one tiny bit of information out of me until I have your whole stupid story. *Everything.* So stop stalling."

Reilly sighed. The woman would not be sidetracked, no matter how hard he tried. "Okay. I *have* been following you." He held up a hand against her immediate protest. "Please, let me finish, since you were so insistent. Yes, I have been following you but it has, most definitely, been for your own protection. We've been concerned about your safety but we didn't want to alarm you, thus the cloak-and-dagger stuff." He paused, sipped his coffee, and struggled with his conscience. How much should he tell her? He wanted to spare her as much anxiety as he could, but at this point it was only fair to tell her what she wanted to know. He sipped again, and regarded her, regarding him. Neither one said anything for a few moments.

Lexie scowled. "Come on, Reilly Ward, don't play games with me. Protection? From what? Or from who? That Seedy Man I flattened with my camera in Central Park, while you were gasping for breath? You were the one needing protection, not me. You're going to have to do better than that."

"Okay, I'll admit that my actual entrance was less than impressive. We are supposed to keep a low profile, you know."

"Any lower and you'd have been underground."

"You really are scoring the points in this conversation, aren't you? Never mind, you have every reason to be upset. Just let me say that there's been some real interest in the comings and goings of your Aunt Lila for the past few months. And by a very unsavory element." He took a long sip of his rapidly cooling coffee, and looked directly at Lexie. "Due to the fact that your aunt owns this building, as well as the antique business downstairs, we're concerned that you may have become a target as well."

Lexie stopped, mid-chew, her expression a mixture of fear and disbelief that Reilly found deeply disturbing. "I . . . I don't understand," she said slowly. "I really don't understand what you're saying. Aunt Lila would never do anything illegal. She won't even park at a meter that still has time left on it."

"Calm down, now. We don't suspect your aunt of anything, Miss Frost, but just because she isn't deliberately doing anything wrong, doesn't mean that she's in no danger." He paused, wounded again by the look of horror on her face. "We have Mrs. Heslop under constant surveillance. She's as safe as if she were here with you. Really. I wish I could tell you more, but right now that's just not possible. Don't worry," he finished, and made a little inward groan at the thought of how lame that had sounded. Apparently, she agreed.

"Don't worry?" Her eyebrows shot upward. "Don't worry? You tell me that my only living relative, the person who is dearest to me in the whole world, is in some terrible trouble that may be life-threatening, and all you can say to me is 'don't worry?' '' Her voice rose sharply as she spoke. "Look, Ward, I don't know anything more now than I did when you walked in here ten minutes ago. You promised me an explanation, mister, and you're not leaving here again until you give me one. A real one, that I can believe." Her eyes flashed almost visible sparks of anger.

Reilly nodded his agreement. This was much harder than he'd expected. Probably the fact that he could not take his eyes off her, and the fact that, for some strange reason, she affected him in a way that no other woman ever had—a way he was far from ready to accept—were interfering with his ability to be objective as he delivered the information that she was so anxious to hear. Maybe a touch of humor would ease the situation. *Worth a try,* he thought.

"Look, since you're so happy to rub in my great lack of jogging ability—and you are a jogging fiend, if you don't mind my saying so—anyway, why not just be relieved that I'm not the one who's assigned to guard your aunt? I mean, who would you rather have looking after your very favorite person—a true, perfectly trained professional—or me? Plain old Reilly Ward? The choice is obvious, I'd say."

"Look, Ward," she began, but he cut her off with a gesture.

"No, I've told you far too much already. You're just going to have to trust me, okay? Please?"

She studied him thoughtfully as she finished her coffee, leaving the rest of her bagel on the tray. "I guess," she said at last, "I don't have much choice, do I? But I do have things to do. Have to be at the shop by noon . . . have to drop off some proofs at *CityArt* and . . ." She hesitated, then looked him directly in the eye. "Tell me straight. Is Lila really all right? And . . . am I? I mean, is it safe for me to do what I normally do?"

Reilly was caught off guard by the realization of how vulnerable Alexandra Frost could be. For just an instant, he glimpsed the soft, warm human being behind all that snappy banter, and he knew she was really afraid. Like anyone else, she had a side that needed reassurance that everything would be all right. If he had his way, that's exactly how it would be.

He grinned crookedly. ''Your aunt's in good hands, Miss Frost. And of course you'll be safe. I'll be right behind you, all the way, annoying the heck out of you. You won't see me, of course, but you'll know I'm there.'' He stopped, smiling gently at the doubtful expression on her face. ''Y'know, I'm likely to get hungry, what with trailing the famous photographer around town all day. What d'you say we have dinner tonight?'' For Pete's sake! Why the heck had he said that?

''Isn't that going a bit above and beyond the call of duty? I mean, I wouldn't want you to have to log any overtime, or whatever it is you guys get when you work around the clock.''

''All part of the job. And if you're having any weird thoughts about it, this isn't a date or anything. It's just two people getting together for something to eat. Think of it as making my life easier. I'll be able to keep an eye on you after work. I will, however, insist on paying, seeing as it's in my job description.'' There. He'd covered his tracks, laid down a few ground rules, as much to ease his own conscience as to pacify Lexie. Not entirely successful on either count.

''Fine,'' she grumbled. ''I'll go. But I guess it'll be up to you to find me, when dinnertime rolls around. You're not always too good at that, are you?'' Privately, Lexie couldn't help thinking that ''plain old Reilly Ward'' had a lot more going for him than met the eye, and that he was probably underestimated much of the time. And he probably planned it that way. She was willing to bet that this man was every inch the ''true, perfectly trained professional.''

Of course, it didn't help matters that this same man was beginning to grow on her. In leaps and bounds. Not that she'd ever let him see that. Why, she still didn't even have a decent explanation of what he was doing in her life. Not that she wanted him out of her life.

''Touché.'' Reilly pushed himself off the couch. ''Enough socializing. I have work to do, too, so don't let me detain you. And you're welcome for breakfast, by the way. Don't even mention it.''

Lexie had been poised to make a friendly remark but changed her mind. In fact, she didn't have a chance to make any remark at all, as the disheveled Reilly Ward thumped Rufus affectionately on the side and disappeared out the door, before she could even take a breath.

"That man is, without a doubt, the most annoying human being on the face of the earth."

Rufus looked up at her questioningly.

"Oh, don't worry," she said, in a voice tinged with annoyance, "your new buddy's bound to be back. Just try to remember who feeds you and puts up with you, okay?"

Rufus rolled onto his side and grunted.

Chapter Five

"Well, you're right about that, mister. She's the best. Mr. B—he's the boss, y'know—he says we're lucky to have her. He says she'll put Shutterbugs on the map." Tommy Angell heaved a long-suffering sigh. "I have to admit, she does do some pretty incredible work. But don't you tell her I said so."

Lexie smothered a laugh. Tommy's high-pitched whine of a voice wasn't meant for keeping secrets. She'd heard most of his side of the conversation from her perch high atop the ladder in the far corner of the storeroom. Unfortunately, whoever he was talking to was apparently a very soft-spoken type. So much so that, if it hadn't been for that blasted new alarm on the front door, she might have assumed that Angell was talking on the phone. But no. The buzzer's nerve-shattering clatter had scared her half to death when his customer had entered the shop a few moments ago. She'd completely lost count on her inventory, and nearly sent a box of expensive digital light meters crashing to the floor in the process. She would never get used to it, and wrinkled her nose at the whole idea. Whatever happened to those nice, tinkly little bells they used to hang on shop doors? Better to welcome the customers with a friendly jingle than to frighten them all away. But Mr. B had insisted, saying he wanted "them" to know that "we" know that "they" are in the store. That was just after he'd had the mirrors and surveillance cameras installed, and that was just after three other stores on the block had been robbed or burglarized in the space of a few weeks. Lexie shook her head. She'd always figured that the cast-iron bars on the front windows and door were deterrent enough. They made the place a pretty forbidding target. And there hadn't been any trouble with thieves so far—touch wood.

Giving the doorjamb a superstitious pat, just in case, she peeked furtively around the corner. Tommy and his customer had their heads together at the far end of the counter.

She hadn't intended to eavesdrop, at least not at first. But her insatiable curiosity had got the best of her when Tommy had mentioned her name, and she'd hurried to the front, keeping discreetly out of sight behind the storeroom door. She still couldn't hear the customer's words, only a low rumble that told her the person was definitely not a woman. And now they'd moved so far away from the door that she couldn't even sneak a decent look at her prospective client. *Better watch it, Lexie,* she warned herself. If she leaned any farther out the door, she was likely to take a swan dive right into the display case. That'd make a good first impression. Carefully smoothing the wrinkled front of her lab coat, then running her fingers through her hair to give it a little fluff-up, she prepared herself to make a somewhat more dignified entrance.

"Oh, absolutely," Tommy declared, before she'd had time to make a move. "We can do that for you. Nooo problem." Lexie imagined him nodding enthusiastically, tumbling long wisps of blond hair into his eyes. "Ms. Frost would probably want to spend the whole afternoon at the estate. Y'know, getting the feel of the place before your guests arrive."

Estate? Whole afternoon? Her feet suddenly grew roots. That sounded suspiciously like another society wedding, or debutante ball. No wonder Tommy sounded so pleased with himself, she thought, groaning under her breath. He knew how much she hated those assignments. Oh, well. Like it or not, it was probably time she made an appearance. Arranging what she hoped was a professional smile on her face, she stepped quietly into the showroom.

No! An instant of pure fear washed over her like a wave. *It couldn't be.* Heart pounding, she made a hasty retreat, flattening herself against the wall in the storeroom. Trapped. Had he seen her?

She'd managed to catch only the briefest glimpse of the man who now held Tommy Angell's complete and undivided attention. But that glimpse had turned her legs to jelly and stolen her breath away. It was Seedy Man. Or his twin.

"Oh, no. No bother at all," said the unsuspecting Tommy. "I'm sure she'll have some questions, y'know, technical stuff. She's been in the back all afternoon. I'll just go get her."

As the unmistakable sound of Tommy's soft-shoe shuffle grew closer and closer to her hiding place behind the door, Lexie held her breath. He wouldn't let the man follow him into the back, would he?

"Feel free to browse. I'll be right back."

"Tommy," she whispered, "don't turn your back on him." In the next heartbeat, Lexie caught a fistful of Tommy's lab coat, somehow managing to lift the diminutive little man right off his feet as she yanked him through the door. Tommy uttered a thoroughly astonished squeak.

"Lexie! What the—"

"Shhhh!"

"Don't shush me! Let go!" He peered unhappily down the front of his shirt. "I had a chest hair this morning but—"

"Be quiet!" Dragging her still-protesting coworker into the closest darkroom, she locked the door behind them.

"Hey!" Flipping the light switch, Tommy squinted suspiciously at Lexie, then waggled a slender finger in her direction. "I've got a customer, y'know? And Mr. B'd have a fit if he knew we'd left the shop unattended."

"I wouldn't worry about Mr. B right now, Angell. That kind of trouble we can handle. But if your customer is who I think he is . . ."

"What're you talking about? He's okay. He wants to hire you. Said a former client recommended you very highly."

"What former client?"

"I . . . well, he . . . he didn't exactly say. But—"

"Did you get his name?" Lexie pressed her ear to the darkroom door.

"Uh, Smith, I think he said. I wasn't really paying too much attention. At least, not until he started talking about this big affair at his country estate, and . . . what the heck are you doing?"

"Shhhh. I can't hear."

"Can't hear what? For heaven's sake, Lexie Frost, either let me out of here, or tell me what's going on. Mr. Smith's out there waiting for—"

"Smith? He said his name is Smith? And you believed it? Really, Angell, didn't you find out anything about him? What about ID? A business card, maybe? Or don't you care who you're hiring me out to?"

"Hmmph! The man wants a photographer, Lexie, not an automatic weapon. It never even occurred to me to ask for ID. I mean, y'know, he's going to have to give us a credit card, or something, when we write the order. What are you—"

Suddenly quiet, Tommy folded his arms and leaned back against the sink, watching Lexie with an expression of earnest concern. "You're really scared of this guy, aren't you? Gosh, Lexie, I didn't think you were ever afraid. What'd he do to you?"

"I—" Lexie bit her tongue. There was no point whatsoever in dragging Tommy Angell into all of this. The less he knew, the better. "He didn't 'do' anything to me. Not really. It . . . it's just that I . . . I think he's been hanging around. Following me. I've seen him too often, lately. And I really don't want to talk to him, Angell."

"Well, why didn't you just say so?" Tommy sniffed indignantly. "I thought we were friends. I mean, I know we have our little differences of opinion but, y'know, I wouldn't dream of putting you in any danger, Lexie. You do know that, right?"

Lexie forced a smile and gave Tommy's arm an affectionate squeeze. "I know."

"I'll just go out there—"

"*No!* Angell, he's dangerous. I don't want—"

"Don't be silly." Tommy elbowed his way past her and unlatched the door. "He isn't the least bit interested in me, and you know it. I'll tell the man you're stuck in the darkroom with some film. Or, even better, I'll tell him you must've gone out the back way, that I couldn't find you." He smiled bravely. "Don't worry. I'll get rid of him for you."

He was out the door and into the shop in a flash, with Lexie close on his heels. There was just no way she could let little Tommy confront that seedy character on his own. She armed herself with a large feather duster on her way past the broom closet, just in case.

"Well! How d'you like that?" Tommy shuffled to an abrupt halt in front of her. "He's gone."

Lexie tore across the shop and out into the street. No sign of the seedy little man. No sign of agent/protector Reilly Ward, either. "Figures," she grumbled, scanning the street once more before trudging back into the shop. "Never a cop around when you want one. Not that *he'd* have done me any good." In truth, she dearly wished he'd been there, wrestling Seedy Man to the ground. Or, better yet, telling her that the whole, chilling encounter had been a figment of her overactive imagination.

"I checked the storeroom, Lex. All clear." Tommy gave her arm a reassuring pat. "Guess he thought better of it, eh? Probably saw you grab me by the throat and took off. Crazy woman! Run for your life!"

"That'll do, Mr. Angell. I was trying to save you from a fate worse than death. Sorry about the chest hair, though. Really."

Tommy harrumphed. "We won't be mentioning that again, Miss Frost. Years of hard work, and you rip it out by the roots. I should get danger pay." He shook his head woefully, and took the feather duster from Lexie's hand. "And you should go make yourself a cup of tea. You're white as a sheet." He studied her thoughtfully. "If you're really worried about the guy . . . well, d'you think we should call the cops?"

"And tell them what? That I think I might have seen someone I think I might have seen before? And that he gave me the creeps?" Straightening her shoulders, she did her best to ease Tommy's obvious concern. "Creepiness wasn't a crime the last time I checked, Angell. Thanks for backing me up, though. I appreciate it." Lexie smiled and drew a deep breath. "Better get back to the inventory, I guess. I'm almost finished."

"Why d'you do it, Lex?"

"Do what?"

"You know. The grunt jobs. The drudgery." Tommy rolled his eyes skyward and sent his fine hair into orbit with a quick shake of his head. "If I had your talent, I'd be . . . well, I wouldn't be here, that's for darn sure."

"Well, it might have a little something to do with all that spectacular equipment Mr. B lets me use, Angell. That, and a steady paycheck. Talent doesn't pay the bills, you know. And anyway, I'd miss you."

"Yeah, right!" Tommy chuckled, obviously quite pleased by the thought. "We'll see if you remember your Angell when you're rich and famous—oops! Speaking of rich . . . that friend of yours called again. You know, 'Mrs. Central Park West.' She got all hoity-toity and accused me of losing your messages." He sucked on his lower lip. "Guess I did sort of forget about it this time. But, really Lexie, I thought you two were such great friends. Why don't you just call her?"

"You make it sound so easy."

"Well, isn't it?"

She sighed. Tommy was right. It should be easy. But it wasn't. Not these days. "René and I were best friends all through high school and college. I love her dearly, Angell, but . . . she drives me crazy."

"How come?"

"Like you said, she's turned into 'Mrs. Central Park West.' Ever since she married Dr. Singer, she's been on this . . . this quest to get me married off, too. When I said no to Jack, she . . . well, she just never gives up. Always trying to fix me up with the perfect man. And now that she's pregnant . . ."

Tommy regarded her blankly.

"Never mind, Angell. I'll call her. Sooner or later. And I promise to make up a good excuse. I won't claim you didn't tell me she phoned. Okay?"

Zzzzaaaapppp!!!!

The two spun apprehensively to face the door as Mr. B's new buzzer squealed its warning. False alarm. A young couple strolled into the shop, frequent customers who captured Tommy's attention with a cheery wave. Lexie sighed again. *Snap out of it, Frost,* she warned herself, heading back to her inventory sheets. The ever-present, and almost sickening, feeling of helplessness and absolute vulnerability that Reilly

Ward's revelation had brought about was a whole new experience for her. And one she didn't quite know how to cope with. But she had no intention of letting it take over her life.

"Quitting time, Lexie." Tommy Angell poked his blond head around the corner and smiled. "Listen, d'you want me to walk you home? 'Cause I don't mind, y'know."

"Thanks, Angell, but I'll be just fine. There's no way I'm changing my life on account of some seedy little creep."

"Well . . ." Tommy pursed his lips in a dubious frown.

"Well, what?" Lexie hopped gracefully from the third rung of the ladder and tossed her clipboard onto the desk.

"It . . . it's just that . . . well, there's this other guy hanging around out on the sidewalk now, been there for the last hour or so. And I . . . I don't want you getting all worked up again."

"Another guy? Angell! Why didn't you tell me before?" Hastily shedding her blue lab coat, Lexie bolted from the room.

"So?" asked Tommy, following her to the front window. "Is he anybody?"

"Nobody special. Just my date for dinner."

"Oh. That explains it, then."

"Mmm?"

"Well, y'know, it explains why he's hanging around."

"Oh. Right." Lexie drew a deep breath and turned back to the window. Federal Agent Reilly Ward had given up his impatient, back-and-forth pacing in favor of a slightly more nonchalant pose. Leaning comfortably against the front fender of a badly dented gray sedan, he folded his arms across his chest and studied the sidewalk. At least, she thought he was studying the sidewalk. A pair of very dark, octagonal sunglasses concealed his eyes, making it impossible to tell exactly what he was studying. Was it his own feet, or was he standing there watching her watch him? She tried not to smile, just in case. Reilly Ward was definitely worth watching tonight, though. He'd traded in his rumpled, blue button-down shirt and scruffy jeans for a pair of sharply creased khaki pants and a softly textured, natural linen shirt, topped with a light tweed jacket. Most definitely worth watching.

Tommy Angell folded his lab coat into a precise rectangle and centered it on the counter beside the cash register, ready for another day. "Someday," he said, in a playfully teasing tone of voice, "I'm gonna find a woman who'll look at me that way."

Lexie took a giant step back from the window. "What way?"

"Oh, y'know . . . hungry."

"Hungry? Really, Angell! I hardly know the man."

"Uh-huh. Well, maybe so. Maybe so." He grinned mischievously. "Planning on changing all that, are you, Lex?"

"What? I—" Lexie glanced quickly over her shoulder and out the window. Reilly Ward hadn't moved a muscle. "I . . . I should go, I guess."

"Hmmm. No snappy comeback? No witty little insult?" Tommy shuffled across the floor, stopping front and center about six inches from the window to peer curiously out at the man on the street. "I don't think I've ever seen you speechless before, Lexie Frost. More than just a pretty face, is he?"

"Very funny, Angell." Lexie tugged impatiently on his sleeve. "Let's get out of here."

"Like that?" Tommy raised his eyebrows in mock surprise. "Might want to tuck in your shirt, Lex. And maybe run a comb through your hair. That is, unless you plan on scaring the poor man to death."

"Aw, darn." Lexie surveyed her pale reflection in the window, jamming the shirttails of her peach silk shirt into her jeans and gathering her unruly mop of hair into an almost presentable ponytail. "Pretty bad, huh?"

Tommy chuckled. "It'd take an awful lot to make you look bad, Lex. Ready?"

"As I'll ever be, I suppose."

Pausing only briefly, to key in Mr. B's top-secret alarm code, Tommy wrenched open the front door and waved Lexie through with an exaggerated flourish. "Too soon for introductions, I suppose?"

"Mmm-hmm. 'Bye, Angell."

She waited until Tommy had shuffled his way around the

corner before stepping out onto the sidewalk. Agent Ward was still studying his feet. Clearing her throat, Lexie strode briskly toward him. He didn't look up. She kept right on going, right past him and on up the street, finally stopping two doors to the north to stare back at him, hands on hips. He had to be kidding.

"Yoo-hoo," she called, waving both hands in the air. "I'm over here."

Reilly turned slowly to face her. Sliding the dark glasses down the length of his nose, he studied her over the rim with an inscrutably blank expression.

"Not very good at this, are you?" she asked, walking quickly back toward him. "What if I'd been one of those bad guys you're so worried about? You'd have let me get away without a second glance. Without a first glance, even."

"Oh, I dunno. You might be surprised at what I've seen this afternoon, Miss Frost." He grinned, easing the sunglasses off and gesturing briefly with them in her direction. "See these? Special Bureau issue—rearview mirrors, built in. You were never out of my sight. Wanna try them on?"

"Oh, yeah. Absolutely. May I play with your secret decoder ring, too?"

"Well . . . maybe after dinner." He opened the car door, motioning her in with a gallant wave of his hand. "You looked awfully . . . hungry, Miss Frost, standing there in the window a while ago. I'm starved, too. Where are you taking me?"

Stalking across the sidewalk, Lexie threw herself into the front seat of his car and slammed the door, hard. "Hungry?" Wasn't that exactly what Tommy had said? Lexie watched as he folded himself into the driver's seat and turned the key in the ignition. Could he have been listening, somehow? Did he read lips, maybe? Or—

Remembering what she'd been thinking, only moments before, about the watchable Agent Ward, Lexie tried to imagine herself with a "hungry" expression. She wasn't the least bit happy with what she saw.

Reilly leaned close, smiling that lovably crooked little grin of his. "You'll have to tell me where to go, I'm afraid. I haven't got a clue."

Lexie's whoop of laughter seemed to take him by surprise. "Did I say something funny?"

"Agent Ward, I'd be very happy to tell you where to go."

"Ahh . . . touché." A flicker of disappointment crossed his face before he spoke again. "Um . . . Miss Frost, why don't we start over?"

Start over? Lexie didn't know whether to be angry or charmed. The man was endlessly confusing. "I . . . I guess that might be a good idea, Agent Ward. Let's start over."

"You were never in any danger, Lexie." Reilly set his fork on the edge of his plate and met her gaze. "Never."

"How could you possibly know that? You were nowhere to be found. And believe me, Agent Ward, I looked."

"Really? I thought you just locked yourself into the darkroom, and stayed there. Smart move, that. Exactly what you should've done. Although . . ."

Lexie twirled a length of pasta around her fork and waited patiently as he chewed his way through another slice of garlic bread. He certainly seemed to be enjoying his dinner. And apparently he had no intention of finishing that last sentence.

"Although . . . what?"

"Hmmm? Oh! Well . . . it's just that old wood isn't much good against bullets. I doubt the darkroom door would've protected you and Tommy Angell, if Mr. Smith had turned out to be one of our bad guys."

"If?" Lexie nearly choked on her linguine. "*If* Mr. Smith had turned out to be a bad guy? You mean . . . he isn't?"

"Well, no. Other than really bad taste in suits, I'd have to say he's pretty much okay." He heaved a deep, sympathetic-sounding sigh. "We scared off a perfectly good, paying customer, I'm sorry to say."

"We? But . . . I . . . you . . ." Lexie stammered, almost painfully. Reilly Ward was laughing at her. Not outwardly, maybe, but he *was* laughing. She could see it in those brown eyes of his—the knowing twinkle, the adorable little crinkles at the corners. *Hey!* Didn't she have some kind of rule about eyes like those? About not letting them get to her? If she didn't, she told herself sternly, she definitely should have.

"You're really starting to annoy me, Ward," she muttered, avoiding his eyes altogether. "If Mr. Smith, or whatever his real name is, isn't a bad guy, how come he didn't stick around? And how come—Hey! You weren't there. How could you possibly know about Smith? Or Tommy Angell? Or . . . or that I . . . about the darkroom?"

A candle, flickering weakly from the bottom of a red glass bowl in the center of their table, cast eerie shadows across Reilly's suddenly serious face as he leaned toward her. "Well," he said, lowering his voice to a conspiratorial whisper, "it's my job to know things. That's just how it is in the spy biz. We're a highly trained lot, you know. At the Academy. Quantico. So, it stands to reason that you're just not going to see us. Unless we want to be seen, of course."

Lexie sputtered into her glass of Perrier. "Is that so? Well, I seem to remember a certain federal agent who had a whole lot of trouble keeping out of sight. Ward, I think his name was. Couldn't find a thing to hide behind in a whole park full of trees. Or was that just more of your 'spy biz'?"

"That particular incident was cruel and unusual punishment, Miss Frost." He scowled. "Whoever invented jogging ought to be, I dunno, drawn and quartered. At least."

Reilly leaned back in his chair. Despite all her efforts to the contrary, Lexie was beginning to look terribly confused. Confused, and tired, and, beneath all that gutsy banter, very frightened. And he felt genuinely sorry for her. In fact, he was beginning to feel a lot more than just sorry for the raven-haired beauty across the table.

"I *was* there, Lexie," he said quietly. "All day. Sometimes out on the street, sometimes in the lane behind the shop. I was there making certain you were safe. Your little foray into the darkroom with Tommy gave me a chance to get in and hustle the mysterious Mr. Smith away, before he could do any damage."

"Caught you!" snapped Lexie, with a satisfied grin.

"Huh?"

"Caught you in a lie, Agent Ward. You never came into the shop. We'd have heard you. The boss installed a new buzzer alarm, loud enough to wake the dead. And it didn't—" Lexie swallowed, hard. Not only hadn't the buzzer announced Reilly Ward's arrival, it hadn't announced Mr. Smith's departure, either.

"Didn't buzz Smith out, either. Is that what you're thinking?"

Lexie nodded. "I know, I know. More 'spy biz,' right?"

He shrugged. "I will admit that my first thought, when I saw Smith, was the same as yours. That he could've been twins with our guy in Central Park. But he checked out, Lexie. Mr. Smith is, in fact, Doctor Reuben Smith. Orthodontist. Big money, according to his lawyer, anyway. He's got a town house in Gramercy Park, and some fancy estate out near Sag Harbor. Unfortunately, though, Dr. Smith seems to have decided that he really doesn't need a photographer who's being watched by the FBI. Thinks it might put a damper on his party, I guess. Sorry."

"A dentist? Ward, I feel like such an idiot."

"Well, you shouldn't. For the next little while, at least, it's better to err on the side of caution. I wouldn't want anything to happen to you . . . er, that is, not on my watch, anyway." He smiled sheepishly. "Not on anybody's watch, Lexie."

There. He'd done it again. Federal Agent Reilly Ward had called her Lexie again. And those brown eyes of his were twinkling at her. And that lopsided little grin was tugging at her heartstrings. What was he up to? she wondered. Trying to move beyond the role of protector? Trying to gather up all the sparks that seemed to fly whenever the two of them got together, and kindle a full-blown fire? Darn if she didn't hope that was exactly what the man was trying to do.

She picked at the food on her plate, avoiding his meltingly brown eyes, avoiding temptation. *Just stick to business, Frost,* she told herself firmly. But the look on Reilly Ward's face as he studied her in the quickly fading candlelight was decidedly unbusinesslike. And it suddenly felt very warm in the little bistro—very, very warm.

"It's getting late."

His voice was all business and Lexie glanced quickly up at him, across nearly empty plates and a rumpled, red-and-white checkered tablecloth, surprised to find the winsome smile had faded from his lips. Agent Ward had apparently come to the same conclusion as she. Stick to business. He smiled politely and squared his shoulders, abruptly flagging down their waiter to demand the check.

"Er . . . unless you'd like some coffee first, or maybe a cappuccino?"

"Oh, no." Lexie smiled, first at Ward and then at the hovering waiter. "I'm fine. Just fine. Thanks."

"Would you like to come in?" Aw, why the heck had she said that? It sounded like a come-on, and not a very good one, either. "Just for a few minutes, I mean." No matter how it sounded, Lexie was suddenly very unwilling to be alone. "You, um, you could make us another pot of that great coffee of yours."

Reilly seemed totally preoccupied, as if he didn't hear a single thing she was saying. She cleared her throat. "That is, unless you have to be somewh—"

"Wait here." Pushing past her as she slipped her key into the lock, he stumbled into the loft just as Rufus's hairy behind met the inside of the door. The big dog hit the floor—a wriggling puddle of puppy-love at the feet of his new best friend. "Good boy." Reilly gave him an affectionate tickle on the chin. "Everything quiet on the home front, old buddy?"

"You've got to be kidding, Ward." Lexie gave the dog a sour look. Thought he could ignore her, did he? "That sissy? He's afraid of his own shadow. Jack should have thrown in a few years of guard dog training when he gave me the big oaf, I guess, 'cause it sure doesn't come naturally to him. If there had been anyone in here, I guarantee he'd have been cowering under the bed again. Right, Rufus?"

"Oh, I don't know." A single snap of Reilly's fingers brought Rufus to his feet, instantly on the alert. He flashed a satisfied grin in Lexie's direction. "We had a little man-to-man last night. Don't you worry. Old Rufus is on the job."

Lexie snickered. "Right. Old Rufus, on the job. Boy, do I feel safe." She watched as her two would-be protectors checked every square inch of the loft—over, under, behind— even in the closets. Rufus actually seemed to be paying attention, for the first time in his life, and she had to admit, Agent Ward did seem to have a way with the usually stubborn animal. They made a pretty good team.

"All clear, Lexie."

"Lexie" again. She smiled a little encouragement. "How about that coffee?"

"Mmmm, awfully tempting. But I'm afraid I still have a few things to take care of. Always on the job, you know." Reilly breathed a sigh of resignation. She was looking especially fragile tonight, as if she needed a good, long hug. And he knew, if he stayed, that's exactly what would happen. Who was he protecting now? he wondered. Lexie, or himself? "Maybe another time?"

"Sure. Good night, then."

Her voice had a nervous huskiness to it that tugged at his heart, and he sighed again. This was how it had to be. He forced a smile. "I don't blame you for being nervous. It's—"

"Who said I was nervous?"

"Listen, it's understandable. This whole situation is pretty unsettling." She looked about to protest again, shooting daggers at him with those violet eyes of hers. He interrupted. "Here. This is for you."

"What . . . what is this?" Lexie examined the black metal object he'd dropped into her hand. It looked a lot like a small flashlight.

"It's a beeper, Lexie. If you need me, just push that button. Try not to worry. I'll be close by."

"Beep if I need you? Great. Kind of like, 'I've fallen, and I can't get up,' isn't it, Ward?" She stared at the tiny device, finally letting her fingers close tightly around it, as if to keep him close.

Reilly gently touched her arm. Still joking around, all bluff and bluster. She probably didn't think he'd notice that little tremble in her hand. Or the way she was chewing her lip. She always did that when she was nervous. Reilly bit sharply on his own lip. Much more of this and he wouldn't be able to leave. "Everything's going to be fine," he whispered. "Lock up after me, okay?"

Chapter Six

When the phone jangled Lexie into consciousness, she was surprised to discover that she'd fallen asleep with her nose in her book. Too much linguine. "Go away," she muttered as ferociously as she could, and piled a couple of pillows over her head. No good. The ringing went on and on. It would drive her crazy long before the answering machine picked up.

Emerging from her pile of pillows, she groped for the phone and snapped, "Hello?"

"Lexie? Oh, I'm so glad you're home. I was beginning to think you weren't going to answer. I'm awfully sorry to bother you, dear. Truly I am. But I just *had* to have someone to talk to, and you're the only one I trust."

"Lila, what's wrong?"

"Oh, Lexie, my room was ransacked, everything strewn all over the place. And the police were here, and . . . and I acted like a hysterical old lady, and, oh, it's just all such a big mess. And now—and now, just when I had resigned myself to losing my beautiful jewels, the ones for my new designs, I . . . I . . . I . . ." Her voice quavered and seemed about to break into pieces.

"Lila? Now, come on, Lila, no one's going to think that you're a hysterical old lady. Who could be expected to stay calm if their room was wrecked? So? Tell me. What happened to the jewels?" Lexie gripped the phone tighter, twisted a strand of hair around her finger, anything to keep her hands from shaking. Something was terribly wrong. Her wonderful aunt was in danger, and nobody was there to look after her. Her stomach wrenched at the thought of Seedy Man, or some other equally repulsive and ruthless individual, getting hold of

Lila. With enormous self-control, she maintained a slim margin of calm in her voice.

"Come on, Lila," she coaxed. "Tell me exactly what's going on."

There was a faint sound on the other end of the line, and Lila sniffed a little before starting to speak.

"Oh, Lexie, I hope you, of all people, don't think I'm crazy."

"Of course not. You know I don't. Just tell me."

"All right, dear, all right. I . . . I had my bag of gemstones with me—you know, the Mexican ones. I brought them to show Julian. Well, I had hidden them in my usual perfect hiding place. Now don't scold me, I know I should keep them in the safe, but somehow I just never trust those big vaults. I'm sure the hotel people lose things in them." Lila seemed to be gathering strength as she spoke.

"I'm not going to tell you what to do, Lila. I just want to know what happened. Are you okay?"

"I'm quite fine, dear. It's just that . . . well, before the police arrived, I checked the room to see what was missing, and . . . and that's when I noticed that the bag was gone . . ."

"Did you tell the police?"

"Yes, of course I did, dear, although I do believe the officer in charge thought I was a dotty old windbag. Really quite insulting," she added, apparently trying to inject a little of her usual indignation into the remark.

Imagining the look on her aunt's face, Lexie attempted a chuckle. "I'm sure it was, Lila. Go on."

"Yes, dear. Well, Sylvia and I went out antiquing while the police were conducting their search. You remember my friend Sylvia, don't you dear? Of course you do. Well, we were gone for hours, and I was actually able to get my mind off the whole sordid business for a little while. I had tea with Syl and her husband afterward and . . . and then the concierge wanted to apologize . . . and, actually, I've only been back in my room for a few minutes." She paused, seeming hesitant to continue.

"What is it, Lila?"

"Well, you see, it's just that . . . I don't know how to say this without sounding foolish, but . . . the stones are back. The bag is right back in my usual hiding place and not a thing is missing. I know it sounds incredible, but I swear it's true.''

Lexie sat up straight. What kind of thief took a bag of gemstones, then put it right back? Were Reilly Ward's ''bad guys'' setting a trap for Lila, a defenseless old woman who had absolutely no idea what she'd somehow gotten herself involved in? She tried to sound calm. ''Of course it's true, there's not a shadow of a doubt as to that. Did you report it to the police?'' She already knew the answer.

''Certainly not! Those imbeciles already think I'm quite mad. I'm not about to give them any fuel for that fire, thank you very much.'' Lila's indignance, at least, seemed to be completely back in place.

''The concierge offered to give me another room, the Regency suite, as a matter of fact. I just may take him up on the offer. What do you think?''

A million worrisome thoughts ran through Lexie's mind. Lila was more than three thousand miles away. How could Lexie possibly make sure she'd be safe? ''I think a change of rooms is a very good idea, Lila. Or, better still, pack up and get out. I'm sure Sylvia would love to have you come and stay.'' She anticipated her aunt's response to that suggestion, too. Lila wouldn't think of it. The woman was really far too independent for her own good.

''Please, be careful, Lila.''

''Oh, my dear, don't worry. I only called for a bit of a pep talk, you know. Perhaps I'll talk it over with Julian tomorrow. He's always so sensible and down to earth. In any case, dear, I feel much better just knowing that you believe the whole remarkable story.''

Even before they'd finished their good-byes, Lexie was searching the tangle of blankets for the beeper that Reilly had left behind, ''just in case.'' This was definitely the time to use it. Where was the ''true, perfectly trained professional'' who was supposed to be guarding her aunt? This whole awful mess should never have happened.

Her hands shook as she hung up the phone. Where was the

beeper? It had to be somewhere in the bed, she thought, sending pillows and blankets flying off onto the floor. Then she remembered. She'd shoved it deep into her pocket, to keep it close. She fished it out, trembling so badly that the stupid thing leaped out of her hands and rolled under the bed. Lexie scrambled after it, frantically pressing the button again and again. *Where was he?*

Angry and afraid, she slumped onto the couch and discovered, to her surprise, that tears were streaming down her cheeks. She never cried. It was a rule. But right at the moment, she couldn't seem to help herself. What if something were to happen to Lila? The thought was just too horrible to contemplate. And what about the protection that had been promised—

As if on cue, the loft door burst open, and Reilly exploded into the room, gun drawn, his face hard with alarm. The angry thoughts that had been running through her mind just seconds before vanished at the sight of the him. He was scared, too, but not for himself. For her.

"Lexie, are you all right?" His voice was a low, professional growl, practiced and steady. An act. Did she know?

He had listened to her side of the phone call, hearing enough in the first few minutes to be sure that something had gone very wrong in London. His immediate response was a transatlantic phone call to his partner, Phil, Lila's protector. Firsthand knowledge would be the only way to allay Lexie's fears about her aunt's safety. But the sudden blast of noise from her emergency beeper had struck fear into his own heart. He hadn't been paying attention. Had someone broken in while he was talking to Phil? Was Lexie in real danger, or just overreacting to Lila's phone call?

He had leaped from the car, gun in hand. He had charged down the block and through the front door of her building, barely aware of the frightened expressions on the faces of the people he'd bowled over on his way. He had lunged up the stairs and into the loft, with only one thought on his mind— she had to be all right. He would never be able to live with himself if he let it happen again.

"Lexie?" he repeated, almost fiercely this time. *"Lexie!* Are you all right?"

"I—" She seemed unable to say more, making a helpless little gesture with her hands and shaking her head, as if speech had failed her.

In less than a second he was at her side, shoving the gun back into the holster that lay across his chest. "Lexie?"

"Ward, it . . . it's okay. I'm fine. Fine."

Without a word, he pulled her into his arms, held her close. "I'm all right," she murmured, so softly he could barely hear her. "Just . . . frightened . . ."

Brushing his face against the wild tangle of her hair, Reilly took a deep breath and squeezed her even tighter, reluctant to let her out of his sight or grasp and telling himself that he never wanted to feel that kind of fear again. *Ever.* He tried to ignore the small prickle at the back of his mind, but it wouldn't leave him alone. Stepping slowly away, he held her at arm's length, gazing down into wide, tear-filled eyes. A kiss was what she needed—what he needed, too—but it couldn't be. That small prickle he'd felt was his conscience, his professional duty, his reason for being with this wonderful, amazing woman in the first place. And, too, it was a nagging memory of just what could happen when the heart was allowed to rule the mind. Things were definitely getting way too intense and personal with this lady. He relaxed his grip on her and straightened his shoulders. *That,* he thought, *was a close one.*

"Look, Lexie, I'm sorry, I . . ." He stopped, at a loss for words.

Lexie was momentarily speechless as well. One minute they'd been clinging to each other as if, in that contact, they'd found the only safe haven left in the world; the next he was pushing her away, making small talk with Rufus, and looking distinctly uncomfortable.

"Hey there, big fella, did you miss me?"

She was suddenly furious. What on earth had she been thinking? How could she have let herself be so swept away by gentle eyes and a pair of strong arms? The man was practically responsible for the danger Aunt Lila was in. And he was looking sideways at her now, speaking softly and gently, as though dealing with a troubled child.

"Feel like telling me what's going on?"

What's going on? He was supposed to know that, wasn't he? She hated feeling so helpless, so frustrated . . . so angry. She hated the way he was looking at her, the fact that he knew things he wasn't telling. She had a right to know, didn't she? *Everything.* What had Lila ever done to deserve such trouble? And why was Reilly Ward letting it happen?

"How could you let anyone get close to Lila? You said she was safe. You promised she wasn't in any danger. I wish I'd never saved your miserable life that day in Central Park!"

"Lexie . . . Lexie, it's okay. Really." He folded his arms around her again, rocking gently back and forth as she collapsed against his chest. "I spoke to my partner in London, not five minutes ago. Your aunt is perfectly safe. I promise. Now, tell me what's happened to upset you like this."

"You . . . you spoke to him? In London?"

"Mmm-hmm. Everything's under control."

Under control? That was how life used to be, before Reilly and his bad guys. But now . . . she couldn't remember ever feeling so out of control before, or so ashamed. It really wasn't his fault, after all. "Did . . . did he tell you about the robbery? Ward, someone broke into Lila's room at Regency House." In a halting voice, she repeated the story of Lila's ordeal. He listened in silence, his arms still wrapped around her. When she looked up at last, she discovered a trace of the old Reilly Ward humor playing across his face.

"Well now, I guess we can only give thanks that it was my partner, Phil, and not yours truly, who was looking after Lila's safety. He was with your aunt all the time. All the time, Lexie. The room really isn't of too much importance when you compare it to Lila's safety, now is it?"

"No. I . . . I guess you're right. It's just that I feel so helpless and I'm so worried about her. And I don't think you're telling me everything. And . . . and I don't know what to do." She took a deep, shuddering breath and laid her head back on his chest, recoiling as the rough edge of his holster brushed her cheek.

"What's wrong?" he asked. "Don't you believe me when I tell you she's perfectly safe?"

"No . . . I mean, yes, I believe you. For the moment. It's just . . . Ward, I hate guns. I always have. Jack insisted that I learn how to shoot. He even tried to make me keep a gun here." She laughed a little, in spite of herself. "Fact is, I'd probably have shot him a few times. Boy, that man is a pain."

Reilly chuckled. "He does have your best interests at heart, I suppose. But the gun idea was not one of his better ones. Unlike old Rufus here, who was an excellent idea. Right, Rufus?" Patting the dog on his woolly head, he abruptly changed the subject. "Feel like coffee? I hear this establishment serves the best in town."

Suddenly weak, Lexie let herself collapse onto the couch. She wanted very much to be brave and strong, to tell him to leave, that she'd be just fine on her own. But that was proving to be an impossible feat. Her hands were still trembling, like leaves in the wind. And she definitely, *definitely,* didn't want to be alone. "Thanks. Coffee sounds good."

"Well, then, allow me."

Reilly leaned heavily against the kitchen counter. The cheerful spurt-and-gurgle of the percolator, in chorus with the rhythm of the grandfather clock, was almost loud enough to drown out the sound of his own heartbeat. It had been hammering away in his ears ever since that first shrill blast from Lexie's beeper. She still had the thing in her hand, rolling it absentmindedly between her thumb and forefinger, and he wondered what she was thinking. He didn't have to wonder long.

"What were they after, Ward?"

Her wide, violet eyes, still slightly teary, tugged at his heart, and his conscience. "Lexie, I . . ."

"Why can't you just tell me what's going on?"

Watching her clench her fist around that beeper, he wasn't sure if she was about to cry again, or fly into another rage. "I'm sorry, Lexie." He rounded the counter to stand close beside her, shoving both hands deep into his pockets. It was the only way to keep them out of the wild tangle of hair that straggled across her face. "I can only imagine how frustrating this must be for you. But try to understand. The less you know at this point, the better. It's safer that way. Trust me. For just a while longer."

"I do trust you, Ward." Lexie reached for a pillow, wrapping her arms tightly around it and resting her chin on top. "Goodness only knows why, but I do. It's just . . . so . . ."

"Frustrating," he repeated. "I know. And I'm sorry." He sighed. It was almost impossible to maintain any level of professional detachment with this woman. Best to put a little space between them, he thought. And the sooner, the better.

"Listen," he said, striding briskly toward the door. "I need to take a quick look around outside. Just to be sure everything's secure."

A moment of panic flashed across her face, but she didn't say a word.

"I'll be right back, Lexie, in plenty of time to pour the coffee. I promise."

"Sure," she said, wearing a brave face. "Maybe you'd take Rufus out for me? He hasn't had his walk yet."

The big dog scrambled to his feet and bounded happily to the door. "No problem. Let's go, big guy."

Lexie fired the pillow at Reilly's back, just as the door closed behind him. The man had her riding an emotional roller coaster, one minute ready to strangle him, the next wanting nothing more than to feel his arms around her. She paced nervously back and forth across the room, made a brief stop to splash cold water on her face and run a comb through her hair, and then busied herself preparing a tray for their coffee. She'd just finished pouring two mugs full when Reilly and Rufus stumbled back through the door.

"Hey! Now cut that out, you big oaf." The dog's impulsive "happy dance" had Reilly tangled in several feet of leash. Rufus grinned innocently up at his struggling companion.

"Hmmm. Honeymoon's over, is it?"

Reilly grumbled something under his breath and threw the leash onto the counter. "I need coffee," he announced, collapsing onto the couch. "And then . . . aarrghhh! Rufus!"

The dog had parked his enormous self on the foot of his newest friend and proceeded to slobber all over his knee.

"Heads up, Ward!" Lexie tossed him a towel. "Go easy on the big oaf, okay? He can't help himself."

Rufus smiled.

"You two . . ." Reilly chuckled to himself, slapping Rufus on the side as he reached for a cup of coffee.

"Us two, what?"

"You keep a guy on his toes, that's for sure. Mmmmm. Good coffee." Taking another long sip, he studied Lexie thoughtfully, and then asked, "Feeling a bit better?"

She swallowed hard. "Look, I'm sorry for all those things I said before. It's just . . . I was . . ."

"Think nothing of it." He grinned, searching her eyes as though to read what she was thinking. "All in the line of duty. Besides, you had just cause. Don't give it another thought."

He drained the coffee from his mug, set it down on the tray, and rose slowly to his feet, giving Rufus an affectionate pat on the head. "See you in the morning, big guy."

"Don't go!"

Her outburst seemed to take him by surprise. Well, he wasn't the only one. Why was she letting herself fall apart like this? It was so unlike her. "I mean, I . . . that is . . . I just don't want to be here all by myself. Not tonight." She stammered her way through an explanation, all the while trying to avoid those knowing eyes of his. "Could you . . . would you mind staying? The couch has to be a lot more comfortable than that car of yours, or the back step, or . . . or wherever it is you spend your nights. Don't you think?"

Chapter Seven

She yawned, kicking free of the quilts that had tangled themselves around her legs during the night. Mmmmm. The sunshine felt warm. But why was she awake so early? Well, not really awake . . .

Whoa! Lexie sat bolt upright in the bed, modestly snatching the quilts up around her shoulders and staring, wide-eyed, at the two occupants of her couch. The painful details of Lila's phone call, and her own uncharacteristically frantic reaction, flooded her awakening mind like scenes from a bad movie. A very bad movie. And Federal Agent Reilly Ward played a starring role.

He'd certainly performed above and beyond the call of duty last night, she thought, remembering how his strong arms had held her, how his calm, steady voice had reassured her; remembering how close he'd come to stealing a kiss, and how badly she'd wanted him to try. Had it had been as difficult for him to back away as it had been for her to let him go?

After that one awkwardly tender moment, he'd been more than a little anxious to put some space between them. And later, despite his lighthearted teasing about the sleeping arrangements, she knew he'd been hesitant to stay the night. Had he feared what might happen between them? she wondered. Had he spent hours staring out at the night sky, the way she had? Close enough to hear his every breath . . . ?

Yoo-hoo! Earth to Frost! Yo, Lexie! You're just begging for trouble. Knock it off, before you step right in it.

She sighed, stretched, then noisily cleared her throat, but her reluctant houseguest showed no sign of waking up to keep her company. Far from it. The phrase "sleeping like a baby" could have been coined for the man on her couch.

A mischievous grin took shape on Lexie's face as she hung over the side of the bed to retrieve her old Pentax from the bottom drawer of the nightstand. The soft morning light was absolutely perfect for a candid portrait of a man and his dog. The two had stretched out to their full lengths along the big couch—Reilly, half-turned toward her, covers thrown off, clothes adorably rumpled, and one arm thrown around Rufus, as if the big dog were a giant teddy bear; and Rufus, with a blissful doggy smile on his big, hairy face. What a pair.

She snapped a couple of pictures, creeping stealthily across the room for just one more, and then a better angle, finally sneaking past the sleeping beauties to find a telephoto lens and capture a portrait Ward was certain to want to frame for his mother, for Christmas. It was just too cute for words, she decided at last, and wasted a whole roll of film on the new best friends.

Enough, already, she warned herself. This was bordering on sentimental, and the rule about sentimental drivel, and photographs of same, was right at the top of her *"now cut that out!"* list.

Throwing a blanket over Reilly's broad shoulders as she passed, Lexie tiptoed through the sunlit loft, taking a detour past the bed to wrap herself in an old quilt. The last thing she needed was for Agent Ward to see her in her tattered and torn Hawaiian print pajamas—a gift from Lila that looked a whole lot more like fruit salad than sleepwear. She'd just grab some clothes from the armoire, then duck into the bathroom to change before the man even knew it was morning. Might have made it, too, if she hadn't stubbed her toe. "Ouch!"

"Problem?"

"What?" She jumped, startled by the sound of his voice. *Get a grip!* "Oh, no. No problem." *Cool, calm and collected. That's me . . . not.*

Studying him from across the room, she couldn't help but smile at the suddenly wide-awake and twinkling Reilly Ward. It wasn't just a twinkle in his laughing brown eyes; it wasn't just his mile-wide grin that grew broader by the second. The man's whole face had taken on the most happily amused and animated expression.

He rolled lazily off the couch as she watched, and stretched like a bear after a long hibernation. His eyes never left her face and he didn't say another word. Just twinkle, twinkle, twinkle, as if he knew a secret.

"Is, um . . . is something funny?" she asked, her smile quickly fading.

"Well, no. Nothing but the mad-hatter expression on your face . . . and those pajamas." He snickered.

The blanket had slipped off her shoulders, exposing most of the back of Lila's fruit-salad muumuu, split seams and all. She snuggled the cover back around her.

"I wasn't expecting company, Agent Ward, or . . . or I'd have chosen something . . . something more . . ."

She felt an unaccustomed blush heating up her cheeks, and dove for the armoire. Letting a man, any man, affect her this way was definitely against all the rules. "That is, what I mean to say is, that I would've worn something more presentable."

Darn it all, anyway, she thought irritably. She was mad at herself, not at him. But she'd bet that wasn't what he was thinking. Strangely enough, at that particular moment, what Agent Ward might be thinking was very important to her.

"There's nothing wrong with them," he said, very quietly. "I just meant they're a little, well, unusual."

Lexie hid herself behind the double doors of the armoire, considerably relieved to be out of his sight, however briefly. She rummaged through the jumble of casual clothing on the shelves, finally selecting an oversized turquoise T-shirt and a favorite pair of stone-washed denim jeans—comfortable, well worn, and perfect for a lazy Saturday. Snatching up the clothes, she spun, ready to make a dash for the bathroom. Reilly's broad chest stopped her short.

"Ooof!"

"Sorry," he murmured, resting both hands on her shoulders. "Are you all right?"

She clutched the bundle of clothes to her chest as if it were a suit of armor. Those big, gentle hands of his were gliding slowly down the length of her arms and, despite the warm swaddle of blanket, that touch made her shiver. She knew he'd felt it—he must have. Had he also felt the sudden quickening of her pulse? Heard the little gasp of surprise that caught in her throat?

She fixed her gaze on the pitifully rumpled front of his nubby linen shirt and swallowed hard, afraid to look up, afraid of what she might say, what she might feel, if their eyes met.

Reilly made the decision for her, tenderly cupping her chin in one hand and tipping her face upward. He was twinkling again.

"I didn't know you could blush like that, Miss Frost. How old-fashioned of you. Was it something I said?"

Lexie stammered her reply, or tried to. "You . . . I . . . no. It's j-just . . . Drat!"

He brushed a wisp of hair away from her face. "Don't be angry, Lexie. I think you look lovely. Fruit shirt, and all. Beautiful, really. But then, I've been thinking that ever since the first day I saw you." Almost before the words had left his mouth, Reilly's expression changed to one of shock. As if the words had surprised him as much as they'd pleased her. "Oh gosh, Lexie, I'm sorry."

"Don't." She pressed one finger against his lips. "Don't be sorry. I wanted . . . I mean . . . I want breakfast. Are you hungry?"

"I'll say." Reilly breathed a low, rumbling chuckle.

"It'll just take me a minute to get dressed," she said, skipping lightly away. "Then, Agent Ward, I'll make us a big batch of the very best waffles you've ever tasted."

"Mmmmm. And she cooks, too."

"No." Lexie shot him a dirty look. "I make waffles, but I *don't* cook." The dirty look became a grin. "That's what take-out's for."

"Makes waffles, doesn't cook. Right." Reilly grinned back at her. "I'll try to remember that, Miss Frost."

He made a dash for the door. "I'll just grab a change of clothes from the car and then . . . do you mind if I use your shower? C'mon, Rufus, let's take a walk."

They were out the door before Lexie could answer. Chuckling to herself, she slipped out of the Maui pajamas and into her comfortable, Saturday clothes. "I want breakfast," she muttered, certain he'd known what she really wanted. "Nice save, Frost." Ah, well, breakfast would just have to do. Maybe later she'd offer to show him the city. A day on the town might be just what they both needed. A chance to relax and get to know each other, away from the forced intimacy of the loft. Not that she was interested . . . oh, heck, who was she kidding? It was time to face facts. She did want to get to know him. And after that brief moment in his arms, she was absolutely certain that the feeling was mutual.

"Lexie, this is great. Just look at that city."

Reilly was hanging over the rail of the Staten Island Ferry—one of the old, orange triple-deckers—looking as happy as a kid at the circus. And right beside him, paws on the rail, ears flapping, stood Rufus. The big dog looked every bit as delighted as the gentle man who was quickly coming to mean as much to Lexie as he obviously did to the canine behemoth.

"It is great, isn't it? I've always loved riding the ferry." She fished an elastic out of the pocket of her jeans and held it between her lips while she twisted her hair into an impromptu braid. Reilly caught her hands in his. "I like your hair when it blows in the wind. You look so . . . wild. Leave it. Please?"

"Only for you, Agent Ward." Not to be outdone, she stretched onto tiptoes to brush the hair away from his eyes. "Windblown looks pretty good on you, too."

Rufus immediately thrust his giant, hairy head between the two of them and sputtered a curious woof.

"Don't worry, Rufus." Lexie laughed and tussled the big dog's ears. "You're looking pretty good yourself, old boy." He flopped contentedly at her feet and closed his eyes.

"So, Agent Ward, did you know that I used to do harbor tours? I was the girl in the captain's hat, you know, the one with the silly uniform, who stood at the front of the boat and told the tourists what they were seeing." She waved her hand aft. "On the right, you'll see a wonder of modern engineering, the Verrazano-Narrows Bridge. It links Brooklyn with Staten Island and is, by the way, one of the world's longest suspension bridges.'' She spoke in her chirpiest, tour-guide voice.

"Enough, already.'' Reilly slipped an arm around her shoulders, as if it were the most natural thing in the world to do, and grinned down at her. "I don't see any captain's hat, Miss Frost, or cute uniform, either. It kind of spoils the effect, you know?''

"Oh. I see. Well then, I guess you don't want to know that the bridge was named for Giovanni de Verrazano. Or that he was the first European to visit New York. Fifteen-twenty-four, I think that was.''

"Miss Frost? Shut up and enjoy the view.''

For a long moment, only the wind and the waves made a sound. It seemed quite natural, then, to rest her head on his chest.

"Lexie, I—''

She straightened abruptly. "I know. We shouldn't. The job, and all. I understand. Really.''

Reilly watched her brush the hair away from her face, straighten her jacket, shove her hands deep into the pockets of her jeans. He watched, and all he could think of was how much he wanted to pull her close and kiss her. But the woman just wouldn't shut up.

"You probably get this all the time. I mean, I'm not the first woman you've ever had to protect, right? And, well, what with being anxious about what might happen, and, you know, all the extra adrenaline and everything . . . it's okay. It really is. I mean—''

"Shut up.'' Reilly grabbed her with both hands, pulling her close, pressing his lips against hers before she could say another word. And Lexie kissed him back.

"This doesn't happen all the time,'' he said, once they'd come up for air. "This *never* happens. It's completely unprofessional and way out of line and . . . and I don't care.''

"*Lexie? Lexie Frost!!!*''

"*Oh, no.*''

Lexie peeked hesitantly over his shoulder, groaned a very

colorful curse, learned in her "seafaring days," and arranged her face into a carefully guarded smile.

"René!"

"I thought I saw you out here." René Singer waved happily as she strode toward them. There wasn't a single chestnut-brown hair out of place on her perfectly coiffed head, despite the nearly gale-force wind on deck. The woman always could work miracles with a little hairspray, thought Lexie.

René was wearing a pastel blue maternity jumpsuit, obviously haute couture and obviously expensive, that revealed every inch of her blossoming pregnancy. She was also wearing her trademark, oversized dark glasses. But Lexie didn't need to see her old friend's eyes to know that, as she bore down on them, the woman was checking out every inch of Reilly Ward.

Lexie braced for impact.

"You look fabulous!" A quick hug, a kiss on the cheek, and René stepped back to study her friend. "Absolutely fabulous. And Rufus!" Although she tried her best, René couldn't quite bend low enough to tickle his chin. She settled for waggling her bejeweled fingers in front of his eyes. "Roofey, Roofey, Roofey. Did you miss me, big boy?"

Poor Rufus eyed her suspiciously and decided, rather quickly, to ignore her. Turning a couple of tight circles, as if contemplating the wisdom of chasing his tail, he finally settled down for another snooze on the deck. Reilly considered doing the same. It was pretty apparent that, whoever this rather overbearing female was, good old Rufus was not impressed. And so far, he'd found the big dog to be a pretty good judge of character.

"Ward? Are you in there?" Lexie was grinning up at him. "I'd like you to meet my very oldest—"

"Excuse me?"

"Oops, sorry, René. I mean, my very dearest friend, René Singer. René, Reilly Ward."

"Very pleased to meet you, Reilly Ward." René studied him seriously for a moment, slipping the dark glasses halfway down her nose as if a little sunlight might make a difference in the opinion she was so obviously forming, and then extended her hand. "That certainly was a very passionate public display of affection, Reilly." She winked in Lexie's direction, blithely ignoring her friend's scathing glance. "As Alexandra's closest friend, I really do feel I have to ask. What are your intentions?"

"René!"

Reilly choked back a laugh, forcing himself to meet René's disarmingly frank gaze straight-faced. And that was proving much easier said than done, because from the corner of his eye, he could have sworn he saw Lexie stamp her foot.

"It is entirely my pleasure to meet you, Mrs. Singer. And I think my immediate intentions are perfectly clear."

Lexie had to swallow a whoop of laughter when René's carefully shaped eyebrows shot upward.

"Right now," said Reilly, faking a pained expression, "failing a cold shower, I guess the best thing for me to do is to take good old Rufus for a walk around the deck." Reaching for Lexie's hand, he locked eyes with her, leaning almost close enough for another kiss before slipping the leash from her hand. "I'll be back. Don't go away."

"Where did you find him?"

René didn't try to hide the fact that she was admiring Reilly as he sauntered across the deck. Lexie found herself enjoying the view, too. That gray University of Virginia sweatshirt he was wearing showed off his broad, muscular back to perfection.

"Nice." René sighed.

Lexie laughed. "We always did think alike." She gave her friend a proper hug. "Gosh, it's good to see you."

"And about time, too. Although . . ." René turned, as if hoping to catch another glimpse of Reilly. "I must admit, you've got a good excuse. He'd make anybody forget their friends."

"Aw, René. I haven't forgotten you. I think about you every day. I've got a stack of messages at work to remind me, too. Poor Tommy's been in a flap because you accused him of not passing them on. But, Ren, I just haven't had a minute to myself lately. Honest." Lexie eyed her friend from head to foot and beamed a wide, approving smile. "Look at you! You're positively radiant. Pregnancy agrees with you, René."

"You're right. It does." She turned a slow, graceful circle, displaying her ample figure.

"And how's Dr. Singer?"

René looked none too pleased. "Why *do* you do that?" she demanded, planting her hands on her hips in a gesture that made her appear even more enormously fertile.

"Do what?"

"You know. Call Aaron 'Doctor' Singer."

"Do I? Sorry. I wasn't aware . . . well, it is his name."

"It's his title. You don't much like him, do you, Lex?"

"What?" Lexie smiled her very warmest smile and wrapped a sisterly arm around her friend's shoulders. It was time for a little white lie. "Of course I like him. I like him fine, René. I mean, what's not to like?"

The determined set of René's jaw relaxed a bit.

"He's rich, and famous . . . handsome, too. And he makes you happy. I don't know him well, that's all, and . . ." Lexie chewed on her lip, trying her best to look thoughtful while she fought the impulse to make a disgusted face. "And, I guess, maybe I'm just a little bit in awe."

"Well, now I *know* you're pulling my leg." René laughed. "You've never been in awe of anybody, Alexandra Frost. Not in all the years I've known you." She whipped off her sunglasses and dropped them into her bag. "Until now, that is. You're in love, aren't you?" she said, leaning close. "So, how does it feel?"

For just a moment, Lexie was speechless.

"Ah-ha! I'm right, aren't I?" René looked like the cat who swallowed the canary. "What's his sign? I'll bet he's a Taurus. He has Taurean eyes, and a classic Taurean nose. Tell me everything. Where did you meet? How long has this been going on? Is he rich?"

"Definitely not," said a chuckling, masculine voice, close behind them. "You don't get rich working for the government." Reilly smiled at the embarrassed expressions on both women's faces when they turned to look at him. He was obviously beginning to enjoy himself. "Your friend picked me up, Mrs. Singer. Bought me a drink and then invited me up to see her etchings . . . er, photos.'' His arm dropped neatly around Lexie's shoulders and he pulled her close. ''I feel as if I've known her for a very long time. And yes''—he grinned, displaying his profile—''it is a Taurus nose.''

René laughed. ''I think you'll do, Reilly Ward. And you just might be able to keep up with her.''

Chapter Eight

"Can I ask you a question, Agent Ward? A personal one?"

Lexie turned, slowly, to look up at him. Her eyes shone with the soft, flickering light of dozens of candles. Candles which, despite his earlier misgivings, did not appear to have put the place in danger of burning to the ground. They did, however, seem to be adding a few degrees of heat to the room.

"Well, I won't promise to answer, but . . . sure. I guess you can ask."

Wearing a mischievous little half-grin, she lifted a bite of chow mein to her mouth without losing so much as a single noodle. It was, Reilly thought, quite remarkable that anyone not born to it could manage a pair of chopsticks so skillfully. He studied the feast laid out before them on the coffee table, speared a chunk of kung pao chicken with his fork, and readied a glass of water to quench the fire it was certain to ignite on his tongue. Forget the candles. It had to be the spicy Szechuan takeout that had him feeling so uncomfortably warm.

"So? What's this personal question you were so keen to ask me? Change your mind?"

"No way. Just deciding—I've got quite a list, you know." They were sitting side by side on the floor and she shifted, making herself comfortable against the front of the big sofa before she continued. "For starters . . . how old are you?"

Reilly sputtered into his water. "Old enough to know better than to try that chicken again. Kung *POW!*" He dropped his fork and drained the glass dry.

"Well?" Ignoring his red-faced reaction to the peppery dish, Lexie smiled questioningly up at him. It occurred to Reilly that, just maybe, some of the heat he was feeling was thanks to Lexie. A dangerous train of thought to pursue.

"How old, eh? Does it matter?"

"I'll let you know," she said, straight-faced. "How old?"

Reilly grinned. "Pretty darned old, I'm afraid. Care to take a guess?"

"Oh, no. No way."

"Ah . . . the young lady's afraid she might insult me." He chuckled. "Well, right at the moment, Miss Frost, I am seven whole years older than you—but don't do the math just yet." He studied his watch. "Because in exactly two hours and forty-three minutes, I'll be eight years older than you—the big three-four."

"Tomorrow's your birthday? Ward! You weren't even going to mention it, were you?"

"Well, to tell you the truth, I'd pretty much forgotten about it, myself. Until this afternoon, that is, when your friend René mentioned my 'Taurus nose.' "

"Aw, is it always like that?"

"Well, yeah, pretty much. Why? What's wrong with my nose?"

Lexie laughed. "No, silly, not your nose, your birthday. You know, is it always . . . forgotten?"

"Pretty much." Reilly sighed. Not for forgotten birthdays, but for the suddenly sad expression on Lexie's face. "Now, don't you start feeling sorry for me, Miss Frost. I've had my fair share of wild celebrations. It's just that, lately, I always seem to be on the job, or . . ."

"Or what?"

"Or too far from home." This time, the sigh was heartfelt. "My mom always makes a cake, anyway. And the whole family gets together and drinks a toast to my empty chair."

"That's so sad." Lexie moved a little closer, resting her hand lightly on his arm. "Where is home, Ward?"

"Portland."

"Oregon?"

"None other."

"Has it been a very long time?"

"Too long. But in my family, absentee birthdays are the norm, I'm afraid. We're always toasting somebody's empty chair."

"How come?"

"Oh, we're all slaves to our jobs." He paused to drape his arm around her shoulders, resting his chin on the top of her head. "You smell so good," he whispered. "It's like you brought all that sunshine and sea wind home in your hair this afternoon."

"That's a very romantic notion, Agent Ward, but don't change the subject. I want to hear more about your family. After all, you know all the private little details of my life. I think it's time to even the score. Don't you?"

"Sounds fair." He brushed the tangle of hair away from her face, winnowing his fingers through the long, dark strands. "I'm the baby," he said quietly. "Youngest of seven. Three of my brothers and one sister are cops, like Dad, and my oldest brother, James, is in the Marines—serving in the Middle East right now. So, you see, we're pretty much accustomed to missed birthdays and Christmases, and . . . whatever."

Lexie did a quick count on her fingers. "That's six, Ward. What about sibling number seven?"

"Lena?" He chuckled affectionately. "We're not a hundred percent certain that Lena's really a Ward."

"Why not?"

"Astronomy," he said, rolling his eyes as if that particular science, or anyone's interest in it, was a complete mystery to him. "My big sister's a research scientist. A stargazer, really. And a poet. Mom says she got all the brains and all the imagination, and that the rest of us just exist to turn a mother's hair gray."

"Sounds like you're all pretty proud of your big sister."

"Yeah." He smiled. "I guess we are, Lexie. She's posted at that big research facility in Hawaii—you know, the one with the monster telescope. Lena claims there are people who would kill for the chance to do what she's doing."

"I'm impressed." Leaning away from him, Lexie poured spring water into her glass and sipped thoughtfully.

"Next question?"

"You sure?"

"Take your best shot, Miss Frost."

"Well, what about family . . . you know, wives, husbands, kids? Have any of you Wards given your poor, gray-haired mom any grandchildren yet?"

"You bet. I'm an uncle five times already. Pour me some water, too, would you? That kung pao burns!"

Lexie passed him the glass of water and settled back into the crook of his arm. "What about you? No wife or kids in your past?"

She hadn't hesitated to make it past tense, absolutely certain that if Reilly Ward were somebody's husband he wouldn't be letting this magic happen between them. He wouldn't be sitting so close that she could feel his heartbeat; wouldn't be tracing little circles on her neck and shoulder with his fingertip, or sending those shivery little breaths into her ear. Still, she wanted to hear it from him. "Well?" she asked again.

"No. No wife. No kids. No . . ." He rested his head on hers once more, heavily this time, as if that last question had caused him some pain.

"Ward?" She tried to pull away, to look up at him, but the man held her close, folding her tight in his arms. She felt his heart begin to beat a little faster, a little harder. "What's wrong?"

"Nothing, really. I . . . I always figured I'd get married, have kids, a house in the 'burbs . . . the whole nine yards. But . . ."

"But, what?" Lexie felt his sudden tension, sensed the darkening of his mood, and eased her arms around his waist.

"My partner, Phil. He . . . I watched him fall in love, Lexie, and I . . ." Reilly paused, abruptly clearing his throat. "Phil got married three years ago. I . . . I did the best-man thing for him."

"Is Phil the same partner who's with Aunt Lila right now?"

"Umm-hmm. We've been together almost nine years. That's a long time in this business. A long time. I remember thinking that if Phil and Bonnie could just keep looking at each other the way they did when they said their vows . . . they were made for each other. She was so beautiful."

"Was?"

He took a deep breath. "Was," he repeated. Even after two long years, it still hurt. The only way to handle the hurt was by not letting himself think about it. He knew that's what Phil did, too. *Don't think it. Don't say it.*

The two of them never talked about it anymore . . . not since the obligatory sessions with the Bureau shrink. But now this truly wonderful woman who'd curled herself into his arms was waiting to hear it all. He tried again to lose the flinty edge that had crept into his voice, but it wouldn't go.

"They were expecting a baby. We . . . we were undercover, Phil and me. Deep under. But he called home anyway. He had to, he said. I should've stopped him, but it was driving him crazy, not being able to see her. Things were pretty heavy with this case we were on, and . . . and we figured it'd be weeks before we could wind it up. He couldn't wait that long, y'know? It was just one phone call. But Bonnie . . ."

"What? Ward, what happened?"

"They said it was a drunk driver. Said he crossed the line and hit her, head-on. She never had a chance."

He felt Lexie tighten her hold on him, felt a halting breath shudder through her body, an echo of his own, melancholy sigh.

"We, uh . . . we didn't know, Lexie. They couldn't contact us. Phil didn't know what had happened until Bonnie was . . . she was already . . . in the ground." Reilly choked softly on his words. "I'm sorry. It's, um . . . still hard to talk about it."

Lexie lifted her hand to his cheek. "Don't be sorry, Ward. Be angry. Be sad. You're entitled. Why didn't the Bureau send someone to find you? To get you out?"

"It—it's not that easy, Lexie. Things had turned sour on us. We think somebody sold us out—Bonnie, too—never could prove it, though. There was . . . the people we were investigating set a trap, and . . . and we got caught. Phil saved my life. I'm not . . . I don't really remember much about it. Words— faces—I remember being so thirsty . . ."

Reilly reached for his glass of water and drained it dry. "They opened fire on us, left us for dead, somewhere in the desert in New Mexico. Phil got us out, got me to a hospital.

He must've carried me, Lexie. He said later that he wasn't sure how he'd managed to do what he did. I know, though. He was thinking about Bonnie and the baby. Thinking he had to get back to them, no matter what. So he did the impossible. He got us both out. But it was too late.

"I remember waking up in this little hospital room, and . . . and the first thing I saw was Phil. He was just standing there at the window, doing a thousand-yard stare. In shock, I guess. I thought . . . huh . . . I thought he was worried about me. I wanted to tell him that I was awake, that I was okay . . . but I couldn't speak. There were tubes in my nose and down my throat. And then . . . then I realized there was another man in the room. The Director had sent some desk jockey from the Santa Fe office to break the news. Can you imagine? Sending some stranger to tell him? Aw, gee, Lexie. I shouldn't have said that. I'm sorry."

"What?" She pulled away to look up at him. This time, he let her go. "Why?"

"Well, isn't that how it happened when your parents died? Some stranger from the airline showed up and—"

"You know about that?" Her violet eyes widened in surprise.

"Well, like you said, I know all the private little details of your life. But now you know all mine, too. So . . . don't be angry." Reilly ran his thumb along the curve of her cheek as he spoke.

"I'm not angry. I . . ." Lexie rose to her knees, sliding her arms around his neck, leaning close, brushing his lips with hers. "I'm so sorry, Ward. For you, and Phil. And especially for Bonnie and her baby. It's hard to imagine why things happen the way they do, but there is a reason for everything. A purpose. That's something Lila's been telling me for years, and I think . . . I think I'm starting to believe it."

She could make him believe it, too. She could probably make him believe just about anything if she looked at him like that when she said it. Abruptly, Reilly pushed to his feet.

"We shouldn't be doing this."

"I know."

"I'll, um, I'll take old Rufus out for his walk, and then . . .''

Lexie watched him cross the room and open the door. "Reilly?'' She waited until he turned and met her gaze. "I'll leave your blanket and pillow on the couch.''

For one long moment she was afraid he'd refuse, afraid he'd leave her to face the night alone. He didn't speak, just nodded once and closed the door behind him.

"What the heck is that?''

"John Philip Sousa, I think,'' murmured Lexie, sleepily closing her eyes.

"Uh-huh.'' Reilly's groan was barely audible from across the room—drowned out by the rousingly loud music. "Sousa? At eight-thirty on a Sunday morning? I was just starting to get used to the darned clock gonging away every half hour. Who the heck—''

"Shhhh. It's just Buddy, downstairs. The man loves that old Victrola of his—plays it loud to attract customers, he says. Just ignore it. Go back to sleep.''

"Sleep?''

Lexie answered with a soft, drowsy, "Mmmmmm.''

"With that . . . that circus music booming away underneath us? You're unbelievable!'' Reilly pulled a pillow over his head and closed his eyes, trying to shut out the blare of trumpets, the thunder of drums. No use. He was wide awake. Of course, there were worse ways to spend a Sunday morning. Turning his gaze across the room, he watched Lexie sleep until the clock chimed again and "Buddy Downstairs" traded Sousa for *The 1812 Overture.* Enough was enough, he decided, grumbling as he rolled off the couch. Lexie opened her eyes and smiled at him. She seemed about to say something, when Rufus erupted from beneath the bed and made a beeline for the door, nails scrabbling on the hardwood floor. He didn't bark, didn't whine, just pranced around on his toes with his tongue lolling out the side of his mouth. In the next heartbeat, someone rapped sharply on the door.

Reilly lunged for the holster he'd left on the end of the kitchen counter. *Stupid and sloppy!* he thought, mentally cursing himself for failing in his responsibility to the job—and to Lexie.

''Expecting someone?'' he hissed, as she grabbed for her bathrobe and shrugged it on over the fruit-salad pajamas. Her eyes were wide with fright, and riveted to the gun in his hand.

''N-no. But . . . Reilly, whoever it is, Rufus knows them. Look at him.''

He had to admit that the dog seemed almost deliriously happy at the prospect of greeting their unknown visitor, but he wasn't about to take any chances. ''Stay back from the door, Lexie. And be quiet!''

Rufus gave an excited little yelp.

''Hey!'' rumbled a masculine voice from beyond the door. ''That you, Rufus? Where's Lexie? Still sleeping?''

Reilly intercepted Lexie's dash to the door, catching her by the wrist. ''Who is it?''

''It . . . it's just Buddy. From downstairs.'' She tried to twist away. ''Ward, you're hurting me!''

''Talk to him, make sure he's alone—and don't open the door. Understand?''

Lexie nodded, suddenly frightened—more by the dramatic change in Reilly's mood and manner than by the thought that they might actually be in some danger.

''Buddy? Is that you?''

''And who else brings you lox on a Sunday morning?''

''I—I'm not dressed yet, Buddy and . . . and I'm not alone.''

''Oy!'' The man beyond the door gave an embarrassed little chuckle. ''So sorry, Lexie. I wouldn't interrupt.'' His voice began to fade away as he retreated down the stairs. ''Come see me later.''

''Stop him—but don't let him in. Not yet.''

''Buddy?'' Lexie leaned close to the door to call his name. ''Don't go . . . you're not interrupting. Just give me a minute.''

Reilly released her, thrusting the revolver into the waistband of his jeans and carefully positioning himself between Lexie and the door.

''Stay back,'' he said tersely. ''Until we're sure.'' Giving the knob a quick twist, he swung the door wide.

The old gentleman in the stairwell looked up at him and nodded. "Good morning, young man," he said, smiling cheerfully. "I hope I'm not spoiling your plans for this lovely spring morning."

Reilly breathed a sigh of relief as he stepped aside to let Lexie greet her downstairs neighbor, a silver-haired, round-bellied individual, small in stature but long on character, if one could judge by the clusters of laugh lines around his mouth and eyes. "No, not interrupting at all," he said, with a wry arch of his eyebrows. "We were just wondering if the circus had come to town. Thought maybe we'd take in the show."

Lexie nudged him sharply in the ribs. "C'mon in, Buddy. Did you say lox? Bagels, too? Mmmmm." She accepted the brown paper bag from Buddy's hand and tore open the top, inhaling the mouth-watering aroma. "Poppy seed—and still warm." She grinned, giving the old fellow a friendly hug. "Thanks, Buddy. What's the occasion?"

"We need an occasion, now?"

"Of course not. You're welcome any time, and you know it. Buddy, I'd like you to meet Reilly Ward." Lexie turned a brief and scathingly cold glance on Reilly. "This is Lila's business partner, Buddy Fine—or Mr. Mystiques, as we like to call him. The best salesman in New York."

Well, heck, thought Reilly, reacting to the angry glint in Lexie's eyes. She was steamed, all right. Now what? How did he convince the woman that she had to be careful, had to let him do his job? He sighed when she scowled at him again. She wasn't having a bit of trouble finding a smile for Buddy Fine, though, and Reilly felt a moment's regret at his reaction—all right, overreaction—to their visitor's unexpected arrival. He extended his hand. "Very pleased to meet you, Mr. Fine. Lexie's told me some good things about you."

"Make it Buddy, young man. Good to meet you, too. So, tell me all about yourself, Reilly Ward. Where'd you meet our Lexie? How long have you two been . . . er, um, that is . . . Oy!"

"Have a seat, won't you, Buddy?" Recognizing the older man's discomfort, Reilly gave him a reassuring slap on the shoulder. "Lexie wasn't expecting me this early, either. I'll just make us a pot of coffee while she gets dressed. And to answer your questions, or at least one of them, I've had my eye on her for quite some time. It took us a while to realize that we were meant for each other, but she was very much worth the wait." He grinned, giving her hand an affectionate and, he hoped, apologetic squeeze.

Lexie choked back the caustic comment she'd been about to make. Meant for each other? "I . . . I'll be right back. Excuse me." She made a quick raid on the armoire for clean clothes and ducked into the bathroom, locking the door behind her.

"Made for each other?" She mouthed his words again, remembering the look of panic she'd seen in Reilly's eyes when he dove for that gun of his. The man had really believed that she might have been in danger, and he'd been ready to put his life on the line for her. Lexie dressed hurriedly, ran a comb through her tangled hair, and pulled it into a ponytail.

It wasn't the same as with Jack, she told herself sternly. Jack worried over nothing. Reilly had a job to do, and—she shuddered at the suddenly vivid memory of Seedy Man—and good reason to be concerned for her safety. She straightened her shoulders and swallowed her pride. When this was all over, she and Reilly Ward would have a long talk, set down the ground rules in advance. But, for now . . .

"Mmmmm. Coffee smells great," she said, flinging the door wide and striding across the room. "He makes terrific coffee, Buddy. The best." She slipped her arm around Reilly's waist, and leaned close to whisper, "Sorry about . . . well, you know. I really do understand. Need any help?"

"Nope." Reilly beamed down at her, obviously relieved. "We're all set. And I, for one, am starved. Let's eat." He threw an arm around Lexie's shoulders and pulled her onto the couch.

"Buddy was just telling me that he's installed a new security system downstairs," he said, spreading a thick layer of cream cheese on a bagel and topping it with thin slices of salty smoked salmon. "He wants to make certain that your Aunt Lila knows all about it before she gets back."

"So she shouldn't set off the alarm." Buddy rolled his eyes

skyward. "I hate to even think it, Lexie. The woman would . . . oy vey!"

Lexie chuckled at the thought. "Don't worry, Buddy. She almost always calls before she comes home. I'll tell her, I promise. But what on earth made you decide to get an alarm?"

"Insurance," he muttered, brushing poppy seeds off his cherry-red golf sweater and checkered pants.

Lexie couldn't help but smile. It was no wonder that Buddy and her aunt got along so well. Beyond their mutual love of antiques and their keen business sense, the two shared a passion for vibrant colors and wildly patterned clothing. A trait that sometimes made it difficult to concentrate on what they were saying. Lexie bit into her bagel and tried to pay attention.

"They were going to raise our rates," Buddy said with a moan, "so . . ." He rolled his eyes and tossed his hands. "What can you do? Anyway, Lexie, as soon as I figure the blasted thing out, I'll give you the codes." He chuckled. "In the meantime, well, if I'm not there, better to stay out, okay?"

Buddy gulped the last of his coffee and struggled to stand up, grumbling, as usual, about her too soft, too low, overstuffed chairs and how he was going to see that she got some proper furniture one of these days. Of course, he'd been saying that for years, and Lexie was still waiting for the "proper" furniture.

"Going so soon?" She reached for Buddy's hands and hauled him to his feet. "Wouldn't you like some more lox, or another coffee?"

"Don't tempt an old man," he scolded, pinching her cheeks affectionately. *"Mein shayner punim."*

Working the kinks out of his knees, he shuffled toward the door. "There's an estate sale out on Long Island this afternoon—too good to miss, this one. So, I close the shop early. Have to do the whole day's sales before noon." He rubbed his hands together and laughed, as if ready to face the challenge. "Nice meeting you, Reilly Ward."

Rufus bounded to the door, almost bowling Buddy over in the process. "You need to go out, old pal? Lexie, you forget about him again? For shame. Such a good dog."

"We'll be going out soon, Buddy, don't worry. There's a jazz festival in the park today. Thought maybe I'd take Reilly and Rufus to hear some real New York music." She grinned. "I might even take a few photos, you never know . . ."

"Sounds good." Buddy opened the door and let himself out, calling, "Have fun, you two," as he hurried down the stairs.

Lexie turned to find Reilly smiling down at her. "How about it?" she asked. "In the mood for some hot jazz on your birthday?"

He pulled her close. "What was that he said to you? Mein shiner, something?"

Embarrassed, she groaned and rolled her eyes. *"Mein shayner punim*—he says it means . . . 'my beautiful face.' "

Kissing her lightly on the cheek, Reilly whispered, "The man knows a good thing when he sees it."

Chapter Nine

" "Whoa, Rufus! I know you're in a hurry to get home and put your feet up, old buddy, but just try to hang on a minute, okay?"

"I'm impressed, Ward. Around the block is about the farthest he ever wants to go, and then I have to drag him. You're a good influence, I guess."

"This is good? I thought—*hey*! Cut it out, you big . . ."

Lexie laughed at his muttered curse. Rufus had had a perfectly wonderful time at the park. Had even, possibly, enjoyed the jazz, had definitely enjoyed the chili dogs and ice cream, and the small children who had gathered round him as he lay in the shade, thumping his tail on the ground. But enough was obviously enough. The dog was now anxious to get into his comfortable "happy place" and heave a huge, exhausted sigh of relief, even if that meant yanking Reilly's shoulders out of their sockets in the process.

"I think we wore the big guy out, Ward," she said, grinning up at him. "Of course, he had to put a lot more effort into public relations than we did."

"True enough. Probably worked up an appetite, too, with all that walking. I know I did. So . . . um . . . what are you making for our dinner?"

Lexie flashed him an indignant look. "I've told you before, Reilly Ward, that I do *not* cook."

He grinned, somewhat lecherously, at her trim form. *Oh, yes, you do, honey,* he thought. No doubt about it. He was just opening his mouth to say so, when Lexie squeezed his arm affectionately.

"So, did you enjoy your birthday in the park?"

Transferring the leash to one hand, Reilly draped his arm

99

around Lexie and gave her an enormous hug. "The best birthday I've ever had, and that's the truth. As a matter of fact," he said, halting abruptly just outside her door, "I think you deserve another thank you."

"Mmmmm. And I like the way you say thank you." Lexie leaned toward him, head tipped back, lips parted. Then she fell down, hard, on her backside. In a most unromantic way. Rufus had somehow succeeded in wrapping his leash around Reilly's legs and had pushed himself between his two favorite people in an attempt to get things moving. The fact that they had both momentarily forgotten about the dog's impatience, or even the dog's existence, had allowed Rufus to drive a physical wedge between them.

Lexie got up slowly, rubbing her bruised behind and glaring at Rufus. "You couldn't just bark or whine like other dogs, could you?"

Rufus jumped up and licked her face.

"Oh, all right, we'll let you have your way—you big pest. But one of these days . . ." To Reilly she added, "Well, don't just stand there, let the darned dog into the building before he decks me again." She pushed past him to open the door.

"Wait." Reilly's sharp tone of voice stopped her in her tracks, froze the smile on her lips. "Hang on to Rufus for me. And don't come up until I give you the all clear—understand?"

Lexie nodded. His voice sounded cold, every word clipped and efficient, and she hated it. But watching Reilly's tense expression as he eased his gun out of its holster, she understood. He was probably telling himself that he had no right to a happy birthday. No right to fall in love. Agent Ward was back on the job.

He took the key from her hand and turned it in the lock, swinging the door wide and stopping to listen for a moment before he disappeared up the steps.

Lexie glanced over her shoulder, checking up and down the busy street. Everything looked just as it should on a warm spring Sunday afternoon. But would she recognize danger if she saw it? She sighed heavily, remembering the flash of anger she'd seen in Reilly's eyes a moment ago. Anger at himself? At her? At what they'd shared?

"I can't let you throw it all away, Ward," she whispered, bending to pat Rufus on his big, woolly head. The dog was staring up at her as if he thought she'd lost her mind. "We're waiting for Reilly to call us, Rufe. Be good, okay?"

He sounded the official, "All clear," just a second later and Rufus tugged impatiently at the leash, hauling Lexie around the corner and up two steps before she managed to unclip it from his collar. He bounded happily up the stairs to greet Reilly, who stood in the half-open doorway, watching.

"Ward, do you smell something?" She sniffed again and answered her own question. "Yup, there's no doubt about it, that's Chanel. Is Lila here?" She took the rest of the stairs two at a time.

"Lots of suitcases," said Reilly quietly, "but I haven't actually seen your aunt yet. Didn't want to barge in and scare her to death. Shall we? Er, go in, I mean, not . . . well, you know."

Rufus charged past the moment he opened the door, with Lexie close behind. But once inside she stopped short. Reilly had to put on the brakes, fast, to avoid knocking her small form to the ground. Again.

They stared in amazement at the clutter that seemed to have taken over the loft. Lila had obviously brought every piece of luggage she could find when she left England. There had to be five large cases, three small ones, two carry-ons, and an enormous tapestry backpack sort of thing. Lexie chuckled to see that most of the bigger pieces had been piled in front of the darkroom door. A not-too-subtle reminder of Lila's opinion of the place, more than likely.

"Your aunt doesn't believe in doing anything halfway, does she?" Reilly's chuckle erupted into full-fledged laughter as Rufus hauled his weary body up onto the bed and collapsed with a loud grunt. The dog's almost human expression seemed to beg them to just leave him alone to recover, please.

Lexie sighed. "Poor Rufus. Such a rough life you have." She turned and raised one eyebrow quizzically at Reilly. "But, speaking of my larger-than-life aunt, where the heck is she?

It's not like her to be shy, especially when she's just back from a trip. And this last trip was a lulu, unless I'm very much mistaken.''

Reilly was starting to get an uneasy feeling—one he preferred to keep from Lexie until he'd figured out exactly what was happening. Maybe he was being overly cautious—he hoped that was all it was, anyway—but something just didn't feel right.

Keeping his voice as casual as possible, he said, ''Looks like you've got a message on your answering machine. Maybe Lila stepped out for a few minutes and called to let you know.''

Lexie glanced at him and then at her machine. ''I'll bet that's exactly what's happened. Guess they don't call you Agent Ward for nothing.'' She pushed the button and, sure enough, Lila's voice issued forth, so loud and clear that they could almost smell Chanel wafting up from the machine.

''Hello, Lexie dear, I just wanted to let you know I've come back early. I'm at the airport now, and I have to find a porter to take my luggage out to the taxi. You can never find a porter when you need one, I declare.

''Anyway, dear, I just couldn't stay another day in that dreadful place. Far too upsetting. I feel so . . . so . . . well, violated is the only word that really describes the way I feel. Now, I hope you don't mind, but I thought I'd just stay with you for a couple of days— Oh! I think I see a porter with nothing to do. Must dash, dear. See you at home.''

Lexie turned to look at Reilly, a puzzled expression on her face. ''I wonder when she left that message? She's obviously been here, but if she was in such a big hurry to get home, why would she go out again as soon as she arrived? It doesn't make any sense, Ward.'' Her brow furrowed as she followed that line of thought a little further.

Reilly had been furtively checking the loft for any signs of violence and was relieved to see nothing seriously out of place. Knowing that his partner was with Lila, wherever she was, it occurred to him that this might be an opportune moment to give good old Phil a call and see what was going on with the whole Frost-Heslop situation. And giving Lexie something to do in the meantime seemed like a really good plan of action.

"Lexie? Do you think Buddy might be back from his auction? If he is, Lila probably went downstairs for a visit."

"But, Ward, the store was dark, closed up tight. Don't you remember?"

"True. But they'd have some major catching up to do, don't you think? I'll bet they've gone somewhere . . . you know, for a bite to eat, or something. Better than sitting here alone, waiting for you to get home."

"You know, you're probably right. I don't know why I didn't think of it myself. Guess I was overreacting, as usual—go ahead and say it." She ran her fingers through her hair, pushing it away from her face, and grinned up at him. "Well, go ahead."

"Nah, I'm too nice a guy to say 'I told you so.' Sure could use a cup of coffee, though. Why don't you put a pot on to brew?" He gave her a gentle shove in the direction of the kitchen.

The second her back was turned, Reilly had his cellular phone in hand and began punching in numbers. "Come on, Phil," he muttered through his teeth. "Answer the phone. Where are you?"

Before he'd counted six rings, Lexie was back at his side, her face bloodlessly pale.

"You're calling your partner, aren't you? You're afraid something terrible has happened. Ward, *where's my aunt?*"

He held up a hand to silence her as he continued listening to the unanswered ringing of the phone. Something was odd. It was almost as if he were hearing an echo of each ring. And so close by. Something was definitely wrong.

Lexie shook his arm. "Ward? Ward!? Who are you calling? Is it about Lila? Tell me what's going on."

He moved the phone away from his ear without disconnecting the signal. Looking at her with calm control, he said quietly, "Lexie, I'm doing everything in my power to find your aunt. And yes, I am calling Phil. But I'm more than a little concerned that I'm not getting an answer." He looked bleakly at the phone

in his hand, and made a move to turn it off. That strange echo
still bothered him, though. Was he imagining it, or . . . Oh, no.
He knew what it meant. Phil was close by . . . very close by.
But, for some unknown reason, was not able to answer.

"Ward?" Lexie was tugging on his arm again. "Ward, do
you hear another phone ringing?"

He wasn't imagining things. She'd heard it, too. "Come on,"
he said suddenly, "Let's try the elevator. We've got to get
downstairs." Still holding the ringing phone, he dashed the
length of the loft to the old freight elevator, with Lexie close
on his heels.

"But, Ward, what about the alarm system?"

At the elevator, the ringing of another phone was clearly
audible, and obviously coming from inside the shaft. "I've got
a feeling that Buddy's alarm is the least of our worries," said
Reilly, wrenching open the gate with desperate haste.

His sharp intake of breath sent a chill of fright up Lexie's
spine. Pushing past to stare down the shaft, she gave a horrified
gasp of her own as she saw what he was seeing. There, on top
of the elevator, lay a man. But how . . . ? *"Oh, no!"*

Her eyes had begun to adjust to the dim light, and in a dreadful rush of comprehension she saw the flood of crimson that
stained the man's face, matted his thick, black hair, pooled
around his head and shoulders. So much blood. Was he dead?

Reilly didn't hesitate. Without a second's pause, he leaped
into the shaft, landing with a bone-jarring thud on the top of
the elevator.

Lexie watched his frantic search for signs of life, for breath,
or pulse. She heard his short sigh of relief when the man
groaned and tried to move. "Take it easy, Phil," she heard him
say. "I'm here. Just relax. I'll get you fixed up, I promise."

Reilly's voice was tight, controlled, but Lexie felt her own
control slipping away. She had to do something, anything, to
help. But what? Watching as he gently maneuvered his injured
partner into a half-sitting position, she finally found her voice.
"Ward, I . . . I'll call an ambulance."

"No!" His answer was explosive. "Here, help me get him

up onto the floor, then we'll see how he is. We can take him to the hospital ourselves.''

The next several moments were taken up by a great deal of struggling and lifting and muttered cursing on Reilly's part, and growing anxiety on Lexie's. This wasn't happening. It couldn't be. This was Reilly's partner, the man who was supposed to be in charge of Lila's safety. Even thinking about what her aunt might be going through was too terrible, too frightening, to bear.

Fighting panic, she watched as, somehow, Reilly managed to lift his partner, a man larger than himself, a man who was barely conscious, up onto his shoulders and, from there, to heave his awkward burden up and over the five-foot gap to the floor.

As soon as Phil's head and shoulders came up over the frame, Lexie was on her knees, grabbing his blood-soaked jacket and helping drag the man onto safe ground.

Reilly followed, hauling himself up from the elevator shaft. He sat for a few seconds, breathing deeply, staring bleakly at his partner and then at Lexie. Almost tenderly, he removed Phil's now-red jacket, and rolled it up to place under his head.

The silence was broken by a loud moan from the injured man. Reilly leaned closer.

''Phil? Phil? Don't exert yourself. We're going to get you to the hospital. Take it easy, okay?'' Reilly's face was creased with worry as he glanced at Lexie. ''This is bad, isn't it? I mean . . . he's hurt really badly.''

''N-no . . . I'm . . . okay . . . okay.'' Phil reached out and clutched at Reilly's jacket. ''I was right behind her, Reilly. Right . . . behind her.''

''Don't try to talk, Phil, we're going to get you some help. Shhh, don't try to talk.''

Reilly's voice was rough and gentle at the same time, and Lexie felt a huge lump form in her throat. Chewing nervously on her lip, she told herself that, no matter what, she had to keep her emotions under control. Letting herself fall apart again would only make things worse for Reilly, and it wouldn't help Lila one bit.

Taking charge, she said briskly, "Come on, Ward, let's bring the elevator up and get Phil to the hospital. Head wounds always bleed a lot, you know? I'm sure it looks worse than it really is."

Almost gratefully, Reilly hit the elevator button. The noisy cage clanked heavily up to the floor and stopped.

Phil groaned again. "Reilly, listen. Have to . . . have to tell . . . what . . . happened. Please, Reilly . . ."

Lexie and Reilly exchanged glances. "Maybe you'd better let him talk, Ward. Maybe he knows something important— something about Lila." She leaned down to speak soothingly to the man.

"Phil, Reilly and I are right here. I'm Lexie Frost—Lila's niece. We're taking you to the hospital and then you're going to help us find my aunt. You can talk now if you feel like it, but you don't have to, Phil. Everything's going to be okay."

Reilly stared at her in frank admiration. This was one amazing woman. "Let's get him into the elevator," he said, hoisting the inner gate. It was heavy oak, grown stubborn with age, and he forced it wide with a grunt of effort. "Okay. Help me, now."

One on either side of Phil, they were as careful as they could possibly be, but it was obvious that the slightest movement caused the man severe pain. The parts of his face that weren't actually blood-covered, turned fish-belly white with the exertion.

"I was right . . . behind her . . . c-coming into . . . the building," said Phil, weakly. "Surprised them . . . out back, disdisabling . . . the alarm. They—they . . . t-took her, Reilly. Must have . . . thrown me . . . in here. I—I couldn't . . ." With a final groan, he lapsed into unconsciousness.

"I can't believe this is happening. Ward, what have they done with Lila?"

Reilly placed a reassuring hand on her arm but his thoughts raced, trying to figure out the best way to handle the powderkeg situation they now faced.

He was saved from having to answer when the elevator finally clunked to a stop. Easing an arm under his partner's shoulder, he motioned to Lexie to do the same. ''Come on, let's get him out of here. We can't do a thing until we get him to the hospital, anyway.''

White-lipped, Lexie nodded, and silently obeyed his instructions.

Chapter Ten

Afterward, Lexie couldn't remember much of the drive to the hospital. It took place at breakneck speed, of that she was certain. But she'd been too busy cradling Phil's head in her lap, whispering reassurances—as much for herself and Reilly as for him—to watch what was going on around her. Just as well, she figured, as it seemed to her that Reilly must have broken the sound barrier several times during the brief trip.

At the hospital, he'd appeared at the car door with a stretcher and nurses before Lexie had even had a chance to lift Phil's head up from her lap. The next half hour was little more than a blur to her. A blessing, really, she reflected later, realizing she must have been in shock.

She was aware that there was a fair period of time when Reilly was not at her side. She had considered going to look for him, but something told her he'd have wanted her to stay right where she was. And so she had waited, battling fright and exhaustion, finally falling asleep on one of the painfully hard waiting-room chairs. At least, she thought that must have been what happened, because the next thing she knew Reilly was gently shaking her awake and offering her a cup of lukewarm vending-machine coffee.

Rubbing her eyes, she sat up slowly, and took the cup from his hand. "What's going on? Is Phil all right?" She sipped the coffee and made a face.

Reilly gave her a lopsided grin, though not a full-power one. "It'd take more than a knock on the head to put Phil Dibiase out of commission. I told them he fell down the elevator shaft, and I think they may even have believed me. They're stitching him up now. How are you doing?" His brown eyes were dark with worry.

"I think I'll survive."

"Lexie, I can't thank you enough for what you did. You're incredible."

Incredible? She sure didn't feel incredible. She stared at him for a long moment, struggling to clear the fog of sleep from her mind and fighting a rising panic. She had to think clearly, had to do something, anything, to help Lila. But what? "Where have you been?" she demanded. "And where's Lila?"

Reilly shifted from one foot to the other, avoiding her gaze. "Lexie, I had to call the Bureau. About Phil, about the whole situation. And then I had to call the New York office. They're going to—"

"What about my aunt? Doesn't anybody care about her? Ward . . . if this is what happened to the guy who was supposed to be guarding her, *what's going to happen to Lila?*" Her voice rose steadily with each word, until the nurses at the desk turned to look at the bloodstained pair with curious interest.

"Lexie, please calm down." Reilly sank onto the chair beside her and gently took her hand. "I'm going to tell you everything I know, but we have to keep a low profile. Please. It's for Lila's sake, believe me." He was looking at her as if he expected her to fall completely apart on him again. No way.

"I'm fine. And I'm perfectly capable of controlling myself. Just tell me what's going on. *Please.* Before I'm forced to run screaming to the police."

"You can't go to the police; this is Bureau business. We're undercover here, Lexie. You know that."

"What I know is that you're telling me nothing. We're sitting in a hospital emergency room, covered in Phil's blood, and my aunt is goodness-knows-where, having to endure goodness-knows-what. I want action. I want to *do* something!" She balled up her fists and pushed herself away from him, shoving angrily against his chest.

Reilly caught her, pulling her close, whispering her name. "Lexie . . . Lexie, I know you do, and we're working on it. Please, give me a few minutes to explain what I know. We can't help Lila if we panic. We can only help her if we keep clear heads and understand every bit of information we have."

Slowly, she pulled away from his embrace, folding her arms across her chest, leaning back against the hard hospital chair. "So talk. I'm listening."

His heavy sigh spoke volumes. This was hard for him, too. But, difficult or not, she needed to know. *Everything.* She met his gaze and waited.

"Listen, these guys we're dealing with aren't just regular, run-of-the-mill thugs. They're international jewel thieves. On a huge scale. We've been trying to bring them down for quite some time now." He paused, as if looking for the right words to continue. "Well, we had reason to believe that they were using your Aunt Lila as a 'mule.' A person who carries things across international borders, with or without knowledge of the fact. In Lila's case, there's no doubt that she has no idea what's been taking place on her forays to the far corners of the world. That, and the fact that she routinely buys semiprecious gems for her costume jewelry, is what made her the ideal candidate for these people."

Reilly searched Lexie's face for some sign that she understood what he was saying. She was as pale as a sheet.

"Ward, what will they do to her? If she doesn't even know what's going on . . . ?"

He reached for one of her hands, coaxing her arms out of their tightly crossed position, aching to make things right for her again. And he would. In time. But what about now? She had to hate what this was doing to her. Maybe he could at least help her find the strength to carry on.

"Lexie, the fact that she doesn't know what's going on is exactly what's going to protect her until we can find her. Personally, I think your aunt is a whole lot smarter than most people give her credit for. She'll play dumb to buy time, no matter how difficult things may be." He gave her hand a gentle squeeze. "Lexie, she's going to be all right. We'll find her." *I promise,* he added to himself, watching her struggle to control the trembling of her bottom lip.

"I know. At least, I'm trying to believe it. I just feel so . . . so helpless. Like I should have known better, like I should have been able to do more, like I should have warned her. I . . . I just don't know." She faltered, letting her voice trickle off to a whisper.

"Don't do this to yourself, Lexie. There was nothing you could have done to prevent this. *Nothing.* But, believe me, you're getting your 'action.' Even as we speak, the Bureau is scrambling to track down Lila's whereabouts. We're putting a line tap on your home phone and the one at Shutterbugs, we're making inquiries at the airport, and we've got people crawling all over your aunt's room in London. Things are being done."

"Mr. Ward?" A man in hospital fatigues, green with a spot or two of blood, strode briskly toward them. He wore a surgical mask, carelessly pulled away from his young and weary features.

Reilly was on his feet in an instant. "Yes, I'm Reilly Ward. How's Phil?" *So much for keeping it all together,* he thought. Despite his best attempt at "Bureau official delivery," he'd managed to come off sounding just as scared as Lexie. Well, he *was* scared, really scared, of what the answer might be. *Phil had to be all right.*

The doctor smiled faintly. "He's going to be fine. However, he is very weak. He needs to rest and recuperate, but it seems that your friend doesn't wish to partake of our hospitality." He held up a hand to indicate that there was more he had to say. "He thinks he'll be better off going home with you. That is, if you feel you can take care of him."

Lexie nodded earnestly. "We can take care of him. We'll watch him like a hawk. We really will."

The doctor studied them seriously for a long moment. "Well, all right. But if there's any blurred vision, dizziness, or nausea, you get him back here—right away."

Assuring him that they would, indeed, obey his instructions to the letter, Reilly and Lexie followed the doctor down the hallway.

"A wheelchair?" Phil snorted, as Reilly helped him off the bed. "What do you think I am, a hundred years old?" But he didn't say much more, going very pale with just the exertion of moving that far.

Reilly's mouth was a thin line. "I'll bring the car around," he said tightly, and left Lexie to wheel his injured partner to the door.

It didn't take much to convince Phil that he was meant to lie comfortably on the couch, making friends with Rufus, who was monumentally happy to have a new, and captive, audience for his leaning and sighing.

"Better check the answering machine. Looks like you've got a message." Reilly's tone of voice was all business.

Almost fearfully, Lexie pushed the PLAY button, and Lila's voice was instantly audible.

"Lexie, oh, why aren't you there? Lexie, it's me, and—now, I don't want you to worry, but . . . some men have kidnapped me and I don't know where I am. What? Okay, okay. Lexie, they say I have to hurry up and get off the phone but I'll call again, really soon. Oh, and Lexie, they say that under no circumstances are the police to be notified. Remember, dear, no police." Abruptly, the message ended.

"Oh, no." The tears that welled up in her eyes were beyond her control. "I . . . I can't believe this is happening." Sobbing, she let Reilly gather her into his arms, let him soothe her with gentle strokes of her hair. Thankfully, he said nothing. Didn't try to tell her that everything would be okay. Everything was *not* okay. And, right at the moment, she couldn't imagine that it ever would be again.

Phil's voice came weakly from the couch. "Don't worry about that lady. She's a tough one. She'll be fine."

"You listen to Phil," said Reilly, stepping away. "I've got to check in. Our guys are going to want to hear about this."

Lexie listened to his short, one-sided conversation with the Bureau's New York office. She was so tired, so frightened. All she could do was stare up at him, wide-eyed and close to tears again, hating the feeling of absolute helplessness that had swept over her.

Reilly finished the call with a curt, "Right. Will do." But his voice and manner softened as he took her in his arms again.

"Come on," he said. "You need some rest. It's been a long day. We're going to need our wits about us tomorrow."

"Rest? *No.* I . . . we've got to do something. *Anything.*"

"I'm sorry, Lexie. We have to play the waiting game now. And it's about the toughest game there is."

Chapter Eleven

"Pssst. Hey, you asleep, partner?"

Reilly's eyes flew open at the sound of Phil's voice, a pale imitation of his partner's usual gruff bellow. Gently extricating his hand from Lexie's, he pushed the chair away from her bedside, careful not to wake her.

"No," he whispered, tucking his shirttail into his pants as he crossed the room. "Not sleeping. You know I can't sleep when the pressure's on. But you should be. The doctor said you have to rest. What's the matter? Are you okay?" Bending to turn on the table lamp, Reilly squinted uneasily at his partner. The man's craggy face was still startlingly pale.

"Oh, knock it off," groaned Phil, with a touch of the old vinegar in his voice. "I'm fine. At least, I will be, once I get rid of this blasted headache."

"Do you want something for it?" Reilly checked his watch. "It's been nearly six hours . . ."

"Nah. Better save it. I've got a feeling I'll need it soon enough." Groaning, Phil gingerly pushed and pulled himself into a half-sitting position against the softly padded arm of the big sofa. His efforts disturbed Rufus, who lifted his head and blinked curiously at the two men before drifting off to sleep again at the far end of the couch.

"Friendly dog," said Phil. "Sure seems to like you, and so does the lovely lady, if I'm not mistaken."

Reilly shifted uncomfortably from one foot to the other, finally clearing a space to sit on the end of the old pine blanket box. Lexie's magazines wound up on the floor at his feet. "It's mutual," he confessed. "But spare me the lecture, okay? I've already read myself chapter and verse—more than once." He sighed. "Doesn't matter. This lady's special."

114

Phil leaned a little closer, wincing with the effort, but smiling through the pain. "Did I just read the word 'love' between those lines?" he asked, chuckling as he added, "Will wonders never cease."

"Not funny," said Reilly, glancing over his shoulder toward the peacefully sleeping Lexie. What had she ever done to deserve this kind of trouble in her life? he wondered, making a silent vow to see that trouble finished, once and for all. He turned back to Phil. "I promised to keep her safe, but . . . I promised we'd keep Lila safe, too. And I keep thinking about . . ."

Taking a deep breath, he steadied his voice. "Phil, I just can't stand the thought of anything happening to her." *Idiot!* He was suddenly furious with himself. Phil didn't need another reminder of what had happened to Bonnie. Not now.

"Reilly, I . . . it shouldn't have gone down the way it did, you know? I mean, I surprised them . . . thought I did, anyway."

"Phil, I didn't mean—"

"Shut up! I know what you meant. Just . . . just let me tell you, okay?"

Reilly nodded.

"There were two of them, out back. They'd just finished rigging the alarm system. I was sure they hadn't seen me. I drew my gun . . . had them cold . . ." Phil slumped into the corner of the sofa, as if just remembering the day's events had sapped his strength. "There was a third man, Reilly. He hit me hard, from behind. Must've used his gun, I dunno. I . . . I really did see stars for a minute, and then . . . then they dragged me up the stairs. I saw the old lady and—"

"Phil? What? What is it?" demanded Reilly, unnerved by his partner's extended silence and the strange expression taking shape on his face.

"Four."

"What?"

"There had to be four!" Phil lurched upright. "Uhh . . . oh . . ." His face went instantly green. "I shouldn't have done that.'' He groaned. ''Maybe . . . maybe I will take that pain pill now.''

Propping a couple of pillows behind Phil's back, Reilly gently settled his partner into the corner before producing the vial of tablets the doctor had prescribed. ''I guess, whatever this is, it's pretty powerful stuff. The doc said one ought to do it. Want some water?'' he asked, dropping a tablet into Phil's hand.

''I . . . uh, yeah, p-please,'' mumbled Phil, without opening his eyes. ''Or just . . . just shoot me now, okay?''

''Take it easy, partner,'' said Reilly, resting a sympathetic hand on Phil's shoulder and offering a glass of water. ''You'll feel better in a few minutes. I'll be right back—don't go away.''

The answer came in a low groan. ''Very funny.''

Returning moments later with a cold washcloth, Reilly placed it gently over Phil's eyes and forehead. ''It's okay,'' he said, interrupting his partner's murmured thank you. ''Don't try to talk. Just rest. You'll be okay, Phil. You're not dizzy, are you? Or nauseated? Or—''

Phil groaned again. ''Aw, cut it out, will you? I was starting to feel better, but you're making me sick.'' He pulled the cloth away from his eyes and stared weakly up at his partner. ''I'm fine. That pill's working already. Just give me a minute . . .''

''Phil, you don't have to—''

''Want to . . . I remember now, Reilly. There were four.'' Phil managed a halfhearted smile. ''I could've taken the three of them, y'know.''

''We used to tell each other we could take on a dozen armed men and come out on top. Now we're down to three?'' Reilly laughed softly. ''Remind me to tell you about a certain incident in Central Park,'' he said, frowning. ''I'm afraid we're getting too old for all this spy stuff, partner.''

''Speak for yourself, Reilly Ward. I, for one, plan to be—''

The phone's loud ring interrupted the telling of Phil's plan.

''Ward?'' Lexie was on her feet, wrenched from a deep sleep, wild-eyed and gasping for breath.

''It's okay, Lexie, it's okay. You'll be fine.'' Reilly darted across the room to take her by the arm. ''Take a deep breath,'' he ordered, gently smoothing the frazzled mane away from her face before placing the impatiently ringing phone in her trembling hands. "Answer it," he said. "Don't worry about trying to remember what they say; we'll have it all on tape."

Reilly turned on the overhead lights and moved to stand behind her, resting his hands on her shoulders, holding her safe. "Go ahead," he murmured, and held his breath as she spoke nervously into the phone.

"H-hello?"

"Lexie?" Lila sounded faint and far away. "Lexie, is that you?"

"Lila? Are you all right? Have they hurt you?"

"Please, dear, just listen. I'll be fine. They say I'll be fine if you'll just do what they say. What? Okay, I know that. Lexie? They say to tell you again. No police. Promise me, dear. No police."

Lexie clutched the telephone so tightly that her fingers began to ache. Her aunt sounded frightened, but she also sounded remarkably self-controlled, and nothing in her tone of voice suggested that she'd been injured. Yet.

"I promise, Lila. Whatever they say. Just tell me what they want."

"The pink violet," said Lila.

"What? They want the pink violet?"

"No, no, no. Lexie, please listen. *Oh!*"

"Lila?!" Lexie screamed her aunt's name into the phone. She was almost certain that Lila's last exclamation had been a shocked response to some sort of pain. "Lila?" she called again, desperately trying to steady her voice. "Are you there? What's happened?"

"I . . . I'm here, dear. N-nothing's wrong . . . nothing for you to worry about. But Lexie, you have to hurry. Oh, please, just listen."

"I am listening. What about the pink violet?"

"Move the little table, Lexie, and roll back the Indian rug. Underneath, in the floor, you'll find—what? *Oh!*"

"Lila?" The line went dead. "Lila? Oh, Ward . . . what have they done to her?"

"Not enough time." Phil had managed to swing his feet off the couch and now sat looking up at them, grim-faced. "Not enough time for a trace. These guys know what they're doing. Give me that tape, Reilly."

"The pink violet," murmured Lexie, as if in shock.

"What did you say? Lexie? Are you all right?" Passing the tape recorder to his partner, Reilly followed Lexie across the room.

"The . . . the violet," she repeated, turning to stare up at him with tear-filled eyes. "She said . . . Lila said I'd find something in the floor, under the pink—"

Reilly didn't wait for her to finish. He had moved the little teak table and rolled back the rug before the words were out of Lexie's mouth.

"There's a loose board," he said, pulling it free. "Lexie, I can't get my hand through this opening. Too small. You'll have to do it."

Dropping to her knees beside him, Lexie slipped her hand through the hole in the subfloor, groping to the left and then to the right, finally closing her fingers around a soft, leathery mass and pulling it out into the light. It was a small suede pouch, one of Lila's gemstone bags. Quickly unknotting the drawstring, Lexie emptied the contents into Reilly's waiting hands.

"Wow!" they exclaimed in breathless unison.

"Reilly, these stones . . . I don't remember Lila having anything like them before, although . . ." Her voice trailed off as she remembered her aunt's excited description of her new Mexican gemstones. "So perfect looking, you can't tell them from the real thing."

"What?"

"That's what Lila told me, after her trip to Mexico. She said she'd bought some gorgeous stones, a real bargain, and so perfect looking, she swore I wouldn't be able to tell them from the real thing."

"Reilly." Phil held up the tape recorder. "Tough old lady, but they didn't let her talk. We've got nothing yet. You'd better get this thing hooked up again, before she calls back." He glanced uncertainly from Reilly to Lexie and back again. "I'd have to bet they're going to want our Miss Frost, here, to deliver their merchandise.''

Lexie rose slowly to her feet, staring first at Phil, and then at Reilly, whose face had grown frighteningly pale. ''I . . . I can do that,'' she said, striding bravely across the room to stare at the silent telephone. ''Just tell me where.''

Chapter Twelve

"**I** don't like this."

"Reilly, I'll be fine. And anyway, we don't have a choice, do we?"

He stopped his anxious pacing of the room for a moment, fixing his gaze on Lexie. "No. We don't. But you'll do what I say—*everything* I say—to the letter. Understand?"

"Chill out, partner." Phil was on his feet, a bit unsteady, but managing well enough to insist on being a part of the operation. "We've been through all this before. Lexie will be fine. She'll wear the wire. We've planted the tracking beacon in the pouch with the jewels. Our people are ready to roll at a moment's notice." Dropping a hand on Reilly's shoulder, he said exactly what all three of them were thinking. "Why don't they call?" It had been more than four hours.

Reilly took up his pacing again as Lexie turned to stare at the phone. It stayed maddeningly quiet.

"Lexie, I need to sit down," announced Phil, inching his way back to the sofa. "Come here, will you? And sit."

Rufus, who'd been watching from his favorite spot beneath the bed, dragged himself out to follow Lexie across the room. He sniffed hopefully at her hand as she sat next to Phil, and then, as if resigned to the fact that an early breakfast was out of the question, took up position near the door to watch Reilly pace. He yawned loudly, as if the whole situation was making him tired.

"You all right, Phil?" asked Lexie. "Can I get you anything?"

He didn't answer, just slowly shook his head. She imagined him willing the pain to recede, ordering himself to be strong, to stay alert. He was a lot like his partner, she thought, studying the determined lines of Phil's pale, craggy face. A sad face. Sad eyes, too. She tried to imagine him laughing, and found she couldn't.

"This," he said quietly, "is a miniature transmitter." Carefully placing the thumbnail-sized device in Lexie's palm, he continued. "There's an adhesive strip on the back. You wear it inside your shirt . . . er . . ."

He glanced quickly at Reilly, who'd stopped his pacing to stare across the room at them, and gave a helpless little shrug.

"It's okay, Phil," said Lexie, feeling more than a little awkward herself. The man was obviously trying to avoid looking down at her chest. If nothing else, she thought, the topic had at least brought a touch of color to Phil's cheeks.

He took a deep breath and nodded. "Yeah, well . . . you wear the transmitter on the right side—*right.* That's important, otherwise your heartbeat will interfere with what I can hear. Okay?"

She stared at the tiny object in her hand for a long moment, suddenly apprehensive. "I . . . I guess so. But won't they know? I mean, what if . . . what do I do if they find it?" The little tremble in her voice stopped Reilly in his tracks again. She hadn't wanted him to know how frightened she really was.

"They'd have to strip search you to find it," said Phil, "and I don't think that's too likely."

"S-strip search?" Her bravado was circling the drain. "Reilly . . . ?"

"Not a chance." He was at her side in an instant. "They're going to want to move fast. They'll take their gems and let Lila go and that'll be that." He shot his partner a look that threatened bodily harm, then folded his arms around her. "Don't worry."

"Sorry," groaned Phil. "I shouldn't have . . . aw, Lexie, I got hit in the head, you know? It made me stupid." He forced a half-smile. "You'll be fine. They won't do more than check you for weapons. I'm sure of it. But with this"—he touched the transmitter once more—"we'll have every word they say on tape. It'll put them away forever."

"Good," said Lexie, leaning into Reilly's arms, drawing

strength and reassurance from him. Then, closing her hand around the transmitter, she rose to her feet. "Better go put it on, I guess."

"Come alone, Lexie . . . on foot . . . and bring the jewels. You did find them, didn't you, dear?" Lila's voice quavered.

"I found them. Lila? Are you all right?"

"I . . . oh! Six-thirty, Lexie. Battery Park, near Castle Clinton. Look for a black van—come to the back. They say . . . they say that once they've got their stupid jewels, they'll let me go. Ow!"

The line went suddenly dead.

"No trace again," growled Phil.

"What time is it?" Lexie demanded. The grandfather clock answered her question, gonging a slow, steady count of six.

"Ward! We've got to hurry. But . . . what if they see you? What if they're watching the building?"

"If they are, Lexie, they'll follow you when you leave. You've got what they want, remember?" Reilly pulled her close for one last hug. "Phil and I have done this before, you know. Trust us. They won't know we're there."

Reilly and Rufus watched her go from the top of the stairs. Wear something that'll stand out in a crowd, Phil had said. And she'd chosen well, gathering her black hair into a tight ponytail and topping it with a bright-red baseball cap. She wore a red T-shirt, too, tucked into baggy, faded jeans held up by a pair of electric-blue suspenders. The outfit made her look very young, innocent, vulnerable. Was the red T-shirt the same one she'd been wearing that day in the park? he wondered. And was that really only five days ago? He felt as if he'd loved her for a lifetime.

"Lexie?" He spoke her name, tempted to forget all about the job and his blasted duty; wanting nothing more than to run down the stairs and stop her, protect her, before it was too late. But after so many years, the job was too much a part of him. It made him who he was. And anyway, for Lexie, Lila's safety was much more than just a job. She'd been saying all along

that she wanted to "do something." Reilly sighed. She'd got
her chance. It was all up to her, now.

"Be careful," he said softly, as Lexie disappeared through
the door. She didn't look back. Rufus stared up at him and
whined.

"Where is she, Phil? I don't see her, do you?" Slouched
low in the backseat of the yellow cab, Reilly scanned the green
expanse of grass, followed the curve of the roadway, finally
fixing his gaze on a rusty black van. It was idling at the curb
about two hundred yards to the north, just past the entrance to
the old fort known as Castle Clinton. "What time is it?"

"About a minute later than the last time you asked," muttered Phil. "Six twenty-six." He took a sip of coffee from a
paper cup, adjusted his newspaper, and made his own surrep-
titious survey of the area.

"What do you make of that?" he asked, directing Reilly's
attention to a long row of trees on the green lawn opposite the
fort. A lone, black-clad figure, who just moments ago had rid-
den past them on a classic Harley-Davidson, was now flitting,
elf-like, from tree to tree, wrapping the stately old trunks with
ribbons of black and gray.

"Who knows," said Reilly. "Some freak doing his thing.
Let's hope he minds his own business."

"Only in New York," said Phil with a groan, sipping the
coffee again and shifting uncomfortably in his seat. Playing the
part of an off-duty cabby was about as much exertion as he
could take.

"Hey!" Phil sat up a little straighter. "Get ready, partner.
Lexie's close. I just heard her cough."

"There!" Reilly heaved a sigh of relief, leaning forward to
watch her—a splash of bright red that rounded the corner and
now ran, full speed ahead, toward the black van. "Slow down,
sweetheart," he whispered through his teeth. "Don't spook
them."

As if she'd heard his warning, Lexie slowed to a jog, then a
brisk walk as she crossed the wide expanse of green opposite
the fort entrance. Reilly saw her brief, curious glance at the

strange goings-on in the trees. He saw her stiffen, then avert her face, breaking into a rapid jog. "What the . . . ?"

"I think she knows the freak," said Phil quietly. "She just groaned."

The black-clad man suddenly skipped across the lawn toward Lexie. He was waving and smiling. The van rolled forward a few feet. Reilly had one hand on the door of the cab, the other on his gun.

"Wait," said Phil. "She's talking to him."

"What? What's she saying?"

Phil shook his head. "It . . . it's okay, I think. Just let me— Shhhh!" Pressing his hand hard against his ear, Phil listened, repeating scraps of the conversation for Reilly's benefit.

"Vincent? Vincent Urbano? I didn't recognize you."

"Alex-ahh-ndra! Didn't I tell you we'd meet again? How lovely to see you."

"I can't talk, now, Vincent. I'm in a hurry."

"But, Alex, I want to show you my project. You could take some photos—oh! You don't have your camera?"

"Please, Vincent, don't. I'm meeting my fiancé and I'm late."

Reilly leaned over the seatback, shielded from view by Phil's newspaper. "You creep," he growled, watching Lexie's struggle to avoid the man's wandering hands.

"Don't make me hurt you, Vincent."

"She said that?" asked Reilly, grinning. "Aw, heck, go ahead and hurt him, Lexie."

"Whoa!" exclaimed Phil. "I think you got your wish."

"What? What did she do?"

"I'm not sure, but look at him go!"

"Well, Vincent Urbano, whoever you are, I'd say you got what you deserved." Reilly watched the lanky man hightail it to the safety of his ribboned trees. He looked back in time to see Lexie step off the curb and stride slowly across the road toward the rusty black van. She stopped, close to the back doors, and straightened her shoulders before rapping sharply on the curtained window. Nothing happened.

"What are they waiting for?" snarled Reilly, his hand on the door once again.

"They're being careful," said Phil. "Calm down. She's fine."

Lexie rapped again, stepping quickly aside when the door swung open.

"What do you hear?" demanded Reilly.

"Shhh. Let me . . ." Phil pressed his hand to his ear once more, and again related scraps of conversation to Reilly.

"Did you bring them?"

"I said I would. But I want to see my aunt first. Lila? Lila! What have you done to her?"

"You wanted to see, you saw. Now get in."

"*No!* Lexie, don't get in the van!"

Phil's hand on his shirt collar kept Reilly in the backseat of the cab, just barely.

"Phil, let me go. We can't—"

"Shut up! I can't hear." Phil closed his eyes to listen. "She's okay. She's talking to Lila . . . Lila's not answering . . . wait, there's a noise, like . . . I think they put a gag on the old lady." He chuckled to himself. "Self-defense. That woman can talk—uh-oh."

"What? Phil? What's wrong?" Reilly stared helplessly at his partner. *"What?"*

The black van lurched into motion, its squealing tires burning tracks of rubber down the road.

"NO!" Not a word, but a fierce, animal sound. *"NO!"* Reilly roared again as he leapt from the cab, gun in hand, already running. He saw the van's back doors fly open, heard Lexie scream as she flew through the air. Instinct kept him running. She hit the pavement with a sickening thud and the scream stopped. She rolled once, twice. The van disappeared around the corner.

"Lexie?" Reilly gasped for breath and called her name again. The small, limp form on the pavement didn't move. He ran faster, heart pounding, lungs on fire. It was like a bad dream. He ran and he ran, but felt he wasn't getting any closer. *"Lexie?"*

Vincent Urbano, the evil-looking little elf, was running, too. Reilly saw him cross the road. Saw him bend over Lexie, touch her hair.

"Freeze!"

Urbano froze. Reilly had put every ounce of his remaining strength into that word. He sank to his knees at Lexie's side, scraping his gun on the pavement. Lexie moaned. Urbano backed slowly away.

"I'm here . . . Lexie, don't try to move. It's okay. I'm here." Reilly slipped his gun into its holster and bent over her, carefully checking her arms and legs for any sign of broken bones.

"Reilly?" Lexie moaned again, then opened her eyes. "Reilly? Don't let them go!" She lurched upright, into his arms. "Oh, please . . . we have to stop them. Let me . . . let me up. Ohhh . . . uhhh . . ." It was the nausea that stopped her. Rolling onto hands and knees, Lexie retched convulsively. There was nothing in her stomach to come up. It had been hours since they'd remembered to eat.

"I—I'm sorry," she moaned, slumping into Reilly's arms again. "They said—they said I brought the wrong stones. Lila was frantic . . . she . . . oh, Reilly, I'm afraid they'll kill her."

Phil's yellow cab squealed to a stop, just inches away. "Is she okay?" he asked, limping toward them with Vincent Urbano in tow. "Oh, boy," he said quietly, when Lexie looked up at him. "Let's get you to the hospital."

"No! Phil, where's my aunt?"

"Our people are on it, Lexie. The beacon is working. They'll get her. We need to take care of *you* now." Reilly was lifting her gently, carrying her to the cab.

"What should I do with this?" asked Phil, still holding Urbano by the scruff of his neck.

"Oh, Vincent," said Lexie. "I—I'm so sorry. Phil, please, don't hurt him. This is Vincent Urbano. He . . . he's an artist. We've worked together. I'm sorry, Vincent. I can't explain right now, but . . ."

Urbano smiled. "Alex-ahh-ndra, I had no idea your life was so vivid! We really must do lunch, and please, bring your friends."

* * *

"She's fine," said the young doctor. It was the same young doctor, a bit wearier and sprouting a healthy growth of stubble on his chin, who'd treated Phil only twelve hours before. "Just scrapes and bruises," he continued. "The nurse is cleaning her up now."

The doctor scratched his bristly chin, knitting his brow as if he had a puzzle to solve. "About this elevator of yours, Mr. Ward. Two accidents so close together . . . maybe—"

"Oh, don't worry about that, Doctor. It's all been taken care of," said Reilly, drifting toward the nursing station, doctor in tow. "I think you've seen the last of us."

"Well, I—I certainly hope so . . ."

Reilly smiled to himself when the nurse on duty thrust an armload of patient charts under the nose of the beleaguered young doctor. Another minute or two and he'd have forgotten all about the suspicious elevator and its two unfortunate victims.

Chapter Thirteen

" "T hey h-hurt her, Reilly. Hit her, I think. Her face . . . I c-can't get it out of my mind." Lexie choked back a sob. "I j-just wanted to touch her, to give her a hug, you know? B-but they . . . they wouldn't let me near her. And her eyes . . . Oh, p-poor Lila."

Squeezing her own eyes shut, Lexie tried to block out the awful image of her aunt, huddled on the dirty floor of that rusty black van, tufts of silvery hair stuck fast to her tear-dampened face, yellow headband hanging limply around her neck. She tried to block out the memory of Lila's cries, too. Muffled by the duct tape that covered her mouth, the feeble sounds had reminded Lexie of a frightened animal. And she could hear those sounds even now.

"Oh, please," she sobbed, giving in to the fear and the pain. "Reilly, we have to help her."

"We will," he said firmly, sinking onto the bed beside her. "We will. *I promise.*" He held her gently, aching to pull her close but afraid he might hurt her. There was hardly an inch on her body that wasn't battered, or bruised, or scraped.

When she sobbed again, Rufus edged closer, resting his head on Lexie's knee and whining softly. She made no move to comfort him, and the big dog turned his questioning gaze on Reilly. *Do something,* he seemed to say.

Do something. But what? Reilly turned, briefly, to look at Phil. His partner was pacing the room, cell phone in hand, stopping every few feet to gaze out the window as if the answers they all sought might somehow appear in the glowering rain clouds that crowded the evening sky. It was as good a place to look as any. They were no closer to a rescue now than

128

they had been twelve hours ago when those creeps had thrown Lexie from the back of the van.

Remembering that moment, Reilly felt his heart clatter against his ribs. He would never forget the sound of Lexie's scream, cut short by a sickening thud as her body hit the pavement. From that moment on, everything, *absolutely everything,* had gone wrong.

Agents from the Bureau's New York office had homed in on the beacon Phil had planted in the lining of the pouch that held Lila's gemstone ransom. The wrong ransom. It had taken the team less than ten minutes to locate the rusty black van, abandoned on Avenue D, empty except for the worthless assortment of stones left scattered across the floor. Lila and the cartel's hired thugs had vanished without a trace.

They'd had to wait far too long for Lexie's X rays and treatment at the hospital. Nothing broken, thank goodness. Except maybe that feisty spirit of hers. She'd fallen apart completely when they'd told her that Lila was still missing.

Reilly rested his head against hers and sighed. He never wanted to see that kind of misery in her eyes again. The fear and uncertainty were much harder on her than enduring the physical pain of her injuries. And while she'd never said it, he knew she had to be blaming him. Why not? He blamed himself. Another botched job. But not another lost life. Not yet, anyway. Lila was still very much alive.

The old lady had left a second message on Lexie's machine, only minutes before their return to the loft. "Twenty-four hours, Lexie. That's all they'll give us. They say we'd better get it right this time, or . . ." Lila had tried to be very brave, but at that moment she'd let a little sob escape—a heart-wrenching cry that had sent Lexie right over the edge again.

The message had ended with a promise that Lila would call back soon, and a repeat of the "no cops" warning. She said her captors had seen Lexie speak to a man in the park. They'd threatened to execute Lila on the spot if they saw him again, or anyone else they didn't like the looks of. *Curse Vincent Urbano, anyway,* thought Reilly.

"Why hasn't she called?" Lexie stifled another sob, clutch-

ing the phone in both hands as if she could squeeze a ring out
of it. And ring it did. Loud and shrill. She nearly jumped out
of her skin.

"Lila?"

"Nope. 'Fraid not, Lex. It's just me. Why the heck aren't
you at work? Mr. B's been lookin' for you."

"Angell, I . . . I can't, not tonight. Please, just tell him I'm
sick or something, okay?"

"Sick? Lexie, what's wrong. You sound terrible."

"I'm fine, but . . . please, Angell, just cover for me. I'll explain later."

"Do you need help?" Tommy's voice rose in panic. "Is it
that guy? Is that creep hanging around again? Gee, Lexie,
should I call the cops? Just . . . just hang up right now if you
want me to call the cops."

"No! Angell, no police. It's not that. It . . . it's personal.
Please, be a real angel and cover for me. Tell Mr. B whatever
you think he'll believe. I'm okay, honest, but I've got to hang
up now. Can't tie up the line any longer."

Tommy made no response.

"Please, Angell, tell me you're okay with this."

"Well . . . I guess. But, whatever you're up to, be careful."

The phone rang again the moment Lexie hung up.

"Lila? Is that you?" she demanded, holding her breath until
the answer came.

"Lexie? Oh, my dear, thank goodness. I was afraid—"

Her aunt abruptly stopped speaking, but Lexie didn't have
time to panic. In the next instant she heard Lila's voice again,
a bit fainter, as if she'd turned away from the phone.

"Don't you dare!" Lila was saying. "You threw my dear
niece out of a moving vehicle, you . . . you big brute! And I
intend to make sure she's all right. Now get your paws off me,
or . . . or you'll never see your precious jewels again."

"Lila? Lila, I'm fine, really. Please, please don't make them
mad at you." Even as she pleaded with her aunt to be careful,
Lexie breathed a sigh of relief. If Lila could still talk back to
her captors, she was going to be just fine.

"You're sure, dear? We were moving so fast. I was certain—"

"Just some scrapes and bruises. Nothing to worry about. *Honest.* But what about you? Are you feeling all right?"

"Don't you worry about me, dear," said Lila firmly. "I'll be fine."

"That's good, Lexie," hissed Phil from across the room. "Keep her talking long enough and we might get a trace." He had already set the wheels in motion to do just that, and waited for word, cell phone to his ear.

Lexie nodded. "I'm so sorry, Lila. I checked as soon as I got home, but there's nothing else in your hiding place under the floor. *Nothing.* I even went through your luggage, but . . . Lila, you have to help me. I don't know where else to look."

"Oh, dear," said Lila, sounding strangely composed. "You know me, Lexie, just a doddering, forgetful old biddy. I can't imagine—Oh! Ow!" she shrieked, her voice fading away from the phone again. "Get your hands off me, you big oaf! I'm trying. Just give me a minute."

Abruptly the line went dead.

"Nothing!" Clearly frustrated, Phil stalked across the room to sit on the end of the bed, absently resting his hand on Rufus's big, hairy head. The dog sighed audibly.

"She was trying to tell me something," said Lexie, sitting up a little straighter and groaning with the effort. "Lila would never call herself a doddering old biddy. And as for forgetful . . . no way. She's sharp as a tack, keeps the whole Mystiques inventory in her head, never has to look up a phone number or an address, and she always knows exactly where her jewelry samples are." She glared at the telephone. *"Call back!"*

The next five minutes passed as slowly as an hour. Lexie wasn't consciously aware of holding her breath, but when the phone rang again she found herself gasping for air. "Lila? H-hello?"

"Yes, dear. Now just listen. They won't give me much time." Lila's tone was clipped and efficient. "Remember I told you about the idea I had for the new necklace designs? Well, while I was in London, I found someone to help me with the prototypes. We made two. Buddy was going to market them for me. Maybe the real gems are in one of them. There might even be some in both. The thing is, I can't remember where I put them. Just . . . can't . . . remember . . .''

Lila's tone of voice had changed. Suddenly she sounded a lot like the feeble old woman she'd claimed to be. Alarmed, Lexie sat bolt upright, throwing her legs over the side of the bed and clutching the phone to her ear. "Lila?"

"It's a Scorpio trait, you know, my dear. Always forgetful. I . . . I'm sorry, Lexie, but what can I do? It's in the stars. Scorpio, you know. Scorpio. You'll just have to keep looking, I'm afraid. Oh, deary me—"

Once again the line went dead.

"No good," said Phil grimly. "They're timing the calls. We'll never get a trace at this rate."

Reilly scratched his head. "Did any of that make sense to you, Lexie?" He'd been listening to the last few seconds of conversation, his head pressed close to hers.

"Clues," she said quietly, struggling to her feet and hobbling across the room. "She was giving me clues. None of it sounded like Lila. All that stuff about Scorpios being forgetful . . . there's just no way. She thinks astrology is a lot of bunk. You should hear some of the arguments she and René have had . . ."

"Lexie?" Reilly sprang to his feet. "What are you thinking?"

"René. Reilly, she was trying to make me think about René. But why? Lila couldn't have given her one of the necklaces. I mean, how? When? Those creeps took her right after she got home."

"Describe this René person," said Phil, "and come sit down, before you fall over."

"I'm fine," said Lexie, pushing his hand away. "Now that we're doing something, I'll be just fine."

The two men followed her into the kitchen, watching as she pulled a bottle of water from the fridge and tried to unscrew the cap. She winced in pain, unable to make her badly scraped hands obey.

"Let me," said Reilly, gently guiding her onto the couch. "Do you want something for the pain?"

Sighing, Lexie shook her head. "No. I'm okay."

"About this René," prompted Phil.

"She's an old friend. An amateur astrologer. Big on horoscopes and all that stuff. Reilly's met her."

"Yeah, and she's pretty good, too. Recognized my Taurus nose from twenty paces."

Lexie laughed in spite of herself, then groaned, holding her ribs. "Ow. That hurts."

"Taurus, what?" Phil looked thoroughly puzzled.

"Nose," said Reilly. "Never mind. René Singer is not someone you'd easily forget, partner. For one thing, she's enormously pregnant, and—"

"Pregnant?" Phil sat heavily on the end of the couch. "Dark hair? Big sunglasses?"

"That's her," said Lexie. "But how . . ."

"Lila ran into her at the airport. Literally." Phil chuckled. "I got almost close enough to eavesdrop on their conversation, but I had to back off. Perfume war."

Lexie laughed—and groaned—again, imagining Lila's fog of Chanel meeting René's cloud of Obsession. But it all made sense. If Lila had given one of the prototypes to René, she'd never come right out and say so. Not in front of those thugs. She was trying to protect René and the baby.

"The old lady was rummaging around in her bag at one point," said Phil. "She could have given something to your friend, I suppose."

"I'll call," said Lexie, trying to stand but discovering, to her surprise, that Buddy had been right about the furniture all along. Too low, too soft, too darned hard to get out of.

Reilly stopped her. "Take it easy, will you?" He brushed the tangle of hair away from her face. "You sure you're okay?"

Lexie caught his hand and held tight, at least as tight as her scraped and aching fingers would allow. "I'm fine. Stop worrying. Just hand me the phone and I'll call René."

"Here, use mine," said Phil, passing the cell phone to Lexie. "Better keep your line open, just in case Lila calls back."

Pushing himself off the couch, Phil steered his partner toward the kitchen. "How about some coffee?"

"Yeah, I guess . . ."

"The old lady'll be just fine, Reilly. She's a tough old bird. We'll get them, next time."

Next time? It was all he could do to stifle the groan that rose in his throat as he watched his partner pour coffee into three mugs. "I . . . Phil, we can't ask Lexie to do that again. What if . . ."

"We won't have to ask her, Reilly. We won't be able to stop her. They're going to expect her to make another drop and she, well, she'd do anything for her aunt. You know that. All we can do is be there to back her up."

"Like we did last time?" Reilly clenched his fists. "How do we keep her safe?" He lowered his voice to a taut whisper. "It feels like a setup, Phil. Reminds me of New Mexico. And if we do manage to get her through this, how the heck do I leave her when it's all over?"

"Leave her? Reilly Ward, if you leave her you're a bigger fool than—"

"But I can't ask her to—"

"To what? To love you?" Phil shook his head. "Too late to stop that, I'd guess. Too late for both of you." He took a deep breath, as if steeling himself to endure what he was about to say. "Listen, partner, you've got to stop living in the past. We both do. What happened to Bonnie, well, we'll never know for sure if it was the phone call that led them to her. I think . . . I'm afraid they'd have found her anyway. I mean, they knew all about us, right?"

Reilly nodded. It would be so much easier to let themselves believe that. And maybe, just maybe, it was true.

"I'll tell you one thing, though. I wouldn't trade that year Bonnie and I had together. Not for anything. And Reilly, if you're lucky enough to find that kind of love . . . don't walk away, partner. You'll regret it for the rest of your life."

"Reilly? What's wrong?" Lexie hobbled into the kitchen

and leaned against the counter beside him. "Is there something you're not telling me?"

"No, Lexie. No more secrets. You know what we know." Reilly slipped his arm around her shoulders. "Just rehashing past mistakes. Things shouldn't have gone down the way they did this morning, Lexie. I—"

"It wasn't your fault." She met his gaze and slowly shook her head. If she knew it, why didn't he? If only she hadn't been so hard on him, all those bumbling-agent cracks. "Those stones looked real to me, too. And if those thugs hadn't used a jeweler's loupe to examine them, we might have gotten away with it."

Reilly let that pass without comment, moving across the room to stir cream and sugar into their coffee. "What did René say?" he asked, setting a steaming mugful on the counter in front of her.

"She's not home. I talked to the maid, Maria. That's why it took so long. Her English is about as good as my Spanish. But from what I managed to figure out, René and Dr. Singer left the city hours ago, planning to spend a few days at their place on Fire Island. I tried calling, but I guess they're not there yet." Lexie turned to stare over her shoulder at the grandfather clock. It was almost seven-thirty. She was trying her best to stop thinking about how quickly Lila's time was running out, but every sweep of that pendulum was another second lost. "I left a message, but René probably won't think to check the answering machine at the beach house. We'll have to keep trying, keep calling. I feel so useless."

"What about the other necklace, Lexie? And this person in London? The one who helped with the prototypes?" Phil had been listening to the tape of Lila's phone call while Lexie and Reilly talked.

"Julian," said Lexie absentmindedly. "She wouldn't have left the necklace with him, though. I'm pretty sure she'd have wanted Buddy to have it, but . . ."

"Julian?" Reilly said the name as if it left a bad taste in his mouth. "Julian St. James?"

"Yes. But, how . . . oh, no." Lexie felt her knees grow weak.

Was Julian involved with the cartel? Not really a friend at all? It would break Lila's heart when she found out.

"We've never been able to prove it," said Phil. "He's a sly one, this St. James. But when your aunt went to visit him, well, that pretty much cleared up any mystery as to their modus operandi."

"What's wrong?" demanded Reilly, watching Lexie's face grow pale.

"Well, what about Buddy? You—you don't think he . . . I mean, Lila always gave the prototypes to him. It was the first thing she'd do after a trip. She always showed him any special stones she'd found, too. What if he's involved?"

"Take it easy," said Reilly. "He's clean. We checked him out weeks ago. Could be he's got the other necklace, though. Do you have his home phone number handy?"

"Yeah. In my book by the bed. Should I call?"

"I'll do it," said Phil, pausing to touch her hand. "You look beat. Try to get some rest. You're going to need your strength to finish this, Lexie."

"Rest? I . . . I can't rest." Lexie took one sip of her coffee and poured the rest down the drain. "I just keep thinking about Lila . . . how small and frightened she looked."

Pacing across the room, she stopped to stare out the window. It was beginning to rain. Giant, random raindrops that splattered against the windowpanes and reminded her of tears. That's what Lila used to call them. Crocodile tears.

"Come lie down," said Reilly, guiding her onto the bed. "You don't have to sleep, just rest and let me hold you." Folding his arms around her, he shifted beside her, careful not to hurt her, until she'd nestled herself against him. "We'll get through this, Lexie," he murmured, close to her ear. "You and Lila are both going to be all right. *I promise.*"

Chapter Fourteen

Reilly matched his breathing to Lexie's—an old trick of his mother's, designed to make the other party drift off into blissful sleep. Not that anything approaching blissful sleep was likely to come to Lexie until this nightmare was over. But a short, restless nap would at least give her a chance to stop thinking for a while. Carefully, gently, he breathed to her rhythm until she gave a ragged gasp and fell into a fitful slumber.

Mom always did know best, he thought with a wistful sigh. How long had it been since he'd thought about the old days—all those happy times back in Portland? A very long time, he decided. But now here he was, practically wallowing in fond memories of home and family. This case—no, this woman in his arms—had him wanting the same for himself. Home and family. It was something he'd never considered possible, until now. Until Lexie Frost.

Taking care not to disturb her, Reilly slipped his arm from beneath her tiny form, and pulled the big comforter closely around her. Silently, he rolled off the bed, and made his way to the kitchen. It was just a few minutes past eight, but already the loft was nearly dark, thanks to the steady spring rain that pattered softly against the windows, drowning out the city sounds from the street below.

Leaning against the counter, nursing a cup of strong coffee, Reilly watched the shadowy form of his partner as he paced like a caged cat, back and forth, back and forth. Gripping his cellular phone, white-knuckled, Phil cursed under his breath with every step.

Reilly sipped moodily, and pondered life—his life. A pretty lonely life, if the truth be told. He knew that Phil was right about moving forward, about letting go of the past. Bonnie's

137

death had happened a long time ago, nothing could be changed, nothing could be proved, it could only be accepted. Phil was also right about living your life in the moment, enjoying every second of it, because you just never knew what might lie in wait around the next corner. Life was full of surprises. So why waste the precious moments in front of you, brooding over a useless ''what if?'' theory?

Maybe Phil was right about Lexie, too. Maybe a person could only reasonably expect one chance at true love in a lifetime. If that was the case, Reilly was feeling ever more certain that Lexie Frost was his one chance. He drained his cup and sighed softly.

Phil stopped pacing and moved to stand beside his partner. ''Feeling bad because you couldn't make it all go away for her?'' He chuckled. ''Me, too.'' Stretching, he gingerly touched his head. ''Man, that aches. Hey, it's gonna be okay, pard, I'm just going nuts because I can't get hold of this Buddy Fine character. Take it easy.''

''I know. You're right.'' Reilly shook his head. ''Huh, you always are.''

The sharp ringing of Lexie's phone immediately focused their attention on the situation at hand. Reilly dove on the instrument before it could ring again.

''Hello?''

A slightly nasal voice, tinged with surprise so apparent that Reilly could almost see the raised eyebrows, said, ''Hello, Jack? Is that you?''

''No, it's not. Who's calling?'' Reilly wasn't about to waste time on niceties when Lila might be trying to get through to them.

''It's René. But who . . . hey, wait a minute, is this that nice Mr. Taurus I just met?''

Reilly sighed with relief. ''Yes, Mrs. Singer, it's Reilly. Thank goodness you called back. I need to ask you what may seem like a strange question. Did Lexie's Aunt Lila give you anything the other day? A package or anything like that?''

''What is this?'' demanded René in a voice tinged with suspicion. ''What kind of question is that, Reilly Ward? Come to think of it, how do I know you're even who you say you are? Let me talk to Lexie. *Now.*'' Her tone was harsh and ear-ringingly shrill.

He hissed out a breath through clenched teeth. "Fine, I'll wake her up," he said curtly, laying the phone down none too gently as he strode across the room.

"Lexie?" Bending carefully over her sleeping form, Reilly whispered her name and ever so gently touched her shoulder. "Lexie," he said again, "René wants to talk to you."

Lexie moved a curtain of hair from her face, wincing with the painful effort involved. She seemed to be struggling with comprehension.

"Ward?" she asked sleepily. "What . . . what did you say? I don't . . . I can't understand what you're saying." She tried to sit up, and uttered a sharp cry of pain.

Reilly instantly moved to help her, sitting beside her and gently putting an arm behind her back for support. Brushing his lips against her hair, he said, "The phone, Lexie. You need to come to the phone. It's René. She wants to talk to you."

Suddenly Lexie was wide awake. "How could you let me sleep? Did Lila call again? Ward, what did I miss?"

Her voice was taut with anger and fear, and Reilly felt a lump form in his throat.

"No, Lexie, Lila didn't call. You didn't miss anything. Come on now, and talk to René. Maybe she can shed a little light on the whole situation." He smiled ruefully. "I tried, but she sure won't talk to me."

With Reilly's help, Lexie hobbled to the phone, stumbling over a sleepy Rufus, who yelped in protest.

Phil handed her the phone, still rigged with the tiny micro-phone that allowed him to eavesdrop and record. He flashed an encouraging grin, adjusted his headset, and leaned back against the counter to listen.

Lexie made a face as she pulled the receiver close to her ear. There wasn't a single part of her body that didn't scream with pain every time she moved. She pushed the thought from her mind. Her discomfort was nothing compared to the terror and pain that poor Lila was being forced to endure. How could she have let herself fall asleep? Shaking off the guilty thought, she sank onto the end of the sofa and spoke urgently into the phone.

"René? I thought you'd never call back! What took you so long?"

"What? Lexie Frost, I don't know what your problem is, but I called as soon as I got your message. Honestly! This is supposed to be a getaway for me and Aaron, you know. Can't blame us for not checking the machine the instant we arrived."

Lexie mentally cursed herself. René had every right to be annoyed. She took a deep breath and forced a note of calm into her voice. "Sorry, René. I didn't mean to yell at you. It's just that . . . René, this is really important."

"Important? I'll say it's important. You've been keeping secrets, Lexie Frost. Imagine my surprise to hear Mr. Perfect Taurus answering your phone in the middle of the night. All I can say is it's about time that you got yourself—"

"René! This is not about Reilly. It's about Lila."

"Well, you don't have to yell. What do you want to know?"

Lexie took a deep, shuddering breath. Forcing herself to speak calmly, she said, "Did Lila give you anything yesterday, when you met her at the airport?"

"Well, she always brings me something, doesn't she? We're practically family, after all. Now, let me see," René sounded as though she were ticking things off on her fingers. "She brought me a silk scarf. Oh, and some Obsession—she knows how much I adore it, and you can never have too much perfume."

Phil snorted, a wordless opinion of this last statement.

"Anything else?" Frustrated, Lexie was afraid she might give in to a scream at any moment.

"Let me think," said René slowly. "Oh, wait a minute. Yes, she did give me something else. A necklace she'd designed. No wonder I didn't remember it right away—it was absolutely ghastly, not my style at all. But, I didn't want to hurt her feelings, so I took it, naturally. Why, is it important?"

Lexie gasped. "Yes, René, it is important but I can't explain right now. Please, please, just tell me where the necklace is."

"Oh." René thought for a second. "Well, as I say, it was absolutely ghastly. I gave it to Maria."

"What?" Lexie almost choked. "You gave it to the maid?!" Calming herself, she asked, "Does she still have it, do you think?"

"As far as I know, she does. She seemed to think it was quite attractive but, then, there's no accounting for taste. And there's certainly no need to yell. Honestly, Lexie."

"I'm sorry. But we have to get that necklace. Where is Maria now?"

"Well, she's at the penthouse in town, of course. Where else would she be? I'll be back late tomorrow, Lexie, if you want to drop by."

"We can't wait that long. We're going to have to go there tonight." Lexie was impatient now, ready to dash out the door. "We're leaving as soon as I hang up the phone. Call me tomorrow, okay?"

"But, Lexie, you don't speak Spanish; how will you make her understand you?"

"I don't know. We'll just have to wing it. Maybe you could call and explain, speed things up for us. Give it a try, okay? Thanks a million, René, I'll talk to you soon. 'Bye." And Lexie hung up before René could say another word.

"That's it," said Lexie, her voice raspy from stress and lack of sleep. She pointed a finger toward an imposing turn-of-the-century apartment building, elegantly restored, with polished brass doors and a row of laughing gargoyles lining the balustrade.

Reilly double-parked, blocking a shiny red Volvo and giving Lexie a helpless shrug as he pulled the keys from the ignition.

"Don't worry," she said, "everybody does it. We'll be long gone before they get around to towing your old wreck."

"Okay, folks, this is for the money," said Phil, as he helped Lexie out of the passenger seat. "Does the doorman know you, Lexie?" He assumed a smiling face and wished the doorman a good evening as they crossed the sidewalk.

"No handouts for panhandlers," the uniformed man said tersely. "Move along now. Don't want any trouble."

Reilly nudged Lexie forward and whispered laughingly in her ear, "So much for the 'unforgettable' Lexie Frost, award-winning photographer."

She elbowed him in the ribs, immediately regretting the move as it caused a spasm of pain to run through the entire right side of her body. At the sound of her groan, the doorman glanced again in their direction.

"Look," he said, "if the young lady is ill, I can call an ambulance. Otherwise, move along." He turned his attention to a car full of immaculately groomed partygoers, complete with full-length gowns and tuxedos.

"He's right, you know," muttered Phil. "We're a pretty motley crew, what with my black eye, and Lexie's scraped-up face and Quasimodo walk. Not to mention your questionable attire. It's a wonder the guy hasn't called the cops already."

"What d'you mean, questionable attire?" Reilly examined his blue shirt and gray tweed jacket with a dubious frown. "What's wrong with this?"

"Oh, come on." Phil laughed. "We could dress you up in a brand-new suit, and whammo! It'd look slept in."

Reilly glared at his partner. "Oh, yeah? Well—"

"Uh, guys?" Lexie gave them both a nudge, ignoring the pain in her side, and battling a nervousness that threatened to erupt into something approaching hysteria. She forced herself to speak calmly. "D'you think, maybe, this little discussion could wait?"

"Right," said Phil. "Time for a Plan B."

Reilly studied the pavement for a long moment. "Okay, Phil, why don't you come up with a way to distract the guy, while we get in?"

"No can do, pard. These fine men are trained to detect that sort of ruse. No, there's only one possible plan, and Lexie here is the only one who can pull it off."

Lexie looked at Phil as if he'd lost his mind. Didn't he realize that Lila might be trying to call at that very moment? She could almost hear the hollow ringing of the phone in the empty loft.

They were FBI agents, for heaven's sake. Why didn't they just show the man their badges? Unless . . . what if they weren't really who they said they were? What if—

No. She drew a deep breath and forced herself to stop. She was a wreck, and she was letting her imagination run wild. Indulging in senseless paranoia wasn't helping. Not one bit. "B-but, why me?" she asked, mentally cursing the tremble in her voice. "Couldn't you just flash your badges and get it over with?"

"Calm down," said Phil, giving her arm a sympathetic squeeze. "That's Plan C. If we can maintain our cover, so much the better."

"So, what is this wonderful Plan B of yours? What do you want me to do?"

"Why, you beg and plead, of course. Tell the man the truth—well, not the whole truth. Just tell him you left something at your friend's apartment, and you need to get in to retrieve it."

Lexie looked at him uncertainly. It was a pretty lame Plan B, as far as she was concerned. But, she reminded herself, time was wasting. Shaking off the hands of her companions, she approached the doorman. "Excuse me. Could I speak to you for a moment?"

The man looked at her warily. "About what?" he demanded, appearing to soften a little as he studied her face. Maybe the tears she was fighting so hard to hold back would work in her favor. She hoped so, anyway.

"I need to get up to Dr. Singer's penthouse. His wife is my best friend, and I left my . . . my . . . necklace there when I visited yesterday."

The doorman looked her up and down. She knew he had to be taking in the tousled hair, the scratched face, and the total lack of jewelry. She wondered if he might at least give her points for coming up with a good story.

"Look," he said, "Mrs. Singer isn't home at the moment. It's only the maid there. If she knows who you are, then I'll let you in." He glanced doubtfully at Phil and Reilly, who were standing back at a respectful distance, eyes averted, waiting for Lexie to pull this off.

"Oh, thank you so much. Maria will know who I am. Please ring up, I'll talk to her." Inwardly, Lexie uttered a fervent prayer that René would have phoned already, and told Maria what to expect. She sighed. Knowing René, it was probably wishful thinking.

The doorman was holding the phone out to Lexie. "The maid wants to speak to you," he said wonderingly.

Gratefully, Lexie put the phone to her ear. "Maria? It's Lexie. Lexie Frost. Please, let me in."

There was a short burst of Spanish, then Maria replied in halting English. "*Sí,* Señorita Lexie. Come. Come up. *Lo siento*—so sorry!"

In the elevator, Phil burst out laughing. "Did you see the man's face?"

Reilly allowed himself a ghost of a smile. "Now maybe we'll get somewhere."

"Come on, guys, this is the top floor; Maria should be waiting for us." Lexie was impatient and pushed ahead of the men, limping down the hallway with great determination. The two looked at each other, shrugged, and followed. What happened next would be entirely up to her.

Softly but impatiently, she tapped on the door to the apartment. Just as she was lifting her bruised hand to knock again, the door was jerked open by a small, dark woman in a flowered apron. Her hair was pulled back into a sleek, fat bun, and her arms were white with flour. She looked at Lexie with a smile of recognition, and waited.

"Hello, Maria. Er, I mean, *hola,*" Lexie began.

"*Hola,* Señorita Lexie."

The smiling woman gestured Lexie and the two men into the apartment. It was obvious that she hadn't the faintest idea why they were there. But Lexie knew that Maria was a patient individual, and probably used to the odd comings and goings of René's friends. She looked to Reilly and Phil for help. "Do either of you speak any Spanish?"

Reilly shook his head and turned to his partner. Phil looked sheepish and said, ''Well, I picked up a couple of words when I was down in Mexico with Lila. I'll see what I can do.'' He frowned. ''We don't exactly have a lot of time.''

Clearing his throat, as if that might help him to speak better Spanish, he bowed slightly to Maria. ''Er, *¿habla inglés, señora?*''

Maria perked up at the use, however halting, of her native tongue. Her answer was less than comforting, though. *''No, señor. No inglés.''*

Phil groaned and looked despairingly at Lexie and Reilly. ''My Spanish is limited at best. It won't be beautiful but, maybe we can get her to understand.'' He turned again to the maid.

''Señora, um, *el collar?''* He made a circling movement around his neck, to indicate the piece of jewelry in question, but the woman simply stared at him in wonder.

''No comprendo,'' she said slowly, *''¿El collar?''*

Phil took another deep dig into his memory bank, brightening slightly as he remembered a key phrase. *''Sí, el collar. ¿Dónde está el collar?''*

Understanding seemed to come to the woman, and she hesitated, narrowing her eyes a little as she asked, *''¿Por qué?''*

Phil tried again. *''¿Por favor, señora, dónde está el collar?* We need . . . we want . . . *la policía . . . el collar?''* he repeated, at a loss for further words.

Maria looked sharply at Lexie. *''¿Es policía?''*

Phil explained. ''She wants to know if I'm a cop. Maybe this time we'll have to show our badges.'' He looked troubled.

Reilly was already reaching for his wallet. Almost in unison, they proffered their badges, and Maria's eyes went wide as her flour-dusted hand flew to her mouth. *''Policía!''* she exclaimed, and scurried down the hallway, leaving the three to wonder if she intended to call the *policía* herself.

''Oh, thank goodness,'' breathed Lexie. Maria was coming back to them, holding a large and gaudy necklace in her hands. She delivered it to Lexie, smiling shyly at the two men.

''Oh, *gracias, Maria, gracias,*'' Lexie's eyes began to fill with tears. René was right, she thought. The necklace really was quite dreadful. But it was also the one thing that might bring Lila back to her alive. And that seemed to give it a special beauty all its own. *"Gracias,"* she murmured again.

The three moved quickly toward the door. *"Adiós, Maria. And gracias,"* said Phil, giving a broad wink to the woman, who blushed furiously.

Lexie impulsively turned back to give Maria a hug, getting covered with flour in the process. "Yes, *gracias* again, Maria. *Adiós.*"

Reilly saved his sarcasm for the elevator. "Well, you two can look at promising careers in the United Nations. Meanwhile, I have to say, just for the record, that Lila's necklace is one of the least attractive pieces of jewelry I've ever seen. No offense, Lexie."

She smiled wearily. "None taken. The important thing is that we have it, and now we can get my aunt back."

The two men exchanged guarded looks and said nothing. They both knew that Lexie's life was about to get a lot more complicated and dangerous than it already was. A lot more. And there wasn't a thing either one of them could do to protect her.

Chapter Fifteen

"Is it you?" Buddy wrenched open the shop door before Lexie had a chance to knock a second time. "Come in, come in all of you," he ordered, waving them through with a "hurry up" gesture. "I got a phone message, and—"

Words seemed to fail him at the sight of Lexie's bruised and battered face. "Oy!" he exclaimed, raising both hands to his mouth in horror. "Vat happen? Vat happen to you, and ver is mein Lila?"

Buddy's accent grew thicker and more pronounced with every word he spoke. Knowing the man as well as she did, Lexie understood that such a lapse could only mean one thing. Buddy was about to panic. He'd be absolutely useless if that happened.

"Calm down, Buddy," she said softly. "I'm okay, I just had a fall. And Lila's going to be fine, too. But we need your help. Please, try to stay calm."

"Calm? You vant I should be calm?" Buddy turned up the volume with every question and, spinning to face Reilly, latched onto his sleeve with a vicelike grip. "Vas dat you who called me, Reilly Ward? I came as soon as—"

One eyebrow curled into a questioning arch as he studied the dark-haired stranger who'd been standing so quietly at Lexie's side. "Who is that one?" he demanded, indicating Phil with a quick jerk of his thumb.

"My partner, Phil," answered Reilly. "He's the one who left the message on your machine."

Phil nodded, extending his hand to the stout little man. "Phil Dibiase. Did you find the necklace, Mr. Fine?"

"I did," said Buddy, with a slow, serious nod of his head. "Lila left it for me. Dropped it right in the mail slot, she did."

147

He fished a gaudy piece of jewelry out of the pocket of his equally gaudy houndstooth pants. ''Worthless, the stones. But, ah! Such a talent, my Lila.'' Brushing a tear from the corner of his eye, Buddy beamed up at his three visitors. ''Is beautiful, no?''

''What about this one, Buddy?'' Lexie had tucked Maria's necklace safely away inside her jacket, holding it close to her heart on the trip back downtown. Somehow, having it near had made her aunt seem closer, too. But now she pulled it out and placed it gently in Buddy's hands.

''Hmmmm.'' Holding the necklace up to the light, he ran his fingers over the stones and frowned. ''I need the loupe,'' he said suddenly, and charged off down the aisle with Lexie, Reilly, and Phil close on his heels.

''Hmmmm,'' he said again, adjusting the loupe and bending low over his worktable.

''What?'' demanded Lexie. ''Buddy, are the stones real or not?''

Buddy straightened abruptly, looking somewhat comical with the jeweler's loupe still lodged between his fleshy cheek and broad, bushy eyebrow.

''Very real,'' he said, widening his eyes and letting the loupe drop into his hand. Looking first at Lexie, then at the two men who stood close behind her, he took a deep breath and repeated himself. ''Very real. And very valuable, too. Like nothing my Lila ever brought to me before.'' He aimed a stubby finger at Reilly's face and jabbed the air to emphasize his words. ''You tell me now, Mr. Reilly Ward. The truth. Vat is going on?''

Pulling his badge from his jacket pocket, Reilly placed it on the table in front of the older man. ''FBI, Buddy. I'm afraid Lila's been involved in something—''

''Vat?'' Buddy's wide face flushed a brilliant crimson. ''My Lila vould never—''

''No, Buddy, it's not that.'' Lexie caught his trembling hand between both of hers. ''Some men, bad men, have been using Lila to smuggle gems. She didn't know anything about it, though. We're certain of that. Anyway, Reilly and Phil have been on the case, trying to prove what was happening, trying to protect us, but . . ."

She groaned, fighting tears and wishing there was an easy way to tell him. "I . . . I'm sorry, Buddy—"

"No. *I'm* sorry," Reilly interrupted, sounding utterly defeated. "We blew it, Buddy." Slipping his arm around Lexie's shoulders, he held her close as he continued. "They've got Lila. And they want their gems back before they'll let her go. Now that you've identified the real stones, we're going to make sure they get what they want."

The color drained from Buddy's cheeks—red to pasty gray in a single heartbeat. "Is . . . is she . . . ?"

"Lila's fine, Buddy. Just scared, like the rest of us. But we'll get her back for you, safe and sound. I promise."

Phil nodded agreement. "First things first, though," he said. "We'd better get Lexie upstairs. Lila should be calling soon."

For nearly an hour, Lexie had pretended to be asleep, curled into the big armchair, eyes closed, one hand on the telephone, every nerve on edge. Why hadn't Lila called?

She longed to be doing something—anything. Even pacing the room would be better than this. She wanted to scream, just throw open the window and scream at the top of her lungs. But here she sat. Reilly had insisted that she get some rest. She'd tried. It was pointless. The metered voice of the grandfather clock filled her mind with thoughts of time. Time wasting. Time counting down. Time running out. A mellow gong marked the hour. It was five o'clock.

She stretched, gingerly testing her sore muscles. Everything ached. The lights were still on in the kitchen, but it was dark in the rest of the loft, thanks to an early-morning rain that clouded the sky and hid the sunrise. She could see two shadowy forms on the couch, Phil in the corner closest to her, with a hairy knot at his feet that had to be Rufus, and good old Buddy at the far end, snoring loudly.

Had Lila been able to sleep? she wondered. Probably not. Knowing her aunt, she'd have to bet that the dear old lady had been wide awake all night—terrified, but trying not to show it.

Probably complaining, doing her best to make sure that her captors were every bit as miserable as she. *Be careful,* thought Lexie, mentally willing Lila to heed the warning. *Be careful . . . and pick up the phone.*

Pushing herself out of the chair, she hobbled across the room to stand at Reilly's side. He was sipping what had to be his fifteenth cup of coffee, and studying a rumpled map of the five boroughs that he'd spread across the kitchen counter. Sliding her arms around him, she rested her head on his chest and breathed a shuddering sigh. "Why haven't they called?"

"They're smart, Lexie. And cautious. They risk exposure every time Lila speaks to you."

"But, Ward, they said twenty-four hours and it's been nearly—"

"It won't be long now."

His words were clipped, his voice harsh and distant. Lexie pushed herself away. Was he angry? Why? What could have happened? What had she done? Staring up at him, feeling hurt and confused, she read the truth in his eyes. It was fear, not anger, that raged within.

"Don't be afraid," she said quietly, reaching up to touch his cheek. Whiskers rasped against her fingers, a sharp reminder of just how long they'd been waiting. "It'll be okay."

"Hey, that's my line." Pulling her close again, holding tight, as if he'd never let her go, Reilly whispered something else, in a voice so quiet she could barely hear the words—words that stole her breath away. She thought she heard him say, "I love you."

I love you. Had he meant to say it aloud? she wondered, losing herself in the warmth of his embrace. *I love you.* His lips felt cool against her forehead . . . warmer as they sought her mouth . . . fiery when he claimed the kiss she wanted more than breath itself.

He could make her forget, this man who said he loved her. The fear, the danger, seemed to fade into the distance, as if the world beyond his arms had ceased to exist. She might even forget all those promises she'd made to herself, all those new rules for life after Jack. She had vowed to be strong, independent, successful; to make it on her own. She didn't need a man to feel her life was complete. But this man . . . this wonderful man, kept surprising her with glimpses of a different sort of life—shared love and laughter . . . and respect.

Ignoring the painful scrapes and bruises that covered her body, she held him even closer, letting the phone fall onto the counter as she twined her arms around his neck. Pure pleasure fed the soft moan that rose in her throat. And then he was gone.

"Aw, Lexie, I'm sorry." His words became a groan as he pulled away. "Did I hurt you?"

"What?" She struggled to catch her breath as her mind tumbled back into reality. "No. No, you didn't hurt me. You . . . you made the hurt stop. You made everything stop, for a minute, anyway." She stepped closer, coaxing his arms back around her, resting her head on the solid wall of his chest. It was useless. Their peaceful moment was lost. "Y'know what?" she asked.

"What?"

"Reality is greatly overrated."

The phone rang before the words were out of her mouth. Loud, shrill, and demanding, as if to prove her point. Lexie lunged for it.

"Wait!" Reilly and the suddenly wide-awake Phil spat the word in unison.

"Let Phil get set up," said Reilly, covering her hand with his as the phone jangled again. "And you need to keep her talking this time, Lexie, so we can trace the call. Do whatever you have to do, but keep her talking."

"I'll try . . . Phil?" She watched him trip over Rufus, fumble with his cell phone; she held her breath while he punched in a series of numbers, groaned aloud when the phone in her hand rang a third time, and then a fourth. Rufus whined, retreating to his safe place under the bed. Buddy, thankfully, was still sound asleep. "Now? . . . Phil?"

"Okay," he said, nodding as he activated the voice recorder. "Pick up."

Lexie snatched the phone to her ear, mid-ring. "Lila?"

"Yes, dear. It's me."

"Lila, are you all right?" She was almost afraid to hear the answer. The voice at the other end of the line sounded so terribly weak, so frail. "Lila?"

"I . . . I'm very tired, my dear. And hungry. These beastly creatures haven't fed me."

"What? They haven't fed you? Oh, Lila, I'm so sorry." How long had it been? Lexie's hands clenched in anger at the thought of what she'd like to do to her aunt's captors, if only she had the chance.

"Well, not unless you consider pepperoni pizza fit to eat."

"Pizza?"

"Can you imagine? My dear, I'd rather starve!"

Lexie smiled in spite of herself. Lila was beginning to sound a bit stronger and, as she'd suspected, had obviously been giving her captors some grief. Good for her.

"You're doing fine, Lexie, just great," said Phil. "Keep her talking, we're almost there."

"Have you at least had something to drink, *Aunt* Lila?" She threw in the title, hoping Lila would take the hint and do her part to drag out the conversation.

"Yes, dear. I absolutely insisted on bottled water. You can't imagine the color of the stuff that comes out of the taps— *Ow!*"

"Lila?"

"I-I'm all right, my dear. B-but . . . they say I'm wasting time."

"Did they hurt you?"

"D-don't worry, Lexie. I . . . I'm fine. And I'm counting on you, my dear. Did you find the prototypes?"

"Yes, and Buddy says the real gems are in one of them. What now, Aunt Lila? What do I do next?"

"Got it," said Phil, flashing a thumbs-up.

"Don't tell her," warned Reilly, whispering close to Lexie's ear. "Lila might tip our hand. Just keep her talking."

"Lila? What now?"

"Half an hour, Lexie. They want you to walk north on Broadway. They say they'll find you this time." Lila drew a sharp, audible breath. "Oh, my dear, please hurry. And come alone, or—"

Abruptly, the line went dead. Lexie stood as if frozen, the phone still pressed against her car, until Reilly pried it loose from her hand. "Lexie? Are you all right?"

She wanted to say yes, wanted to look him straight in the eye and tell him that everything was under control. But even if she'd been able to find her voice, telling him that would have been a lie. Her heart was drumming against her ribs, so loudly she could hardly hear herself think. And her hands had begun to tremble.

"Lexie?" he repeated, gently cupping her chin in his hands.

"I'll be fine," she said at last, trying her best to avoid meeting his gaze. She could feel his tension, could hear it in his voice. She couldn't let him know how terrified she really was. "I can do this, Reilly. I'm ready, but just . . . just hold me, please. Just for a minute."

Reilly closed the space between them in an instant, folding her safe in his arms, holding her so close that their hearts seemed to beat as one. She felt his lips brush her forehead. "I'll be right there with you," he said quietly. "Every step of the way. C'mon, now, we've gotta move. Phil, did you get the stuff?"

"What?" Lexie stared up at him. "Ward, what are you talking about? They said to come alone."

"You will be alone. I'm going first."

"No! Reilly, if they see you . . ."

"If they see me," he said, accepting a brown paper bag from Phil's hand, "they won't think anything of it. They won't even bother to look."

Lexie watched as he pulled a raggedy old overcoat out of the bag and shrugged it on. It was several sizes too big, its frayed hem drooping almost to the floor, sleeves falling well below his fingertips. A fake beard, matted and scraggly, and a battered, brown felt hat pulled low over his face, completed the disguise.

Reilly grinned. "See what I mean? Guys like this just blend into the background in this city. There's one on every corner.

I'll be half a block in front of you all the way, doing my bag man routine.''

''But—''

''Lexie, don't argue,'' said Phil abruptly. ''You're not going in alone. Reilly will be on the street, and I'll be in the cab. We'll both be able to hear you, so talk to us, okay? Let us know what you see, what you think.'' Opening his briefcase, Phil selected a tiny microphone, identical to the one she'd worn the day before, and placed it in Lexie's hand. ''You know what to do with this, right?''

''Uh-huh.'' She stared at the tiny object as if in a trance. She knew what to do, but her feet wouldn't move. Looking up, she saw Reilly slip a tiny listening device into his left ear, threading the wire down under his shirt. He clipped an almost invisible microphone to his collar then, and connected both wires to a transmitter/receiver that he'd fastened to his belt. Engrossed in the process, he seemed completely unaware that she was still in the room.

''Let's go,'' said Phil firmly, gripping her shoulders and pointing her toward the bathroom. ''We need to move, Lexie. Wear something bright again, okay? And hurry.''

Hurry. That's what Lila had said. The thought of her aunt set her feet in motion and she flew across the room, catching one last glimpse of Reilly before she closed the bathroom door. He was tucking a very large gun into the folds of that enormous coat. She felt her blood run cold at the thought that he might actually have to use it.

As Lexie passed the corner of Broadway and Grand, the steady, drizzling rain gave way to a torrential downpour. Turning up the collar on her yellow slicker, she quickened her pace a bit, peeking out from under the brim of her hat to scan the street. She could see Reilly, huddled in the doorway of a building halfway up the block. But for the two of them, the sidewalk was empty.

Glancing quickly over her shoulder, she located Phil's yellow cab, idling at the curb two blocks to the south. *So far, so good,* she thought, shoving her hands deep into the pockets of her coat. The rain was relentless and cruel, like sharp little needles that stung her cheeks and stabbed the pavement, making a firecracker sound against the yellow oilcloth fabric of her raincoat and hat.

"Can you hear me?" she asked, suddenly afraid that the downpour would drown out her voice. She breathed a sigh of relief when Reilly stepped out onto the sidewalk, dropped his shopping bag, and then stooped to pick it up. He nodded briefly in her direction before beginning a slow shuffle up the street. Behind her, a horn honked once, twice. "Okay, Phil," she answered. "I hear you."

She scanned the street again, aware that she hadn't a clue what to look for. Would they be driving another van? On foot, maybe? Or holed up in one of the buildings? Lowering her head, Lexie spoke quietly. "I don't know what I'm looking for, guys, but so far I haven't seen anything funny. Except for a grown woman dressed like a duck and talking to her chest, that is."

That should give them both a good chuckle, she thought, wishing she could find something to laugh about, too. Instead, she thought about Buddy, about the terrified look on his face when they'd awakened him to say good-bye. She thought about Reilly telling her to be careful, making her promise that, this time, she would not let them make her get into their van, or whatever they happened to be driving; that she would stay on the sidewalk; that she would trust him.

She could almost hear him whispering those words again, too. *I love you.* Why hadn't she answered? She couldn't deny what she felt. Shouldn't try to deny it, especially not now when they were walking into the greatest danger she'd ever faced. And Reilly was ready to protect her with his life. Suddenly, she wanted him to know that she'd heard him. She wanted him to hear those words, too. He had to hear. What if she never had another chance to tell him?

"Reilly? About what you said before . . . in the kitchen. I . . . I want . . ." She looked up, saw him shuffling along the sidewalk, slow and steady. He stiffened at the sound of her voice, turned, kicked at something on the pavement, and looked directly at her for an instant. The words stuck in her throat. What if that wasn't what he'd said? What if she'd imagined the whole thing? She'd make a fool of herself, and embarrass Reilly in front of his partner. "I want . . . that is . . . just . . . just be careful, okay?"

He raised a hand to the brim of his hat before he turned, and then, falling back into his shuffling gait, Reilly plodded off up the street. She watched him and wished she could hear what he was thinking. Wished she'd had the guts to tell him the truth.

Things would be different once Lila was safe, once this whole awful business was over. There would be time to figure things out, time to discover their true feelings. But suddenly she feared it would never be over. It seemed as if she'd been walking forever—definitely more than half an hour, she was certain of that. What if they'd seen her talking to herself . . . what if they'd seen Reilly or Phil? "It's been too long. Do you think they know?"

Reilly suddenly backtracked, stepping off the curb to pick up a pop can discarded in the gutter. He polished it on his sleeve and dropped it into his bag, turning to stare back at Lexie again, through the rain. She could almost hear him telling her to keep going, to be strong.

"Okay," she said quietly. "Don't worry. I'm okay, just nervous. Where are they?"

Crossing Union Square, Lexie looked up through the pouring rain to read the time on the clock tower. Just after six. The morning rush hour was well under way, but the sidewalks were still nearly deserted, thanks to the steady downpour. "Where are they?" she whispered again, abruptly choking off her words with a cough. A long, black car with dark, tinted windows cruised past, hugging the curb. It slowed to a stop a short distance up the street.

"It's them . . . I think," she said, faking another cough, then lifting her head to look directly at the car. No more mistakes. She wanted to be certain they would recognize her.

Lexie stayed close to the buildings as she moved slowly past the big car. The driver kept pace, inching up the street as if daring her to run. Was it them? Or was some other pervert stalking her now? She felt her hands begin to shake and forced herself to stand still, turning slowly to face the car as the back door flew open.

"Get in."

She couldn't see the speaker, but his voice was a low growl, coarse and menacing. Lexie flattened herself against the storefront and shook her head. She could see three vague shapes inside the dark car. Maybe one of the shapes was Lila. Maybe not.

"Where's my aunt?"

"She's right here. *Now get in.*"

"No!" From the corner of her eye, Lexie could see Reilly shuffling back down the street toward them. "You let my aunt out, now. Then I'll give you the necklace."

A pair of feet, two hands, and then a dark, angry face materialized from the gloomy interior of the car. No wonder she hadn't been able to see him, she thought. Everything about him was dark. He was dressed in black from head to foot, knit cap, jacket, turtleneck, pants, even his hands were gloved in black leather, and his face was an unhealthy gray. He glared at her, dark eyes beneath thick black brows, and lurched across the sidewalk. "Don't play games with me, little girl. Just do what I say and nobody gets hurt."

Reilly was closer now. Close enough that Lexie could hear the scuff-and-slosh sound of his shoes on the pavement. The dark man didn't seem to notice, or didn't care. Reilly was just another vagrant, just part of the scenery.

"Don't make me use this," growled the man, letting her glimpse the object hidden in the pocket of his jacket.

A gun! She had to warn Reilly before it was too late, before he got any closer.

"You won't shoot me," she said, surprised at how clear and steady her voice sounded. "You don't know where the necklace is."

"What?" Dark Man's eyebrows lurched upward. "You brought it with you. That was the deal."

Reilly was only inches away now, still shuffling, staring down at the sidewalk.

"Your deal," she said bravely. "I'd have to be stupid to trust you, wouldn't I?"

"Why, you little—"

Lexie saw the black-gloved hand reach out to grab her shoulder. In the same instant, another hand appeared, thrust under Dark Man's nose, palm up. The hand wore a dirty, fingerless glove.

"Got a dollar, mister?" asked Reilly, in his best bag man voice. "Sure could use a hot cuppa Joe."

"Get lost, you bum," growled Dark Man, giving Reilly a two-fisted shove. "Get lost, before you get yourself hurt."

Lexie wasn't sure how he managed it, but somehow Reilly succeeded in planting the barrel of that big gun he'd hidden under his coat right in the middle of Dark Man's stomach. "Freeze," he said quietly, "and hand over the gun, before *you* get yourself hurt."

Reilly stepped quickly in front of her, using Dark Man as a shield against his cohorts in the car. "Take his gun, Lexie."

She did as she was told, holding the weapon as tightly as her trembling hands would allow. For the first time in recent memory, she was actually glad that she'd listened to Jack— though she was certain this wasn't what he'd had in mind when he'd insisted that she learn how to shoot.

Phil appeared then, in a flash of yellow with squealing tires. Angling the taxicab into the curb, he lurched to a stop, blocking escape for the occupants of the black car. A blue van wheeled in behind him, disgorging four agents in FBI jackets, guns drawn. They pulled two men from the car and led them away as Reilly snapped cuffs on the still-glowering Dark Man.

"Where's Lila?" In all the confusion, it seemed as if they'd forgotten about her. Panic-stricken, Lexie screamed the question again, in a voice she hardly recognized as her own. *"Where's my aunt?"*

Phil checked the car and slowly shook his head. Dark Man was staring at her, silent and smug. He knew exactly where Lila was, and she would make him tell. Suddenly she was screaming, pointing his own gun at him and screaming. "Tell me where she is, *right now,* or I'll shoot. I swear, I'll shoot."

"What? What is this?" Helpless, the man looked to Reilly. "You can't let her . . ."

Lexie watched his dark face grow pale. Her hands weren't trembling anymore. She was holding his gun as if she'd fired it a hundred times before, and her aim was true. *"Tell me!"*

From the corner of her eye she saw Reilly reach out to her, but she sidestepped, avoiding his touch. "Maybe you'd better tell the lady what she wants to know," he said, sounding icily cool and calm. Meeting his gaze, Lexie knew it was all an act. She read the question in his eyes. *You wouldn't really pull the trigger . . . would you?* At that moment, she honestly didn't know.

"Lexie, we've got her!" yelled Phil, crossing the sidewalk in a single bound. "The phone trace paid off. Our people found Lila."

His words took a moment to sink in. "You . . . you found her?" Suddenly weak, she felt her hands begin to tremble again.

Cautiously taking the gun from her hand, Phil draped his arm around her shoulders and gave her a gentle squeeze. "Lila's safe," he said quietly. "It's all over now."

"So, um . . . you were bluffing . . . right?" Reilly rested his chin on the top of her head and waited.

Lexie didn't answer him right away. She couldn't. Bluffing implied rational thought, and she'd been anything but rational with that gun in her hands. But would she really have pulled the trigger? It was a question she didn't want to consider, an act she didn't want to believe possible.

"Lexie?"

She sighed. Apparently Agent Ward wasn't going to quit until he got his answer. "I don't know," she said at last. "I just wasn't thinking. I kept picturing Lila . . . how they might have hurt her. I was crazy, I guess. Out of my mind with worry. I wanted to make him talk. But . . . no. I don't think I could have shot the man."

Shifting in Reilly's arms, she grinned up at him. "Sure gave him a good scare, though, didn't I?"

"Honey, believe me, he wasn't the only one who was scared."

"Oh, yeah?" Lexie snuggled a little closer, adjusting the blanket they'd pulled around themselves when they'd curled up on the couch.

"Er . . . ahem. Sorry to interrupt you two," said Phil, appearing unexpectedly in the doorway, cell phone in hand.

"Not half as sorry as I am," grumbled Reilly, watching his partner cross the room. "What happened to that comfortable bed and warm bath you wanted? I thought you went to find a hotel."

"Yeah, well . . . something came up. How's your aunt, Lexie?"

All three of them turned to look at Lila, sound asleep in Lexie's big brass bed. "She'll be fine," said Lexie. "More insulted than injured, I think. But, boy, was she hungry! She had me send out for pasta Florentine and ate most of Buddy's, as well as her own."

"Where is the old boy?" asked Phil.

Lexie chuckled. "Lila sent him home. I really think he wanted to take her with him, but she told him she'd probably sleep for a week. Then she took one of her pills and mellowed right out—didn't even complain when Rufus joined her on the bed. The two of them have been dead to the world ever since."

At the mention of his name, Rufus rolled one eye open and gave his tail a lazy thump before drifting back off to dreamland.

"Lucky dog," said Phil. "Listen, I really am sorry about this, but . . ." He stared at the ceiling for a moment and shuffled his feet.

"Well?" demanded Reilly. "What's so important that it couldn't wait till morning?"

"We, uh, we got a call."

A call? What did he mean by that? wondered Lexie, not at all sure that she wanted to know the answer.

"When?" Reilly's voice, suddenly grim, made her shiver. She couldn't understand anything they were saying. Was it some kind of code?

"Now," answered Phil. "We're on the four-fifteen."

"Blast." Reilly's arms tightened around her as he breathed the word.

"I'm sorry," said Phil, giving a helpless little shrug as he turned to face them again. "Really sorry." And then he was gone, across the room and out the door as quickly as he'd come.

"Reilly? What's wrong? What did he mean? Why—"

His fingers, pressed against her lips, stopped the questions. "I didn't want this, Lexie. I thought we'd have some time . . . I thought . . ."

His voice was soft and gruff at the same time, with a catchiness about it that tugged at her heart. One look at his face answered all of her questions. She was losing him. The call was to take him away. He was leaving.

"Lexie, I . . ." Reilly struggled with words that seemed to tangle on his tongue.

"It's all right," she whispered, trying to be brave. "I knew you'd have to go . . . just not so soon." She could see the pain in his eyes, feel it in his touch as he traced her lips with his fingertips. This was hard for him, too.

"I hate this," he said at last. "I feel like there's so much unfinished between us, so much I want you to know."

Lexie sighed, moving closer, finding shelter in his arms. "It's not like you're going to the ends of the earth," she said quietly. "I mean, Washington's not that far away. We can still—"

"But I won't be in Washington. Not for a while, anyway. It's another assignment, Lexie. And I won't be able to contact you." His arms tightened lovingly around her. "You do understand that, don't you?"

She nodded, unable to speak. She understood perfectly. It was his job, after all. Tomorrow, he and Phil would be putting their lives on the line again. For somebody else, this time. Blinking back tears, she made her decision. She wouldn't tell him. Not now. It wouldn't be fair. If he knew how much she loved him, he would also know how much it hurt her to let him go. And he would worry. She couldn't let that happen. His mind belonged on the job, one hundred percent, not wandering, not thinking about her.

"I understand. Just promise me you'll be careful, Reilly. And maybe, when it's over, you could call and let me know you're okay.''

''Count on it,'' he said, losing his fingers in the tangle of hair that tumbled around her shoulders and across his chest. It was soft and wild, just like the woman in his arms. He needed to remember this moment, and all the wonderful moments they'd shared. He needed to remember the sparkle and flash of her violet eyes, the delicate rosewood scent that clung to her skin. More than that, he needed to tell her the truth, that he loved her with all his heart and soul, that only death could keep him from coming back to her, if she'd have him.

But how could he ask her to wait? This new assignment might take weeks, even months, to complete. And when it was finished, there'd be another, and then another. He wouldn't wish that kind of life on anyone. The waiting, the uncertainty, never knowing when he'd be coming back—*if* he'd be coming back.

''I should go,'' he said gruffly, pressing his lips against her forehead, then bending for one last kiss. It was short, bittersweet, strangely awkward after all they'd shared. He felt Lexie tremble. Was she crying? Cupping her chin in his hands, he met her gaze. She looked so small, so terribly frightened, but she was trying her best to hide it. He smiled, aching to ease her mind. ''Don't worry,'' he said. ''I've got Phil to watch my back. And he's the perfectly trained professional, remember? I'll be fine.''

''I know you will,'' she whispered, gently touching his cheek before he turned to walk out of her life. ''So will I.''

Chapter Sixteen

Lexie pressed her face against the cool glass of the window and sighed deeply. She had been standing, looking out over the rooftops, for almost an hour and it was definitely time to shift into action. She sighed again. Why was it so hard to get herself in gear these days?

Reilly had been gone for over a week. Nine days, to be exact. Well, eight days, seventeen hours, and . . . She turned just in time to watch the minute hand on the old grandfather clock fall into place at ten twenty-five. Eight days, seventeen hours, and twenty-odd minutes. How unlike her to know such a thing . . . or even to think of such a thing.

Why was she letting this happen? What about all those rules of hers? Rules that had kept her strong and focused for as long as she could remember. Rules that had seen her through the good times and the bad. *Times a lot more devastating than this,* she thought, remembering a long-ago day when her whole world had fallen apart around her—both parents lost in the blink of an eye when their plane struck the side of a mountain. But even then, barely seventeen and suddenly all alone, her rules had kept her going.

Don't let them see you cry. Never let them know what you're thinking. Don't put your trust in anyone but yourself. Don't let anything get to you—not ever. She'd broken every one of those rules for Reilly Ward. And what had it gotten her? Oh, sure, their last embrace had been full of unspoken promises. But now she felt certain that Reilly had said all that he meant to say to her. His job had brought them closer than they'd had any right to be, and she knew that he'd had to pull away. From the case, from the location. From her.

Groaning softly, so as not to wake Lila, who was sleeping—

again—Lexie turned away from the window and walked quietly to the kitchen. Her aunt had managed to sleep around the clock in the days immediately following her rescue, and still insisted on naps at least twice a day. The woman was a regular Rip Van Winkle, unlike Lexie, who'd barely slept at all since Reilly left. And it showed. Even Tommy Angell had noticed. Fatigue was slowly but surely wearing her down. Trouble was, whenever she slept, she dreamed of Reilly. Better to stay awake. Coffee, that would help.

Rufus got up silently—unusual for him, not even a grunt or a thump of the tail—and followed her across the room, his big fuzzy face turned mutely upward. His expression was almost quizzical. What, he seemed to be asking, was wrong with this picture? He sat beside her as she leaned against the counter, and offered her his paw.

"Aw, Rufus . . ." Another rule out the window. Bursting into tears, she knelt down to wrap the big dog in an enormous hug. "Aw, Rufus," she sobbed, "I can't even make coffee without thinking about him. And you don't want to go for a walk without him. And he's probably never coming back. And I—I . . . I don't want to feel like this."

The dog pressed his black nose against her neck in an almost human display of concern. Lexie sobbed until she'd exhausted herself, finally releasing her hold on poor Rufus when she realized that his furry neck was totally soaked with her tears.

She let herself slump back against the counter. The foolishness of the situation didn't escape her, even in her hopelessly unhappy state. She gave the dog a halfhearted grin, and rubbed his ears affectionately. "We make a fine pair, don't we, big guy? He's gone away, done what he came to do, and we mope around like a couple of sorry old maids."

That image brought Lexie, almost instantly, to her feet. She grabbed the coffeepot as though it were a living creature that she'd have to subdue. "Right. Enough of this nonsense. What do you say, Rufe? Should I make a pot of coffee for me and our favorite aunt, and maybe a piece of toast for you?" She drew a deep breath. "We're going to be fine!" This last was delivered with considerable vehemence, as she tried to convince herself, and the dog, of its veracity. *"Just fine."*

She almost believed it, too. Until the rich aroma of coffee reminded her of Reilly again. Maybe he would come back. Someday. When, though? The one phone call she'd had from him since his departure had been an absurdly abrupt one from a pay phone at the airport. He'd probably felt that it was the decent thing to do, in light of all that had happened between them. "See you soon," he'd said. Well, maybe so. But would it ever be the same between them? Now that she was just Lexie Frost, photographer, and he was Reilly Ward, federal agent, off on another case. Maybe helping out another damsel in distress. She choked down a sob. *No. Don't do that. Not that.* "Really," she said again, "I'm fine."

"Lexie, dear, I do believe I smell coffee." Lila made a grand entrance from behind one of the Chinese screens, dressed in a brilliant orange silk robe, with a sky-blue headband holding her hair in place. "You really are an angel, dear. You must have read my mind while I was sleeping."

Lexie busied herself with getting out the mugs and cream for their coffee, carefully hiding her puffy face and tear-reddened eyes from her aunt.

"Whatever is the matter, dear?"

Darn! How could she possibly know that something was the matter? Lexie cleared her throat, steadied her voice, hid her face behind the refrigerator door. "Not a thing, Lila. Sit. Coffee's almost ready. I'll bring you a cup."

"Well, dear, if nothing's wrong, why are you hiding yourself in the icebox?"

"Just getting us some cream, Lila."

"The cream is already on the tray, Lexie. Look at me, dear."

Darn again. For as long as she could remember, she'd never been able to put anything over on Lila. The woman had some kind of radar where emotional upsets were concerned. Squaring her shoulders, she turned to face the music.

"Oh, Lexie, you've been crying."

"No, really, Lila, I'm just tired and stressed out. You know, with everything that happened, it . . . it was just such an ordeal. I guess it's starting to catch up with me.''

"Ha! You might fool some people with a line like that, my dear, but do try to remember who you're dealing with. If I can survive the 'ordeal,' and be prepared to get on with my life, then you can most certainly do the same. Come on now, we both know it's that lovely man. You're heartbroken that he's gone away. And nobody could blame you the tiniest bit. Let's sit with our coffee and talk about it.''

"Oh, Lila, that was just a case of getting caught up in the moment,'' she lied, trying to disguise the little catch in her voice by clearing her throat again. That was really all it was. Just the heat of adventure, the thrill of a dangerous situation. From the corner of her eye she saw Lila shake her head in obvious disbelief. Lexie lifted the tray and motioned her aunt into the living room.

Settling herself on the couch, Lila propped her feet up on the blanket box and smiled gently at her niece. "You know, dear, sometimes it happens that we fall in love with the wrong man, or we find the perfect man and the timing is all wrong. I think—and I'm very wise about these things, you know—I think that your Reilly Ward truly is the perfect man for you. Do try to have a little faith.'' She reached for her coffee and dribbled a double dose of cream into it.

Lexie chewed on her lip. "Oh, come on, Lila, you're just partial to him because he and Phil happened to save your life. Not that I won't be eternally grateful for that,'' she added hastily. "I mean, sure, he's a great guy, but men like Reilly get caught up in the excitement and the danger. He has no reason to pursue a relationship. That's just wishful thinking on my part. I will admit that I can't help wishing, no matter how strong I like to think I am.'' She lifted her mug and took a long sip of coffee. "Why is life so complicated? I feel as if I'm ten years old again.''

Lila laughed her trademark tinkling-bell laugh. "Lexie, dear, that feeling never goes away. Why, I still feel that way, and that's why I'm finally going to take dear Buddy up on his charming offer of a getaway trip to the Catskills. It's so romantic, and he's very sweet and considerate. Who knows, I may even marry again.'' She sighed contentedly.

Lexie stared at her aunt as if she'd suddenly grown another head. ''You're going to do what?'' she asked faintly. ''You might even what?''

Lila nodded. ''You see, dear, life is full of surprises. There's always time for love and romance, and we can be happy in our lives if we just accept the fact that happiness is there for us. You might want to give it a try.''

''Since when did you become such a profound philosopher?''

''Oh, it's not philosophy, it's just life. And I've already lived a wonderful life; I think I'll start another one.'' She looked fondly at her niece. ''You have so much time ahead of you, dear, why not relax and enjoy yourself? Things are working out so well for you.''

''Working out well?'' *What planet was Lila living on?* ''Lila, my life is a mess.''

''Well, you look at it any way you like. But that's not the way I see it. You're an extremely well-respected photographer. I brag to all my friends about you, you know. Tiny, temporary setbacks in your personal life shouldn't throw you into depression. Cheer up, dear, I've got some juicy news.''

Still boggled by the thought of Lila and Buddy running off for a romantic tryst, and possibly even considering marriage, Lexie was glad to be diverted, however temporarily. ''I'll bite. What's the news?''

''It's Julian. We've discovered that he's really a dreadful crook on a rather large scale. Do you know that he was at least partly responsible for what happened to me? Yes, it was his idea to have your aunt turned into a 'mule,' of all creatures. I'm sure I have the terminology correct, and I am terribly unimpressed by the picture it brings to mind. A mule, indeed!''

''Oh, Lila, it's only an expression. It doesn't reflect on you personally,'' said Lexie, grinning weakly. ''So, I guess it's safe to assume that good old Julian will be spending some time behind bars?''

''Yes, dear, and I can't say that I'm at all upset about it. In

fact, the knowledge that he absolutely detests vertical or geo-
metrical patterns makes me feel even better about his stay with
all the other criminals.'' She grew thoughtful. ''He always
hated any kind of stripes. It serves him right. You see, Lexie,
there is justice in life. You just have to wait to see it,
sometimes.''

''So it's really all over, then?''

Her aunt nodded, a satisfied smile lighting up her face.

Lexie felt brighter than she had in days. ''Let's go out for
lunch, Lila. Kind of a celebration—my treat.''

''Oh, I'm sorry, dear. Truly, I am. But, you see, I've already
made arrangements to leave with Buddy this afternoon. We
want to get up to the mountains before sunset. Isn't that just
too romantic? So I have to spend the next couple of hours
packing and getting organized. You understand.''

Lexie felt as if all the air had been let out of her balloon at
once. She put on a brave face, though. ''Of course I understand,
Lila. It's just that . . . well, I just thought . . . I thought that,
maybe once you managed to wake up, we'd have a few days
to spend together, that's all.''

Lila leaned forward and patted her hand. ''And we will, dear.
Another time. I promise.'' Briskly, she got up and took her
mug into the kitchen. ''I have to get started now. I may be
every bit as fabulous as I was in my younger days, but it takes
me a little while longer to get ready.'' Giving a sly wink, she
was off to haul her big suitcase onto the bed and start packing.

Lexie sipped moodily at the dregs of her coffee. It was obvious that she couldn't count on Lila to keep her busy. She was
going to have to handle that herself. Now was the time to dust
off those rules and start living by them again. *Never let anything keep you down.* That was a good one to start with.

''I'm going to take Rufus for a run,'' she called, almost
cheerily. ''I'll be back in about an hour, so I'll see you before
you go.''

''Fine, dear, enjoy yourself. And please, do tire the hairy
beast out. Then maybe I'll be able to get my cases out the door
without him slobbering all over them.''

Rufus bounded across the room, jumping up against Lexie

as she tried to open the door. ''Down, you big idiot,'' she said affectionately, after pushing him aside for the third time. ''How the heck are we going to get out of here if you keep trying to knock me over?'' She patted his fuzzy head and clipped on his leash. ''Okay, big guy, let's go.''

Rufus was, as always, terribly enthusiastic to get out of the apartment, then equally enthusiastic to get back inside once he'd sniffed the great, exercise-filled outdoors. Lexie, however, was determined. She'd been idle much too long, hiding out in the loft, avoiding the park and the gym, using her bumps and bruises as an excuse. Well, enough was enough. The bruises were healed and it was time to get moving. Walking briskly, she chirped encouragement to her lackadaisical companion as he lounged at the end of the leash, some six feet behind her all the way.

It had all been so different with Reilly. Happy walks, arm-in-arm, with Rufus jogging alongside, joyfully keeping pace with his new best friend. Now, here she was, playing ''drag the dog'' again. She hauled on the leash, steering the big oaf toward the park. Reilly had certainly made an impression, she thought. It seemed there was nowhere that was empty of memories, even though their time together had been so fleeting.

Through the dense fog of her thoughts, she gradually became aware of a car horn honking insistently behind her. Not that there weren't hundreds of car horns honking almost constantly, but this one seemed to be following her. For an instant she was terribly afraid, visions of guns and dark strangers flashing before her eyes. She gathered up the leash, pulling Rufus close and preparing to run, dragging him behind her all the way, if necessary.

''Hey, Lexie,'' came a familiar voice. ''Lexie! Hey, over here! Halloo!''

She turned, half-disappointed, half-relieved, to find Jack Gillespie hanging out of the window of his Mercedes.

''Oh, hi, Jack, what are you doing here?''

''On my way to lunch. How about taking the hound home and coming along with me? I'm going to El Gordo's . . . your favorite.''

For a brief second, time stood still for Lexie. Then, turning her back on her aching heart, she smiled brightly. "Sounds great, Jack. You'll have to pick me up in half an hour, though. I want to say good-bye to Lila and change my clothes."

Jack's eyes lit up. "Hey, any time you say. I'll be there." He paused, inching the car forward into traffic. "You know that all the good tables will be taken if we don't get there in half an hour. I'll pick you up in twenty minutes." With a cheery wave, he pulled away.

"What have I done?" she wondered aloud. Lunch with Jack? Talk about asking for trouble. Still, she never could resist El Gordo's. Turning, she dragged the still-reluctant Rufus back home.

"Sorry, Jack, what did you say?" She'd been wondering what Reilly would think of the spicy Mexican dishes served up in what had once been her favorite restaurant, and then wondering if Lila and Buddy had left the city yet. Their good-byes had been hasty. She'd managed to avoid any mention of Jack Gillespie, thanks largely to the fact that her aunt had been totally preoccupied with her own plans. Lexie had changed and brushed her hair, pinning it back off her face with a couple of fan-shaped clips, without giving much thought to the whole procedure. She hadn't even really noticed what she'd put on, until Jack had pointed out how much he'd always liked her in that particular shade of blue. Unintentionally, she had dressed in a way that had the man thinking she was trying to please him. What a classic faux pas.

"Lexie, you're miles away. I was just saying how wonderful you look, and how great it is to be back in our favorite spot. Together. I couldn't be happier." Jack was positively beaming.

"Thank you, Jack. I . . ." She tried to smile, but the look on his face—so happy, so hopeful—tied her stomach in knots. It would be very wrong to let him think that things were going to be different between them. She had examined her feelings, but there didn't seem to be a darn thing left over for Jack Gillespie. "I guess I'm just a little preoccupied. Sorry."

"Perfectly understandable, considering all the stress you've been under. I worry about you, Lexie, you know that. And this last escapade just goes to prove that you're not safe living on your own. Not safe at all.''

Just like old times, thought Lexie, half expecting him to start clucking like a fussy mother hen. ''Jack,'' she said quietly, ''the fact that I live on my own had absolutely nothing to do with what happened to Lila, and you know it.''

''Yes, well, maybe so. But if you'd had a husband to look after you, they wouldn't have taken such awful liberties. A woman on her own is an easy target. There are way too many freaks out there.'' He sipped thoughtfully on his ice water and soberly shook his head. ''Way too many freaks,'' he repeated.

''Oh, really, Jack. You always could exaggerate. I see nothing's changed.'' Life with Jack. It was all coming back to her now. Too many freaks—oh, please.

''Alex-ahh-ndra! So wonderful to see you again!'' As if cued to make an entrance, Vincent Urbano sidled up to the table. ''I've missed you at the gallery! Ah, well. Life, that is to say *your* life, is always so vivid, so full of surprises. It is sooo good to see you, Alex-ahh-ndra.''

''Uh, Vincent, this is . . .'' Lexie started to introduce Jack but was cut off in mid-sentence as Urbano took her hand and lifted it ceremoniously to his lips. She pulled away as soon as she politely could, doing her best to avoid causing a scene. But, in spite of her efforts, it seemed that everyone in the room had turned to watch. Even away from the gallery, Vincent Urbano had a way of attracting attention. Maybe it had something to do with those outrageously tight purple leather pants of his.

Jack was incensed. Apparently he had no qualms at all about causing a scene. ''Now, look here, you . . . you . . . whoever you are. You can't just come waltzing in here, annoying people when they're trying to have lunch. It's totally inappropriate. You'll have to leave or . . . or I'll have you thrown out!''

Vincent raised his eyebrows. One at a time. *''Par-don-nez-moi?''*

''Jack, this is Vincent Urbano. He's an artist . . . I'm sure you've heard of him. I shot his MOPA show.'' Leaning across the table, she whispered, ''Get a grip, will you, Jack? He's just a little eccentric. He's not about to hurt anyone.''

Vincent smiled happily. ''You see, Mr. Man, Alex likes me. Perhaps I'll join you.'' While he looked around for a chair to draw up to their table, Lexie looked at Jack. His color was rising rapidly. She was going to have to do something. And quickly.

Standing, she reached across the table and grabbed his hand. ''Jack and I were just leaving, Vincent. Sorry. It was lovely to see you, though. Really.''

''What? B-but . . . I . . . hey! Lexie!'' Jack sputtered one protest after another as she dragged him out onto the street. ''I just wanted to have a quiet meal with you,'' he said at last. ''We should have had that creep thrown out on his ear—had every right, you know. Now what are we going to do for lunch?''

Lexie had a sudden flashback to lunch in the park with Reilly. ''How about a chili dog?'' she suggested, only half-joking.

The look of horror on Jack's face made the joke a very brief and one-sided one.

''You know, Jack, I'm feeling awfully tired all of a sudden. Would you mind very much if I took a rain check?''

''Of course not,'' he said, making a valiant attempt to hide his disappointment. ''You get some rest. How about tomorrow night, around seven?''

''Well, it's not really . . . that is, I—I have to work tomorrow, Jack, until closing.'' What the heck was the matter with her? Why didn't she just say no?

''I'll pick you up at the shop, then. Say, nine-ish? That'll still give us plenty of time to catch up.'' As if the matter were settled, he bent to give her a quick peck on the cheek before helping her into the car.

Nine-ish? Lexie stared disconsolately out the window. Rock bottom. That's where she was at, all right. Letting Jack Gillespie tell her what to do, *and* when to do it. Time for a new rule. Something about getting a spine and using it.

* * *

It was time to get a grip. Time to get busy. Those films of Jazz in the Park were still waiting in the darkroom. There might even be something she could sell to one of the monthly "scene" magazines.

Banishing all thoughts of Reilly and Jack to the far corners of the loft, she shut herself in the darkroom and got to work. Before long, she felt almost like her old self. Not enough to hum in her off-key way, but definitely better than she'd felt for days. The shots of the concert were great, if she did say so herself. Full of motion and color. Full of life.

She looked briefly at the last contact sheet, fresh out of the fixer, and felt a sob rise in her throat. The first few shots on the roll were of Reilly and Rufus, playing in the park. How could she have forgotten? Jazz in the Park was his birthday treat. Real New York music. She had caught him off guard, smiling pensively as he listened to the music, and laughing at Rufus when the big dog had jumped up on him.

Lexie stood and stared at the photos for a long time, until her eyes were too full of tears to see them clearly anymore. "Way to go, Frost," she said, trying to find the lighter side of things. "Too many tears. They're watering down the developer."

She cleaned up the darkroom, wondering if she'd ever be ready to develop those other shots of Reilly, those Saturday-morning, sleeping-like-a-baby shots. Sentimental drivel, she'd called it at the time. Pushing that roll of film to the very back of the shelf, she turned off the light. There was really nothing more for her to do, and suddenly she felt totally wiped out. Maybe, at last, she'd be able to get some sleep.

The phone was ringing as she opened the darkroom door. Could it be him? she wondered, sprinting across the room to catch it before the caller hung up. "Hello?" she said softly.

"Hello," answered a woman's contralto voice. "Am I speaking to Alexandra Frost?"

Lexie sat up straight. She had no idea who this person might be. "Yes," she said, "This is Lexie Frost. Who's calling, please?" Her heart thumped. She was inexplicably convinced that Lila was in trouble again.

A warm, low laugh allayed her fears. "Oh, thank goodness. I've gone through half the Frosts in the book trying to find you," said the woman. "Lexie, you don't know me, but my name is Lena Ward. I'm Reilly's sister."

Lexie felt a pounding in her head, heard a rushing sound like the waves of the ocean. Reilly's sister!

"Lexie, are you there?"

It took almost superhuman effort to focus her attention. "Yes, I . . . I'm sorry, yes, I'm here. B-but, Lena, is Reilly all right?" She held her breath, felt her heart flutter to a sickeningly painful stop.

"Oh, I'm sure my little brother is just fine. He always manages to find his way out of difficult situations—some sort of divine protection or lucky star or something. We're not exactly sure, but we don't worry about his safety all that much. And you don't need to, either."

Lexie's heart settled back into a tentative rhythm. Why was Lena calling her? She was almost afraid to ask. "Where is he now?"

"Well, that's why I'm calling, Lexie. Reilly and Phil got called away on a top-priority mission. We're fairly sure that they've finally got a line on the people responsible for . . . well, you know, for Bonnie. . . . Anyway, we think they may be in New Mexico. Reilly never says too much, but I just felt I had to call and talk to you."

"I really appreciate it, Lena. It's been over a week since he left, and . . . I was kind of wondering . . ."

The warm laugh sounded again. "Reilly sure is crazy about you. Knowing my brother, though, he probably didn't get around to telling you. He, um, he kind of opens up to me most of the time, and he told me that he loves you and that he can't wait to get back to you to tell you so in person."

"He told you that?"

"Um-hmm. He said a lot more than that, as a matter of fact. But I don't want to embarrass you. Not until I can see the expression on your face for myself, anyway."

"Oh, Lena, I love him, too," confessed Lexie, astounded that she'd actually said the words. And to a stranger! "I really do. More than you can possibly imagine. I just wish I'd been able to work up enough courage to tell him before he left. I hope I get the chance.''

''I'm sure you will. When my brother wants something, he always perseveres until he gets it. And he is head over heels in love with you. I'm so happy for both of you, Lexie. And I'm dying to meet you. Have you ever been to Hawaii? The flowers here are so beautiful in the summer. Perfect time for a wedding.'' The voice seemed to be musing now, planning ahead.

''Wedding? What wedding?'' asked Lexie.

''Oh, I don't know, just whatever wedding happens to come along.''

Lena sounded so relaxed and easygoing. As if there could be an earthquake in her backyard, and she would just look out the window and say, ''Darn, we'll have to re-dig that garden.'' Lexie liked her already.

''Thank you so much for calling, Lena. You can't imagine how much better you've made me feel.''

''Don't mention it, hon. I know just what it's like to have no idea what's going on in a man's head. Kind of messes up your day, I think. Anyway, I have to get back up the mountain. We're tracking a new object, you know. Maybe it's that lucky star that's watching out for Reilly.'' Lena laughed again, as if she knew exactly what Lexie was thinking. ''Don't you worry. He's fine. And we'll talk again, really soon. Hopefully it'll be face to face. 'Bye now.''

'' 'Bye,'' murmured Lexie, feeling not so alone and lonely anymore. After all, she thought, those same stars that Lena was going up the mountain to watch were shining down on Reilly in New Mexico, or wherever he was. And in a few more hours, they'd be shining down on her, too.

Chapter Seventeen

"Y'got it all wrong, y'know."

"Huh? What the—?" Reilly mentally cursed himself. He was slipping. Heck, he'd downright bottomed out. Tommy Angell was standing beside him on the sidewalk. Elbow to elbow. Close enough to touch. People *never* got that close without him noticing. "Er... did you say something? Were you talking to me?"

"Well, I don't see anybody else nearby, do you?" replied Tommy, with a quick toss of his head that sent his pale blond hair into orbit. He patted it back into place. "You're that agent-friend of hers... Ward. Am I right?"

He nodded.

"Well, you got it wrong," he repeated. "About Lexie, I mean."

Reilly regarded the little man. Got it wrong? Judging from what he'd seen in the last few minutes, that didn't seem too likely. And what could Tommy Angell possibly now about it, anyway? Surely Lexie wouldn't have confided in him... would she?

He glanced up the street again, just in time to watch her disappear around the corner with Jack Gillespie at her side. Jack's hand was resting comfortably in the small of Lexie's back. As if it belonged there.

"I'll bet she hates that," said Tommy, shoving both hands into the pockets of his blue Shutterbugs lab coat.

Was the little guy being sarcastic? wondered Reilly. Or did he really know something worth telling? "Where're they going?"

"P. J.'s, I think. Lexie didn't want to get dressed up." The devilish twinkle in Tommy's eyes was unmistakable as he leaned closer to ask, "Gonna follow them?"

"Maybe. But what have I 'got wrong,' Mr. Angell?"

"It's Tommy. C'mon in the shop, will ya? Mr. B'd have my head if he knew I left the place unattended." He turned abruptly, running long fingers through his hair to keep it in place, and did a fast shuffle across the sidewalk.

Reilly watched him go. Was Tommy right? he wondered. Had he misinterpreted the smile that had blossomed on Lexie's lips when Jack walked through the door? Or the way she'd touched the man's arm when he bent to kiss her? Or the fact that she'd *let him* kiss her?

A minute sooner, and it would have been him walking through that door and into her arms. He remembered the rush he'd felt at the sight of her—every good emotion he'd ever known; and then the awful crash, that sickening feeling, like a fist in his gut, as he watched her walk away with Jack. Got it wrong? Wasn't it more likely that after her taste of life on the wild side, Jack's straight-and-narrow ways had begun to look pretty good? He could hardly blame her. Maybe she was better off. Maybe he had no right . . .

"You comin' in, or what?" demanded Tommy. He was standing in the doorway, hands on hips, frowning.

Or what? That was the question, all right. Should he make it easy for her? Just turn and walk away? Disappear forever? The fist in his gut grabbed hold and twisted. He couldn't walk away. Not without knowing. Sighing, he followed Tommy into the shop.

"So, Mr. Angell . . . er, Tommy . . . tell me what it is that you think I've got wrong."

"Well, y'know . . . about that stockbroker ex-fiancé of hers. The high and mighty Mr. Jack Gillespie." Tommy leaned on the counter and shook his head. "Poor Lex. She moped around here all afternoon, stewin' about their dinner date. Said she should've just said 'no' to the man, instead of letting him talk her into something she didn't want to do."

"You mean, they're . . . she's not . . ."

"In love?" Tommy grinned. "Oh, Lexie's in love, all right.

Head-over-heels, unless I'm very much mistaken. But not with Mr. Gillespie. And you can take that to the bank.''

Reilly shifted uncomfortably. He had the distinct impression that he was being teased, not something he particularly enjoyed. Six brothers and sisters—all older—had seen to it that he'd had more than his fair share of teasing growing up, good-natured and otherwise. He studied the little man's smug face for a long moment, then forced his voice into something approaching Bureau official delivery. "Okay . . . then, who?"

"She won't tell." He shrugged. "Well, y'know, Lexie pretty much keeps things to herself. But I can guess. I'm a very good guesser, hardly ever wrong—hey! Where're you goin'?"

"I don't have time for games." Reilly stopped, halfway to the door, and turned slowly back to face Tommy. The little man looked utterly astounded, possibly even a bit frightened. *Good,* he thought. The tough-cop act was having the desired effect. It was only a shame that Phil wasn't around. They could have run a classic good cop/bad cop scam on the little guy. "I thought you had something to say, Mr. Angell. Apparently I was wrong."

"N-no, wait!" stammered Tommy. "I . . . it's . . . it's . . ."

"It's what?" Reilly took one step closer, relaxed the stern set of his jaw, let a little warmth creep back into his voice. "You were saying?"

"It's Lexie. She . . . she's been miserable . . . ever since that thing with her aunt . . . ever since you left."

"Miserable?" Reilly moved back to the counter, unnerved by a sudden pang of guilt.

"I've tried to get her to talk about it, you know, friendly-like, but . . . well, she just keeps saying she's tired." He gave a little snort of disbelief. "Oh, she's tired, all right. I mean, that's what happens when you don't sleep, you know? But . . ."

He looked up, obviously craving a little encouragement. Reilly held his tongue. If he gave in, started coaxing the information out, bit by bit, this could end up taking all night. Better to just wait, let the awkward silence work for him.

"Well," said Tommy, sounding somewhat deflated, "I caught her crying once. She tried to deny it, of course."

Of course, thought Reilly, choking back a smile. That was one of those rules she'd told him about. *Never let them see you cry.* He waited.

"And today . . . well, she told me she was only going out with Gillespie so as to break it to him gently. You know, that she wouldn't be seeing him anymore. That . . . that she's in love with somebody else."

"She said that?"

"Well . . ." Tommy wrinkled his nose. "Not in so many words. But, hey, you don't work with somebody for three years without getting to know them, y'know. I saw all those faraway looks she tried so hard to hide. I saw the tears, and the dark circles under her eyes. And you . . . you . . ."

Reilly took a step back and squared his shoulders. Timid no longer, Tommy Angell seemed to be working himself up to something. He half expected the little guy to get physical, maybe reach across the counter, grab him by the collar. He tried not to smile.

"You made her love you, Ward. Oh, yeah. I saw the way she looked at you . . . told her I was gonna find a woman to look at me like that. And I will, too. Someday." A flush of red crept up the back of Tommy's neck and spread across his face as he stepped from behind the counter. "I'll tell you one thing for sure, mister. When I do find a woman who loves me, I won't go running off on her. Won't leave her to wonder. How could you do that to Lexie?" Balling his hands into tight fists, he inched closer. "Well?"

"Calm down." Turning his back on Tommy's ire, Reilly paced the length of the shop. Had she really taken it that hard? Worried herself sleepless? Why hadn't he told her the truth? Oh, sure, she still would've worried. But she wouldn't have had to wonder.

Turning, he strode back to the counter, studying Tommy's face as he drew near. "Lexie knew I'd have to leave, once her aunt's case wound up. We both knew it. And it wasn't easy for me, either."

Why was he baring his soul to this angry little man? Simple, he thought. For the same reason that Tommy was angry. Because he cared about Lexie, too. It appeared an apology was in order. "I, uh . . . I'm sorry . . . for the hard time, just now. And thanks, Tommy. For filling me in. Guess I'd better get moving. Where is this P. J.'s?"

"Oh, you don't want to go there." Tommy glanced at his watch. "If everything went according to plan, our Lexie's on her way home by now, and Mr. Stockbroker is officially an ex-ex." He grinned widely. "You do remember where she lives, right?"

"Look at that moon, Rufe. And all those stars. D'you think Reilly can see them? Hmmm?"

"I see them, love," he whispered, adjusting his headphones and slouching low behind the wheel of his old Ford. That bug he'd planted was still transmitting. Loud and clear. He really should have retrieved it before he left, but with everything else that had happened in those last few hours . . . well, it hadn't exactly been at the top of his "to do" list. It didn't really matter. The thing would run out of juice soon, anyway. For now, though, he was glad to be able to hear Lexie breathing, yawning, softly sighing. She had to be lying in bed, he thought. Looking up at the stars through that skylight of hers. When she yawned again, he let himself picture a long, luxurious stretch.

"C'mere, you big oaf."

What the—? Heart pounding, he lurched upright. Had she spotted the car? Was she talking to him? No. Just the dog. Talk about wishful thinking.

"Don't worry. I'm not going to cry on you. And Jack won't be back to bother you, either. Never again. So just . . . just go to sleep. C'mon. Snuggle up. Oh, Rufus. I . . . I'm . . . so . . . tired. So . . . very . . . ti . . . mmmmm . . ."

When sleep stole the last of her words away, breaking the connection between them, Reilly slipped the headphones off and let them rest around his neck. Oh, how he wanted to touch her, to hold her. He wanted it so much it hurt. Instead he gripped the steering wheel, rested his head against the cool glass of the side window, and tried to steady his breathing.

He could see her, in his mind's eye, wearing those fruit-salad pajamas of hers, lying on her side with one arm tucked under her head . . . and all that wonderful black hair fanned out across the pillow. So close. He could walk across the laneway and let himself in . . . wrap her safe in his arms . . .

No. She'd already had a miserable day—a miserable week. Make that month. What she needed at the moment was a good night's rest. Tomorrow would be soon enough. He could wait that long to hold her, to tell her all the news. And then, if she'd have him . . .

"Hey, lady! C'mere, will ya?"

Juice Louie stepped out from behind his brightly canopied pushcart, wiped both hands on his apron, and then pointed directly at Lexie. He was laughing, as if he'd just heard a really good joke.

"Who, me?"

"Yeah. You. C'mere, will ya?"

"I'll be right there, Louie, just let me . . . aw, Rufus!" No longer content to lounge around at the end of his leash, it seemed the big dog had found a new way to annoy her. He was a good ten feet up the hillside, sniffing hopefully at the trunk of an old sycamore tree. Lexie groaned, hauled on the leash, but Rufus had become an immovable object again. What was so darned interesting about that tree, anyway?

Louie grinned. "Nice day, eh, lady?"

"Sure is. It's—*Rufus!* Don't eat that!" What on earth had the big oaf found this time? Now he'd probably be sick before they got home. "It is a beautiful day, almost like summer—*Rufus!* I said, don't eat that!" Lexie groaned again. This was absolutely the last time she'd bring the canine behemoth to Central Park. "Sorry, Louie. Did you want something?"

"Yeah," said the boy, laughing again. "Man say, give you this." He offered her a huge bottle of frosty-cold papaya juice, then cleared his throat, as if about to make a speech. "Man say, lady with big, brown, stubborn, woolly dog need a drink."

"Man? What man?" Suddenly the situation felt all too familiar. "Louie? What—no, I don't want a drink. What—?" She scanned the hillside, suddenly certain she knew why Rufus was so interested in that tree. But the big dog was nowhere to be seen. *"Rufus? Reilly!"* Lexie yelled their names at the top of her voice as she reeled in the dog's leash and watched the empty clip bounce across the pathway toward her. She jumped when Louie touched her arm.

"Man . . . ha . . . man say, tell lady he's been working on . . . on his approach." Poor Louie was almost doubled over with laughter. She wasn't likely to get any useful information out of him in that condition.

"He say, he . . . he ain't no pervert. Ha!" Message delivered, Louie turned and trundled his cart away from her down the path.

"Hey! You can't—Louie, which way did he go?"

"I'm right behind you, Miss Frost," came the gentle reply. "And still managing to annoy the heck out of you, it would seem."

Reilly's breath felt warm against her neck. And definitely annoying, in a wonderful sort of way. Instead of turning, she closed her eyes, leaned back against his broad chest, let him fold his arms around her. His lips brushed her ear, then her neck. "It's good to be back," he whispered, and the words shivered through her like a forbidden touch.

"How'd you like to take me home, Miss Frost? So we can say a proper hello."

"First things first, Agent Ward." Turning to face him, Lexie twined her arms around his neck. "Kiss me."

"Yes, ma'am," he said, leaning almost close enough. "But you should know . . . I might not be able to stop."

Stop was exactly what he did, though, gazing down at her with one of those heart-stopping, lopsided grins, his meltingly brown eyes twinkling up a storm. Lexie called his bluff.

"This is New York City, Agent Ward. Central Park. I doubt anybody'd notice. So . . . what are you waiting for?"

Reilly laughed. A low, chuckling, warm-blanket sort of a laugh that wrapped itself around her as his lips brushed hers. His arms tightened in a hug that lifted her right off her feet. "Mmmmm, you feel so good."

Abruptly, Reilly released her, holding her gently at arm's

length. "First things first, Lexie. How are you, anyway? Are all those bumps and bruises healed?"

She nodded. "I'm just fine. Now that you're here, that is. And Lila's good as new, too. Maybe even better than new. You won't believe what she's up to."

"Wouldn't have anything to do with our friend, Buddy Fine, would it?"

"How'd you know—Reilly Ward, you haven't been spying again, have you?"

"Who, me?" Now was not the time to confess his late-night eavesdropping, he decided, watching her violet eyes flash dangerously. "Just perceptive, that's all. I saw the way the man looked at her . . . a lot like the way I look at you, I'd imagine."

Rufus chose that moment to let them know they'd ignored him long enough. He tried the old wedge trick, shoving his head between their legs. When that didn't work he tried a growl, then a bark, finally jumping up to press his cold nose against Reilly's neck and drag his tongue across Lexie's face in a sloppy kiss. She made spitting noises as she pushed him away. "Okay, okay, we haven't forgotten about you, you big pest."

The dog grinned up at them, obviously overjoyed to have his two favorite people together again. "Here," said Lexie, scratching his hairy chin. "Come get your leash on. Now behave, okay? Good boy."

"What about you, Reilly?" she asked, slipping her arm through his as they strolled off down the path. "How've you been? And Phil? Where is Phil, anyway? Did he come with you? Are you here on another case? How long can you stay? And what about Bonnie? Did you finally figure it out? Reilly, do you—"

"Whoa! One question at a time, please. But how . . . how'd you know we were . . ."

"I had a long talk with your sister yesterday."

Reilly stopped dead in his tracks. "With my . . . with Lena?"

"She's terrific, Reilly. I liked her right away."

"She called you?"

"She said you'd told her all about me, and that she couldn't wait to meet me, and . . ."

Reilly glanced sideways at her, afraid to even imagine what his big sister might have said. "And . . . what?"

"Oh, just girl talk."

Reilly groaned, suddenly grateful that the two of them didn't own fax machines. Lena probably would've sent one of those naked baby pictures from the family album. Come to think of it, Lexie had more than a few embarrassing shots of him in her collection, too. "C'mon," he coaxed. "What did Lena tell you about me?"

"What makes you think we talked about you?" she asked, laughing. "Don't worry. Your sister didn't tell me anything I didn't already know. She didn't want me to worry, that's all. And she told me she was pretty sure the case you were on had something to do with Bonnie's death. Was she right?"

"Well, sort of," said Reilly, pulling her toward a park bench. He draped his arm around her shoulders as they sat. "We were back in New Mexico. The A.D.—sorry, the Assistant Director—knew we'd want to be part of the team when it all went down."

"Can you tell me? Is . . . is it over?"

"It's over. Finally." He took a deep breath, shaking his head as if he still couldn't believe it himself. "I can't really talk about the details, Lexie. I hope you understand that. But we did finally arrest the creeps who dumped Phil and me in the desert two years ago. The Bureau has had another team undercover for the last six months. This time everything went as planned. They got the evidence we needed to put them away. And Phil and I were there to make the arrest."

"Oh, Reilly, thank goodness." Lexie leaned into his arms for a hug. "Now maybe you and Phil—"

"It's not what you think, Lexie. They had nothing to do with Bonnie's death. We . . . we know that for sure now. It really was an accident." He breathed a sigh that shuddered through his body.

"All this time, Lexie. We blamed ourselves. When we should have been glad he made that call. It was the last chance he'd ever have to hear her voice, to tell her how much he loved her.''

''But, how . . . ? You were so sure you'd been sold out.''

''Oh, somebody sold us out, all right. But it wasn't what we thought. Not somebody on the inside. Not somebody we should've been able to trust.''

''Then, who?''

''An ex-con. Phil and I put him away years ago, some petty offense. He was out in three, bummed around the southwest for a while, finally got a job pumping gas in Albuquerque. He was there two years ago, Lexie, when we were undercover. And he recognized us. He was the one who sold us out. Used the information to buy his way into the syndicate . . . anyway, we put him away again. For a long stay, this time. So, it's over.''

''I'm so glad. What a relief it must be for Phil, for both of you.''

He nodded, straightened his shoulders as if to shake off the past, and smiled down at her. His slightly cryptic expression, and the sudden tension in his arms, told Lexie he was about to say something important.

''What?'' she demanded, when the silence grew too hard to bear.

''I was just considering my answers to the rest of your questions, Miss Frost.''

''I see. And were you planning to keep them to yourself?''

''You want your answers, do you?''

''Mmmm-hmmm.''

''Okay, here goes. Fine, thanks—him, too—Brooklyn, I think—yes—no—as long as you'll have me.'' Reilly drew a deep breath and tried not to laugh at the puzzled expression taking shape on Lexie's face. ''Don't tell me you've forgotten the questions?''

''I . . . as long as I'll have you?''

''She forgot the questions, Rufus.'' Reilly rolled his eyes dramatically. ''What do you think? Should I tell her?''

Rufus woofed encouragement.

''Don't tease,'' warned Lexie, giving the dog a sour look.

''I'm feeling just fine,'' Reilly said with a laugh, beginning his recap. "And as far as I know, Phil's fine, too. He's in Brooklyn right now, scouting out cheap office space. Yes, we did drive up together, and no, we're not on another case." He paused for effect. "We've resigned the Bureau, Lexie. Decided we're getting too old for the spy biz, so we're going into business together—Dibiase and Ward Investigations. We might even have need of an ace photographer from time to time. What do you think?"

Lexie was staring up at him, openmouthed and, for once, utterly speechless. It was obvious she didn't know what to think.

"So . . . as to your last question, I can stay just as long as you'll have me, Miss Frost. Do you think there's room for one more in that loft of yours? I'm quiet . . . good with animals . . . clean up after myself . . ." He stopped. The bewildered expression on Lexie's face was slowly becoming a smile. Maybe she just needed a bit more incentive. "Honest, you'll hardly know I'm there. I, um . . . I don't need much closet space, and . . . oh, yeah, I cook, too. I'd make somebody a heck of a husband. So? Lexie?"

The smile became a laugh as Lexie threw her arms around his neck. "Welcome to New York, Agent Ward. Now, shut up and kiss me."